Death du Jour

Death
du Jour

LOU JANE TEMPLE

BERKLEY PRIME CRIME, NEW YORK

THE BERKLEY PUBLISHING GROUP
Published by the Penguin Group
Penguin Group (USA) Inc.
375 Hudson Street, New York, New York 10014, USA
Penguin Group (Canada), 90 Eglinton Avenue East, Suite 700, Toronto, Ontario M4P 2Y3, Canada
(a division of Pearson Penguin Canada Inc.)
Penguin Books Ltd., 80 Strand, London WC2R 0RL, England
Penguin Group Ireland, 25 St. Stephen's Green, Dublin 2, Ireland (a division of Penguin Books Ltd.)
Penguin Group (Australia), 250 Camberwell Road, Camberwell, Victoria 3124, Australia
(a division of Pearson Australia Group Pty. Ltd.)
Penguin Books India Pvt. Ltd., 11 Community Centre, Panchsheel Park, New Delhi—110 017, India
Penguin Group (NZ), Cnr. Airborne and Rosedale Roads, Albany, Auckland 1310, New Zealand
(a division of Pearson New Zealand Ltd.)
Penguin Books (South Africa) (Pty.) Ltd., 24 Sturdee Avenue, Rosebank, Johannesburg 2196,
South Africa

Penguin Books Ltd., Registered Offices: 80 Strand, London WC2R 0RL, England

This is an original publication of The Berkley Publishing Group.

This is a work of fiction. Names, characters, places, and incidents either are the product of the author's imagination or are used fictitiously, and any resemblance to actual persons, living or dead, business establishments, events, or locales is entirely coincidental. The publisher does not have any control over and does not assume any responsibility for author or third-party websites or their content.

PUBLISHER'S NOTE: The recipes contained in this book are to be followed exactly as written. The publisher is not responsible for your specific health or allergy needs that may require medical supervision. The publisher is not responsible for any adverse reactions to the recipes contained in this book.

First edition: March 2006

Library of Congress Cataloging-in-Publication Data

Temple, Lou Jane.
    Death du jour / by Lou Jane Temple.— 1st ed.
       p. cm.
    ISBN 0-425-20806-0
  1. Women cooks—Fiction. 2. Cooks—Crimes against—Fiction. 3. France—History—1789-1815—Fiction. 4. Social classes—France—Fiction. I. Title.

    PS3570.E535D425 2006
    813'.54—dc22

                                                                            2005035481

PRINTED IN THE UNITED STATES OF AMERICA

10   9   8   7   6   5   4   3   2   1

*This book is dedicated to my family of friends,
upon whose shoulders I so often stand.
You support me in so many ways.*

ACKNOWLEDGMENTS

This book took some special historical knowledge. Venee Londre, of the University of Missouri–Kansas City, with his skill in French, French history, and French culinary history, showed me the way. If I messed up, it was me, not him.

As usual, Steve and Cathy Doyal could be called upon when needed, as could a host of others: Robert and Sally Uhlmann, Don Benjamin, Lois Chiles, my daughter, Reagan Walker, Margaret Silva, and Cort Sinnes, to name a few. Lisa Queen, my agent, is the perfect example of grace under pressure. Thanks to all.

PROLOGUE

*E*TIENNE *de la Porte slipped out the courtyard door to the arcade. It was the hour, eleven at night, when his household settled down and he could have a moment on the outside without someone calling for him right away. Tonight the master and his guests had taken their supper early, at ten, because they had been invited to a late gambling party. They had departed about fifteen minutes ago. Gambling. He felt his stomach muscles tighten at the thought of it. If only he could say no to it.*

Etienne glanced in both directions, expecting to see his business partner coming toward him, but the passageways were empty. They met twice a week at this time. He folded his arms over his chest and involuntarily tapped his foot, impatient and anxious. He badly needed to liquidate the assets he and his partner had acquired. His gambling debts, many of them held over from his time at court, others recent, had put him in something of a financial crisis. It was very irritating that the largest of these monies were owed to nobility. He would never enjoy paying off gambling debts to a nobleman or, worse yet, noblewoman, even if they were legitimate ones. And the nobility, who never paid their own debts freely, were the worst for threatening lawsuits and jail time and other unpleasantness.

He was able to pinch extra funds from the household accounts, of course. He had learned how to commit that particular form of larceny from experts at Versailles. But he was in need of rather more money than shoeing the mule, as it was called, could bring him. He needed to be done with this nefarious project and liquidate, cash out, and have plenty to live on in comfort for the rest of his life, if he stayed away from the card tables. His partner was so cautious, saying they must wait, that the price they could get for their goods now would rise as time passed and memories got hazy. But Etienne didn't see how he could wait anymore. He'd been thinking, and he had come up with what he considered a slick method for removing suspicion from himself once and for all. Then they would be free to liquidate. If his partner agreed, they could both be rich men in a month. Etienne heard footsteps and turned to see his partner walking toward him under the arcade.

MONSIEUR Desjardins put down his pen and rubbed his hands. Lately they hurt, his fingers cramping by this hour at night, which seemed to be the only time he usually had for his bookkeeping chores. They had to be done, though, and it was his responsibility to do them. Luckily the master didn't expect him to also keep records for his business. There was an accountant for that. He had heard other maîtres d'hôtel complain about how they had to do the accounting for both the household and their master's business interests.

Suddenly, there was a loud noise, seemingly from the room across the hall. M. Desjardins got up and swiftly went into the entry area right outside the office. The room across this area was Fanny's bedroom now and she had gone to spend the night at her parents' home so no one should be in there. He opened the door abruptly but all was dark and silent. M. Desjardins considered getting the oil lamp from his desk or lighting the candlestick he knew was on Fanny's chest, but rejected those ideas. He hadn't heard footsteps and no one had been down from upstairs for an hour at least. It was almost midnight. Most likely a mouse had pushed something off on the floor as it scurried around the room. Tomorrow he'd see that traps were laid. Or the next day. Tomorrow the whole household had the day off by orders of M. Monnard, the master.

M. Desjardins went back to his desk, sat down, and started to put his accounts away, done for the night. He would have to get up early in the morning, make the coffee, and go to the bakery for the bread. Fanny had reminded him before she left that the bakery would be open only until eleven in the morning tomorrow so that the baker and his family might enjoy the holiday.

He could have ordered Fanny to stay here at her duties until midmorning tomorrow. It would have been within his rights, what with the chef off tonight helping cook for the National Assembly and again tomorrow for all those who had come from all over France to take the oath. But Fanny was the only member of the staff who was a native Parisian and she came from the very neighborhood that had started the whole revolt last year, the faubourg St. Antoine. It wouldn't hurt him to make coffee in the morning, especially if it would keep their household safe and calm. Not that Fanny seemed overly political. He had never heard, or overheard for that matter, her talking about the revolution. But it seemed wise to give her a full twenty-four hours off. And the master was the one who had volunteered his own chef, Henri Brusli, to the cause and insisted that everyone have the day off to participate in the celebration.

The master was good at that sort of maneuvering. Over the last year he had avoided making enemies and kept busy, working for no-

bility and the bourgeois alike, although the nobility didn't seem to be building much in Paris these days, with the government and their place in it questioned at every turn. M. Desjardins picked up his lamp and headed out the door. He was ready for bed. But first he would take his usual stroll around the square. Sometimes he even took two, one before sitting down to do his postings and another when he got cramped and sleepy, as he was now. He was nervous about tomorrow, about this political fête. He hoped it didn't stir up more trouble.

CHAPTER ONE

"I have a present for you," Fanny's mother called. She was changing her clothes behind a carved wooden screen in the bedroom. Fanny's father had built that screen for them years ago. Fanny remembered how pleased her mother had been when he brought it upstairs from his workshop. After that day, the whole family dressed behind that screen, one by one. Fanny's mother also moved the screen to separate the adult sleeping space from Fanny and her brother at bedtime. That was when they all slept in the same room, before Fanny and her brother got their own bedrooms on the third floor.

Now, Fanny realized her parents had probably been using the screen to create privacy so they could have sex. It made Fanny uncomfortable to think they were doing "that" while she slept innocently on the other side of the screen as a child. She still couldn't fathom her parents feeling anything like what she had come to identify in herself as passion.

Martine Delarue came back into the kitchen holding up two necklaces. "I got one for each of us," she said and slipped a blue velvet ribbon around her daughter's neck. On it was hanging a polished piece of rock held in a gold oval.

Fanny pulled the necklace down to her lap. "Wait a minute. Let me see it before you fasten it." She turned it over in her palm and broke into a big smile. "Is it from the Bastille? Everyone is wearing them. I see them at the market all the time."

"Of course," her mother said with satisfaction in her voice. "That damnable place is completely pulled down now and made into paving stones for the muddy streets, with a few pieces of jewelry to boot, though they're probably fake for all the hundreds of Bastille earrings and necklaces and brooches I see about. But I got these from Marie down the street and she knows better than to sell me a piece of bogus limestone chipped off a church over on the Left Bank somewhere."

Fanny put the necklace back around her neck and her mother tied it securely, then Martine leaned down and kissed her daughter on the top of the head, ruffling her hair affectionately. Fanny and her mother had the same dark, thick hair. It was so brown it was almost black. In fact, the two women looked alike: ivory skin, dark hair, and unusual blue eyes the color of turquoise. They were both striking, perhaps Martine more so for the streaks of silver in her hair. Aging well was rare in Paris these days.

Fanny got up and tied her mother's necklace.

"I figured we should have a little bit of the old prison so we could tell our grandchildren about how the people of

Paris took matters in their own hands, way back in 1789," Martine said proudly.

Fanny didn't like to think about that day. She had been frightened and confused by the violence and it still rested uneasily on her mind. Even though she was only an assistant cook, she supposed working in a grand house on the Place Royale could put her in a vulnerable position. She could imagine a crowd coming there, to her house, even though her master wasn't nobility, and killing the lot of them.

All the cooks and maids and other household servants around the square felt the same as she did and they could talk of nothing else for weeks last summer, after the violence at the Bastille. And the politics here in Paris hadn't settled down in the last year—had gotten more intense, in fact, so the homeowners around the square were as nervous as the help.

Why, just the other day her friend Louise, at number five, had been made to pack up and move with her master to his country estate hundreds of kilometers from Paris. To be safe, the master said. Of course, he was a viscount and might have reason to be afraid, although a noble family could be killed in their beds in the country just as easily as in the city. Fanny had heard about bands of farmers who had broken into a noble's country house while he was gone off to court. They supposedly killed the caretakers and took all the fine things, breaking up what they didn't want. Her fellow workers had a laugh about that the other day at the staff meal, trying to picture a fine gilded chair in a hut with dirt floors, or a huge silver platter with nothing but gruel to be served on it. But even though they made fun, it was an uneasy sort of joking that had a subtext of concern for their own skins, citizens though they all were.

The rest of France was a big puzzle to Fanny. She'd been to Versailles once when she was young with her parents, and to Chartres, to the cathedral with her school class, but that was as far as her traveling had taken her. If someone were to tell her she had to go live out in the country somewhere, she would faint.

Fanny took a last sip of coffee and got up. "Are you sure you don't want to go to the Champ de Mars?"

"Of course not. I've done my part. I was over there on Tuesday hauling dirt in a cart like a mule. There'll be a bunch of country boys dressed up in ragtag uniforms talking about the Rights of Man and all our menfolk getting tipsy and making fun of them. And the parade ground will be knee deep in mud by noon. The rain during the night will see to that. Your father went off over there early this morning. He worked a bit on the parade grounds yesterday for a few hours, after he installed some cabinets. I told him I, for one, wanted to celebrate the liberation of the Bastille at the Bastille. Because the rest of the country wants to get in on our party, we have to have the Fête de la Fédération where there's room for country boys to parade around like they were soldiers."

Fanny watched her mother put on her white lace cap and pin a red, white, and blue cockade to the side of it. She was still amazed, and she would have to admit it concerned her as well, at the way her mother had changed in the last year. She hadn't been aware her mother had any political leanings until the Bastille incident.

Last year, after the Bastille, was the first time in her life she hadn't seen things exactly the way her parents did, and while she guessed this was part of growing up, it made her uncomfortable not to have their same views. While she pictured gangs of rampaging murderers come to kill innocents and get a few folks out of jail, her parents felt the crowd had been justified. Fanny's father said he wasn't there himself and she believed him. But he must have heard all the talk in the neighborhood, and Fanny asked why in heaven's name their neighbors, the parents of the children she grew up with, had felt they needed guns and ammunition in the first place. She thought her parents' answers vague. Martine said things like "The king's soldiers were moving in on Paris," and "Our neighborhood actually saved the country by destroying that prison." No one explained to her why the king's soldiers and her neighbors weren't on the same side anymore.

Now her mother bought lockets made of the dungeon to leave to their descendants. Fanny couldn't understand how they saw this whole revolution as a positive move, as most of their neighbors obviously did, when the lot of them depended on the nobility plus rich merchants for their living.

And it didn't end there. Last year, 1789, right after the Bastille fell, Fanny's mother and father had started going to community meetings in the faubourg St. Antoine. After these meetings, they talked about how more "common citizens" should be represented in the National Assembly, about how the Third Estate, which was everyone but priests and nobility, were 97 percent of the population but they didn't have 97 percent of the seats at the Assembly, not by a long shot.

Then her mother did the unthinkable. Fanny still couldn't believe any of it had really happened. In October, Martine marched to Versailles with thousands of other women and they forced the King and his family to move back to Paris right then and there, walking beside the royal carriage, by that time sixty thousand of them. As a little persuasion, they had the royal guards' severed heads on pikes alongside the carriage. The king and his unpopular wife, their son, and their daughter had to look at the heads of men they had known for years, all the way to town.

The king had needed a little persuasion about moving the court from Versailles to Paris, being a person who naturally had trouble making up his mind. But after some of the crowd ran up and down the halls of the residential palace like wild banshees looking for the Queen and vowing they would kill her, the king agreed to move to the palace in Paris in the Tuilleries, which was what the crowd wanted.

Fanny still couldn't believe her mother had been a part of such a dangerous, foolish, and yes, she supposed, brave thing. It made her proud of her mother and nervous for her at the same time. She had tried to get her to talk about it, but Martine was uncharacteristically vague and Fanny was afraid to push her for information because she was afraid of what her mother might tell her. Had her mother been there when those guards were beheaded? Surely, Martine hadn't been involved in anything like that?

Shaking off those worrisome thoughts, which had a tendency to flood into her brain more and more often lately, Fanny pinned a cockade on her own cap and the two women left the house.

The Delarues owned the buildings they lived and worked in. There were two structures, side by side. In the corner building at rue Cotte and rue du Faubourg St. Antoine, Martine had a dress shop on the ground floor. She sold hats and corsets and other handiwork made by some of the wives in the neighborhood, along with her own dresses. Martine's shop was a way for the local women to have a place to congregate and to make their own money. Martine sewed up low-priced clothes for the neighborhood women but made her real income creating expensive outfits for the bourgeoisie and even some nobility. The family lived on the second and third floors of this corner building.

Next door, a larger ground floor space was the Delarue workshop. Philippe and his son, Albert, built their signature furniture with workers and artisans hired to assist them by the job. The Delarues, *père et fils,* were known for their beautiful bookcases and cabinets with inlays of exotic woods. Albert and his wife and young son lived above the workshop on the second floor. The third floor was a dormitory for single male craftsmen. It was used when they had a big job and hired extra employees.

When Fanny and her mother went outside, the excitement of the celebration was palpable on the street. Today was an official holiday of the new government: the Fête de la Fédération created to mark the one-year anniversary of the storming of the Bastille prison. The faubourg St. Antoine was charged with energy that was joyous and slightly malevolent all at the same time. There was an underlying current of danger—this was about revolution, after all—but it did not stop the crowd from laughing and singing and crowding the sidewalks and streets.

The Delarues weren't the only skilled craftsmen in this quarter. Most of the men worked in wood and most owned or co-owned carts they used to make deliveries, which made them much more mobile than the normal Parisian. Today the whole neighborhood was using their carts to go to the festival.

People called out greetings to Martine and Fanny. Carts clogged the streets with mules and excrement. Families had all piled onto the flat, wooden beds, along with wine and food and tablecloths and blankets and extra clothes for the little ones, who always spilled something on their fronts. Everyone was moving, or not moving, in the same direction, west.

The faubourg St. Antoine district was just east of the Bastille. Originally outside the city walls, the quarter retained its independence even though those city walls separating it from Paris were long gone. It didn't take long for the crowd to migrate en masse to the broad expanse where the big prison had stood. To most of the neighborhood, this was as far as they needed to go. St. Antoine residents felt proud of their participation in the destruction of the Bastille and all it stood for. And for today, it was not just a big, empty space, but the emotional heart of the city, awash in color and sound and people. Street peddlers were everywhere, selling food and coffee and wine. Pickpockets and prostitutes were plying their trade, the prostitutes as visually arresting as possible, and the pickpockets as invisible as possible. The only people noticeably absent from the throngs were the clergy, who were unpopular with the new government and increasingly so with the people. Even though most everyone had been raised a Catholic, it didn't take long, nor too many newspaper articles, for citizens to resent the church's status as the First Estate, and certainly resent all the tax exemptions they got. So, the church, and those who wore the uniforms labeling them a part of it, were nowhere to be found this day. They were not missed.

But what one couldn't miss was the sound of music. Every kind of music and musician was represented, from Turkish flute players to Gypsy accordionists to serious string quartets playing Baroque inventions. Those who wanted to dance or sing along or be inspired could all find a tune suited for them. After each song, the audience that appreciated the performance would throw change into an empty violin case or an upturned hat.

Well-to-do merchants laughed with oyster sellers who flirted with National Guard members who were leering at the merchants' daughters. The city had come together for a day.

Fanny and her mother bought a baguette filled with cheese and ham, and red, white, and blue paper fans with slogans of the revolution printed on them. Paris was especially proud of its ice cream. The supplies of ice from Northern Europe made it possible to have frozen confections and iced drinks even in the summer. Fanny and Martine bought paper cups of strawberry ice from a vendor with a big copper vat of it packed tightly in a box of ice chips and straw. Then they strolled over to the river and watched as men raced up greased mainmast poles of fishing boats and merchant ships, falling in the Seine more than they made it to the top.

As much as they were enjoying themselves, they only listened halfheartedly to the speeches. The members of official political committees praised the revolution, and guild presidents paraded with their officers, some with several hundred members of the guild in tow. Fanny and Martine scoffed at this as the Delarues lived in a quarter where guilds were not allowed, a privileged area. In St. Antoine, people were free to practice their trade without paying for apprenticeships and going through a long journeyman period. Technically, no one who lived in one of the "privileged areas" was supposed to do business outside their area, but in reality they carried on business all over Paris, their privileged status serving as an invisible mantle protecting them. For instance, Fanny's father was a gifted cabinetmaker who worked for rich merchants and nobility in every part of the city. A marquis wasn't about to go pick up his own bookshelves, was he, now? No, he wanted them installed in his library without a bit of fuss on his part, except to pay for them, which he would put off as long as possible, Fanny's father always said.

Fanny's mother broke the rules, too. Most of her customers wouldn't dream of coming to her shop in a "trade" quarter of town so she made house calls in the better sections of Paris, measuring, fitting and delivering the finished products.

The city authorities allowed this stretching of the regulations and the illegal actions of the "privileged area" citizens. Supposedly it was to keep the guilds from having absolute power over trade in Paris, giving those who chose not to be a guild member a little additional edge. But Fanny's father reminded his family and neighbors often that if the city officials wanted to, if they didn't need them anymore or thought they were getting too powerful, they could make life miserable for those in the privileged areas, and no one in their family should ever forget that. "Don't abuse the privilege," he always said.

Fanny and her mother sat dangling their legs over the side of the quay. "Mama, has Papa's business picked up? And what about yours?"

Martine shrugged. "It's not as bad as it was last year. Nobles aren't buying or building new houses in Paris, or buying furniture either for that matter, but the bourgeoisie are. And Paris will never stop loving the latest clothes. Besides, the noble ladies can't get rid of their panniers fast enough.

Those hoop skirts advertise the one wearing them is rich and spoiled and is just asking for her head on a pike. So now, everyone wants a slim line with more modest fabrics. I'm actually selling painted linen again instead of brocaded silk. 'Martine, I need something more in keeping with these terrible times,' they tell me. They never suspect their little dressmaker was one of those who brought the king and his pathetic family back to Paris, where they belong. They should never have let Louis the Fourteenth move the whole court off to Versailles in the first place. But we put it right, and brought Louis the Sixteenth home," she said with a malicious chuckle and a gleam in her eye.

Fanny was disconcerted by her mother's cynical point of view. Had she, Fanny, been so softened by eighteen months of living around luxury, that she would defend the king and his silly wife against her mother? No, she knew her parents were good people and what they believed was right.

The king was no better than any other man, and if he wanted respect, he had better be working to help all his people live decently.

"What about you, dear? How is it over at the Place Royale? By the way, I hear there's talk about changing the name of it." Fanny's mother slipped a handkerchief out of her bodice and wiped a smudge of ice cream from her daughter's cheek.

Fanny realized her mother had continued to talk to her while she had been occupied with her own thoughts. "The name of what?"

"The square where you live, silly. They just can't decide what to change it to."

Fanny had heard gossip about this herself, but she wasn't sure why Place Royale was such a terrible name. Most of

Paris was named after kings. She realized she didn't listen to half of what the other cooks and maids said when they talked politics as they walked to the baker's together or visited Les Halles. As much as the events of the last year worried her, she really didn't keep up with everyday politics the way some of the other servants did. She was so busy most days it didn't make a difference to her what the bare square of paving stones named Place Royale was called. Her mother probably knew more about the goings-on in her neighborhood than she did.

The life of the city, all the important things that had happened and were still happening, worried Fanny, but she didn't have the time or inclination to participate in them as her parents were doing. Until something dramatic occurred, something like her friend's whole household leaving Paris, or a day like today, when you were supposed to consider the changes in the running of the country, she hardly noticed what was transpiring outside her kitchen.

She was cooking at a beautiful house on the Place Royale, and that was her whole world right now. That and Henri.

Suddenly a weight pushed against Fanny's shoulders. It was a young woman and a man. The woman was holding on to the man's jacket collar with her hands as she kissed him, and that unbalanced them both—that and the fact that they were slightly drunk. A bottle of champagne was visible in the man's jacket pocket.

"Oh, I'm sorry," the girl said, looking down at Fanny and Martine with a giggle.

Fanny pressed back against the girl's legs. "You want to step the other way. You are pretty close to the edge here," she said, indicating the distance from the ledge of the quay down to the river.

The man turned his attention to Fanny for the first time. "Thank you so much," he said, while moving the woman away from the edge of the quay with one sure movement of his arm around her waist. He looked down at Fanny and smiled. His eyes crinkled with the smile and Fanny observed he was very handsome. She felt a flush of heat on her cheeks and broke the eye contact by glancing over at her mother, who was also gazing intently at the man.

"Oh, yes, thank you," the young woman said as the couple walked away.

Martine studied the couple as they laughed and hugged. "Did you know the city of Paris compiled a book of the names, prices, and addresses of the best prostitutes in the city, just for this holiday weekend? Now isn't that a special service for the men from the provinces?"

Fanny looked back at the man and woman. "Is that who you think that was, a working girl and a man from out of town?"

"Could be," her mother said as she swung her legs around to stand up. She reached down her hand to help her daughter and Fanny took it, trying to be graceful. "I'm all for the girls having a profitable weekend and the men enjoying their time here in Paris."

"Mother, you always steered us to the other side of the street when we walked past prostitutes. I thought you disapproved of them."

"Oh, I did and I still do. I wouldn't wish that profession on my daughter, or even my enemy's daughter, but I can't judge a poor woman trying to make a living. It was your brother I was trying to keep away. He was always very interested in those girls—asked who they were even when he was a tiny boy."

Fanny laughed. "He couldn't wait to have a girlfriend either."

Her mother nodded in agreement. "Albert always loved women. He would have been in plenty of trouble and broke, too, without a wife."

"Tell me true, Mama, have you had a fight with someone in the neighborhood?"

"What are you talking about?" Martine said as she interlocked her arm with Fanny.

"You said 'my enemy's daughter' a minute ago. Who were you talking about?"

Her mother looked surprised and uneasy. "I did say that, didn't I? I can't think what I meant. Let's buy a treat," she chirped, obviously trying to change the subject.

Fanny made a mental note to ask her father if her mother was having a squabble with someone. He always knew everything, especially what you didn't want him to know.

But now she was going to allow herself to be bribed by her mother. If Martine didn't want to talk about enemies who might have daughters, she would have to buy Fanny a profiterole.

IN July, dark comes late in Paris, but Fanny should have left her parents' house a bit earlier than she had. Night had almost fallen as she hurried toward the Place Royale. She had walked her mother home, run into her brother and his family, and played with his son, Charles. They had all enjoyed a bottle of wine together around the table in her brother's kitchen, the little boy falling asleep on his grandmother's lap. Everyone was anxious for Fanny's father to arrive with a report about the big celebration at the Champ de Mars.

Fanny had waited for her father as long as she could and now she was going to have to hurry to get home before dark. It was true that she would be on streets that had hanging candlelit lanterns; some even had been converted to oil lamps. She saw the lights going on in front of her as the lantern lighters made their way through the quarter. But tonight didn't seem to Fanny to be a good night to be out after dark, what with the big celebration and all the wine and beer that had been consumed today. She was sure most of Paris was drunk by now, and drunk people could do things in the dark of night they wouldn't do in the daytime, straight and sober.

Fanny turned right to cut through the passageway to the Place Royale entering under the King's Pavilion. She paused for a minute, slightly in awe, as she always was when she entered the part of Paris that was now her home. Even in the dim dusk light, the Place was elegant, luxurious, and formal. It had the quality of a location you would dream up, not one that actually existed. Thirty-six identical houses formed a perfect square. All the houses were constructed and designed of the same brick with matching stone facings and steep slate roofs. All four rows of houses forming the square were linked by the ground-floor arcade, the square itself paved so that military parades could be held there, a bronze statue of Louis XII on horseback in the center. All four sides reflected the same amount of light, the pale red brick, gray slate, and ivory granite creating the look of a stage set that was glowing from within, soft and alive. It was magnificent.

Fanny started toward her house, number twenty-three, on the northern side of the Place. It was unusually quiet. She didn't pass another soul in the arcade and there was only one family and a few other people cutting across the square. Perhaps the festivities of the day had worn everyone out, or compelled these particular residents to hide behind their walls.

Shouting erupted in the farthest corner of the open square, where two men were talking. Fanny looked around quickly and saw that she was now alone on the street with these two. She would have to pass them to get home. They were just blurry shapes to her. She walked faster and squinted to see if she could pick out their faces, but it was too dark. One of the men turned and began walking toward her, and although she knew it was her imagination working overtime, she felt a shiver of apprehension. Could a little disagreement between two men meters away be dangerous to her? She tried to shake off that feeling. Whatever those two had been arguing about, it was none of her business and had nothing to do with her.

But she couldn't stop watching them, her eyes darting back and forth between the two. The man walking toward her was wearing light-colored knee breeches with a short blue jacket, and he pulled up his jacket collar as he walked. The man still standing in the corner of the square had his arms folded across his chest. He seemed to be trying to decide whether to follow the other man or not. Then he turned and walked in the opposite direction, toward the north side of the square.

When the man in the blue jacket passed into the arcade, he stepped under a vaulted stone arch that held a lantern. He was just a few meters in front of Fanny and the narrow shaft of light from the lantern above fell on his face. Fanny was expecting to see someone she knew. After all, hundreds of people lived behind these doors and she saw many of them every day. Instead of one of her neighbors, she recognized the man as the one she had seen earlier in the day, at the Bastille, with the woman her mother had thought a prostitute. She was still studying his face when they passed, forgetting for the moment that it was unseemly to meet the eye of a strange man. He bowed his head and smiled, that same handsome smile that had so captivated her by the river. She bowed her head toward him slightly and hurried on.

"Good evening, Fanny," the man said after he had passed.

Fanny felt the hairs on her arm stand up. She whirled around but the man had disappeared through the south entrance to the square, the one Fanny had entered moments ago. She wanted to run after him, to ask him how he knew her name, but the passageway between the square and the street didn't have streetlights and it was now pitch dark. She turned back and hurried toward her house, just as the second man opened a door under the arcade and stepped through it. It was the door to number twenty-three, the door to Fanny's own household.

Fanny moved toward her address less quickly, unsure of what waited for her there. It seemed everything familiar today held something unfamiliar within, starting with her own mother. Now the place she had come to regard as home held a puzzle as well. Which of the six men who lived inside the walls of number twenty-three had been arguing with the handsome stranger?

CHAPTER TWO

FANNY woke up still curious about the events of the night before, especially the argument. But she didn't have time to think about it too much. The morning was busy as usual, as it was in all the great houses in Paris.

Number twenty-three, Place Royale, was a hybrid of a house because the owner, Monsieur Monnard, was an architect. In 1605, his ninth-generation great-grandfather, an architect as well, had worked on the construction of the Place Royale. Henri IV had awarded him a house for his efforts, number twenty-three, a house that was still in the family.

So M. Monnard was obliged to keep the general design of the house. This was not a burden as he was very proud of it, and of the contribution of his distant relative to the whole square. For almost two hundred years his family had lived in the same house and someone in every generation had been designing homes and buildings that whole time. And it would continue. His own son worked with him now and also lived at number twenty-three.

The house was one of very few on the square still in the hands of a descendant of an original owner. Because of that, it was the site of many tours of architects, builders, and various city officials wanting perhaps to duplicate the beauty of the Place in other squares, should that be possible and affordable.

But many things had happened in the design and building of houses in 185 years, especially these grand *hotels particulars*. So in addition to retaining the original design, M. Monnard also had to show off some of the new features he could provide his clients. He had built some extra additions to the house that made it a combination of old and new.

The family and public areas of the house were equipped with English toilets, the fancy flush toilets that were all the rage in Paris. There was no citywide sewer system yet so the soiled contents of those toilets went into a metal tank on the subground level of the house and the waste removal wagon emptied it twice a week.

The servants' quarters still had chamber pots, of course, but they could be emptied into that same tank. This modern method of waste management at number twenty-three kept down the stink that permeated the courtyards of other houses on the Place.

They also had hot water for the bathtubs. M. Monnard had built a cistern on the roof to catch rainwater, right next to the chimneys. He'd been careful that it didn't disrupt the symmetry of the roofline. He would never do anything to break the general design lines of the square. The heat from constant fires in the chimneys warmed the water; it was filtered, then piped down to a bathing room with not one but two bathtubs in it. Fanny thought it a wonder.

The servants still used a tin tub and water they heated over the open hearth fire. The men bathed on Tuesdays, the women on Thursdays.

Another example of the patchwork character of number twenty-three was the servants' quarters. Most of the houses on the square still provided their servants with sleeping quarters on the top floor of the house, and indeed the other female household workers in M. Monnard's household slept there. But Fanny slept on the subground level, in the former bedroom of the maître d'hôtel. The subground level was where the storage for the whole house was, the pantries and all the workings of the house. It also held the original kitchen. Fanny slept down there because she was the first one up in the mornings, to kindle the fire in the fireplace and make the coffee and walk over to Rue Vieille du Temple for the bread.

She was able to have this bedroom all to herself because M. Monnard had built a carriage house in the courtyard behind the tall, massive carved doors that opened out onto the Place. It housed a room for gardening supplies and one for harnesses, along with the two carriages—one little phaeton and a larger closed carriage—plus four horse stalls and the horses to go in them. The male members of the household staff had their own quarters over that carriage house. There was a barracks-style room, and a separate bedroom for the maître d'hôtel. The only one who didn't sleep there was Henri, the chef.

The second thing M. Monnard had built in the courtyard was a separate kitchen. Most households in Paris cooked on an open hearth in the fireplace, like the original kitchen inside number twenty-three. Normally, when the cook of a household wanted something roasted or baked, they took it to the bread baker down the street at the boulangerie and paid a small fee to have him perform that service. But M. Monnard was positive more and more families were going to want their own ovens at home. He believed building a separate structure to house the kitchen was the safest solution. No one wanted to go up in flames owing to an oven malfunction on the ground floor of a mansion. So, to Henri's great excitement, M. Monnard built an example of a modern kitchen to show off to his clients. Henri lived above this kitchen, in a big room under the rafters connected to the main floor by a corkscrew staircase.

So Fanny slept down next to the old kitchen, while Henri slept over the new one. It was just as well. If their rooms were nearer, Fanny was sure one of them would crawl into the other's bed more often than they did now. The fact neither was assigned sleeping quarters with the rest of the staff was what allowed their attraction to blossom.

Sexual relations were taboo among servants, reason for dismissal if they were discovered. There were no secrets within a household staff, however, and Fanny assumed everyone knew about their affair. She realized she giggled and smiled way too much when Henri was around. But she couldn't help it. Her job was not as important to her as the feelings she was having for the first time. She was eighteen. It was about time she fell in love. And she innocently trusted the other members of the household to keep their secret. Henri did, too.

Fanny returned home from her daily trip to the boulangerie, her hands full of bread and packages, but as soon as she opened the outer door, Henri grabbed the bread from her. "I can't believe you left without me," he scolded. They normally went together.

Fanny had her usual reactions to being around Henri: extreme discomfort, acute self-awareness, dizziness, tingling in various parts of her body, and the flushing of her cheeks. Henri was tall and lanky, with chestnut brown hair worn long, green eyes, and the most beautiful hands Fanny had ever seen. Fanny always told him he should be playing the piano with those hands instead of using the rolling pin and cleaver. "I thought you might still be exhausted from your weekend and I didn't want to wake you. When did you get home?"

Henri's expression changed. His eyes left Fanny for the first time and he turned and started walking toward the house. Fanny could feel a lie coming. "I don't know. I didn't look at a clock. It was almost dark. I fell asleep as soon as my head hit the pillow. Why?"

"Oh, I just wondered. I saw two men when I was coming home, arguing out in the middle of the square, and I could swear one of them came in here. I wondered whether you had seen him."

The moment when Henri should have replied came and went as they entered the house. He seemed to be searching for words. Fanny sensed his awkwardness and stopped what she was doing to regard him. But the arrival of the maid who attended the master and his wife broke the uneasy silence.

"Oh, there you are. The master is already up and wants his coffee, Fanny," Josee-Marie said with a little stamp of her foot. Josee-Marie was responsible for giving both the master and the mistress their morning trays.

Henri looked relieved to end the conversation. "I'll see you later. Don't forget we have a lesson this afternoon," he said as he put down the baguettes and sacks on the work-table and hurried out the door.

Fanny brewed the coffee. Paris was coffee mad. Coffee houses were where Parisian husbands went to see their friends, conduct business, read the newspapers. At first, wives complained about this new fad, but after several years, it was clear no one would give up their coffee and by that time women were enjoying it as well, and began to serve it at home.

Fanny ground the roasted coffee beans in a crank-operated grinder. She poured boiling water from the kettle that was always hanging on a hearth hook over the grounds, which she'd placed in a porcelain teapot. Then she cut several slices off one of the loaves of bread and placed them in a napkin-lined sliver basket. She fetched a small ramekin of butter out of one of the cool storage rooms, then put all of this on a large silver tray, along with a pot of honey, a small pitcher that she filled with milk warmed over the fire, and a bowl of the precious white sugar that the master favored.

Josee-Marie took the tray and paused at the doorway. "You might as well make another tray. I heard the mistress stirring," she said as she prepared to climb up to the master's suite.

And so went the morning. Fanny hurried from task to task, concentrating on the job in front of her but still trying to watch the rest of the kitchen, as Henri had taught her. She had a capon she was stewing over the hot part of the fire, her cast-iron pot with the bird next to the teakettle on the second hook. She also mixed up an unleavened barley bread that had a cake-like texture. She poured this thick batter in a greased Dutch oven and covered it, placing it in the back of the fireplace where the embers were low. And there were some green beans and zucchini squash that she had bought a couple of days before when the green grocer cart came around. She'd throw them in with the chicken in a while. They should be used up today.

Now she needed to make a cold dish for Henri, for dinner. She soaked and cleaned some leeks, and blanched them until the whites were tender. Then she made mustard dressing for them, whisking together some mustard from Burgundy with grape verjus and walnut oil. She dressed the leeks and let them set to absorb the flavors.

They had delicious tarts at the baker's, and Fanny had purchased one with cheese and chard. That was for the master's table, that and the leeks. The capon and vegetables were for the staff. And the barley bread was for the staff, too. It was much too coarse for the master and mistress but Henri said it was one of the best things Fanny baked. He said her crumb was beautiful. Fanny wasn't really interested in baking, but it was nice to be complimented anytime.

Henri cooked most of the dinner for the master and mistress and their table, with Fanny's help. Fanny cooked most of the dinner for the staff, which numbered eight adults and two boys about ten, who ate more than anyone. Fanny and Henri met every evening about five, after dinner was served, and they discussed the next day's menus, what the mistress and master had ordered, what was available at the markets, then Henri gave Fanny assignments. It was the best time of the day. Although they were rarely completely alone—the whole household staff wandered in and out of both kitchens all day—no one was really paying attention to them. Spending that time together, talking about food, looking at cookbooks and recipes Henri had collected, that was when Fanny had fallen in love, with food and Henri.

After the meeting for the next day, they went through the leftovers and discussed what would have to be made for supper. Usually they could make do with what was on hand, making soup for the staff out of odds and ends, and rearranging dishes for the master's table. The master and mistress ate simply at night unless they invited someone to supper after the opera, which they did often. The master loved the opera.

If there were guests, Fanny and Henri would come up with something fresh to put out for them. Except for special occasions, the staff did not serve supper; rather, the dishes were laid out in the salon or dining room in covered silver containers, along with bottles of wine, plates, and glasses.

The staff ate before and after the real meals, at noon or one, then they ate leftovers after dinner had been served for the master and mistress, around six or seven in the evening.

Fanny was almost ready for this first staff meal. She was just sugaring some peaches that she bought last week. She'd ripened them and had used the best ones for a peach melba for the master's table. The ones with brown spots she had peeled and cut up for the staff. M. Desjardins stuck his nose in the kitchen and she nodded. She knew he would ring the bell up on the ground floor, then step out in the courtyard and ring it again, so Henri and the driver could hear. Today they were eating outdoors, on a trestle table set up by the footmen and M. Desjardins just by the entry door. They could let any deliveries in and eat lunch at the same time. They had a couple of worn-out linen tablecloths they spread over the wooden boards for this purpose, ones with holes and stains that wouldn't do for the master's table anymore. They didn't send them to the laundry every time, using them over until they were too soiled. It was just fine for the staff.

Fanny had pulled apart the capon, discarding most of the bones. She put the meat on a platter and surrounded it with the vegetables. She had some marinated cucumbers and onions, the barley bread, and she'd also made a kind of a pudding with stale bread, cheese, and eggs. And then they had peaches for dessert. Vera, the second maid, had set the table with the old pewter plates and the scratched wine-glasses. M. Desjadins had already put out all the bottles of wine that had been opened but not finished in the last couple of days by the master and his family. That was what the staff normally drank unless there were no leftovers, and then they drank Beaujolais from a barrel the maître d'hôtel kept under lock and key in the wine cellar.

Fanny filled a pitcher with water and went out the delivery door to the courtyard. She put the water by the wine bottles so everyone could combine water and wine to their own liking, then took her place next to Henri at the table.

The household staff was seated according to their station. M. Desjardins, as maître d'hôtel, was at the head of the table. Henri, as the chef, sat at the other end. To Henri's right, Fanny was seated, and to her right was the scullery maid, Henriette, who had the lowest-ranked job in the house. She cleaned and scrubbed and lifted and moved from daylight to dusk. She was responsible for washing all the dishes as well, although Fanny tried to clean up as she went. Next to her was one of the two young boys who ran errands and did all the odd jobs around the house. His name was Simon. Next to Simon, on the left of M. Desjardins, sat the driver, Charles. He was responsible for the horses, carriages, and equipment, as well as driving the family about. Charles was stretched thin with all his responsibilities, and the two boys helped him more often than anyone else. On his right was Jules, the footman, who served at table, acted as handyman, and also rode on the carriage when the occasion warranted having a footman. Next to Jules was Nicholas, the other boy. Nicholas and Simon had originally been seated next to each other, as their lowly station warranted, but they bickered and pinched each other so much that M. Desjardins had separated them. Vera, the second maid, sat on Nicholas's right. Vera took care of the young Master Monnard, the son, and his family, who occupied the third floor of the house. Josee-Marie, the first maid, attended the master and mistress of the household, thus her place of status on Henri's left. That was the ten of them, all with as many duties as they could possibly accomplish in a day. Fanny thought them to be an average number of servants for a house on Place Royale. She knew the nobility had more, and some of the judges, who weren't paid terribly well, had fewer. Fanny couldn't imagine how they could get by with even one person less.

The dinner table conversation today had started with the Fête de la Fédération, which had invariably led to politics. Fanny's mind wandered as other people talked and ate, using their hands for emphasis. She looked around the table. They were a handsome group, well dressed and well fed. It wasn't such a disaster as her parents had thought, her wanting to be a cook.

"Fanny, this barley bread is delicious today," M. Desjardins said kindly.

"Thank you, monsieur," Fanny said, blushing.

"As a matter of fact," Henri said, looking at Fanny

proudly, "would you please make another for the master's table today? I was wrong about it not being elegant enough."

At that moment M. Monnard came through the small door cut in the porte cochere. M. Desjardins sprang to his feet, as did Josee-Marie.

"Sit down, sit down. What a good idea to eat out here today. There is a little breeze and we should take advantage of it. Monseiur, we will do the same, if you please."

"It will be my pleasure," M. Desjardins answered. He remained standing until M. Monnard had entered the house, then sat back down and turned to Jules. "Have the boys help you move this table over by the well and arrange the pots of roses around it. There is one guest along with the family today."

Fanny gulped down her last bite of chicken. "I'll excuse myself then and get to it," she said. M. Desjardins nodded at her in approval and she left the rest of the staff to dally a few more minutes over their wine.

TODAY, as soon as dinner was served at four, Fanny and Henri would disrupt their routine, as they did once or twice a week. They would go to have a lesson on cuisine across the square with Henri's mentor, Etienne de la Porte. Because he respected Henri, Etienne had agreed that Fanny could come along. Chefs from other houses were invited as well and some brought their most promising assistants. Among the household staffs around the Place Royale, it was prestigious to be included in this group of cooks. Fanny was flattered to be involved and she learned more about her craft just being around other cooks, hearing the questions they asked.

It was to one of these sessions they were headed now. Fanny wiped her forehead with a big white napkin as they walked. The subground kitchen was cool, with thick walls and no direct sunlight. The caves for both the wine and the dairy products were there as well as the meat storage. But it was July and the open fire had been roaring, and Fanny spent most of her time with her head bent over it. She felt limp.

"Chef Etienne's master has gone out of the country on business and his mistress and the children went to spend a few days with her sister and didn't require the services of their chef," Henri explained as they crossed the Place. Normally, they had their lessons on Sunday, on Chef's half day off. Today was Monday.

Henri looked as if he had just stepped out of a bath and the barbershop. He didn't appear to be hot and sweaty at all. Fanny wondered if she would ever get to the point where physical labor wouldn't show on her person.

Etienne was the chef of number six, where it was rumored that Cardinal Richelieu, who had lived at number twenty-one right after it was built, had dined and then hired the chef away from his host, the meal was that good.

The doors to the inner courtyard were open and Fanny and Henri stepped in. Etienne was sitting at a table set up in the yard, one of his assistants by his side. He saw Fanny and Henri and waved them over. Another one of Etienne's assistants brought a tray with an iced fruit drink, a carafe of wine, and another of water. Like M. Monnard, Etienne had devised a method of capturing rainwater on the roof of the house, but he had uses for it other than bathing. His cistern was attached to a pipe that drained it down near the kitchen door, and had a metal sieve on the spout to filter out leaves and other materials. Chef put this relatively clean water in shallow trays in the coldest cellar he had. For several months he was able to make ice this way and he kept it through the warmer months in his ice pit lined with burlap and straw.

Chef Etienne said you should never use the dirty ice from the Seine for any liquid refreshments. He said the refuse of Paris was floating in that water and it was barely fit to keep meat from spoiling.

Fanny's household bought their ice from Norway, where it was supposed to come from the mountains, not the cheaper ice cut from the Seine. Ship's transported big blocks of glacial ice down to Paris, then merchants stored it in ice houses and pits outside of the city, selling it to butcher shops, ice cream producers, and great mansions when their own meager ice supplies dwindled.

Fanny was flattered to be offered an iced beverage in July. There were lemon and orange slices floating in it. She poured herself a glass and took a sip, even though the other cooks who were joining them were still arriving and she supposed she was being rude. The water was sweet and tart at the same time, fragrant with citrus and, most important, cold. What a treat. She blotted her forehead once more with her napkin, then folded and tucked it neatly on her apron sash, as Henri had shown her.

"Henri, I have been waiting to hear about the feasts. Tell us everything," Chef Etienne commanded as soon as everyone had arrived.

Since Henri had been asked by his master to help with a special communal feast held at the Palais-Royal the day before the festival, his status in the neighborhood had gone up. In addition, the same team of chefs made a meal for the out-of-town participants at the Champ de Mars.

"The meal for the Assembly was easy. They absolutely wanted it to be as simple as possible. It couldn't resemble a banquet at Versailles by any stretch of the imagination. The whole idea was that men could be equal sharing a common meal."

"So, what did you prepare?" Etienne asked.

"We used the kitchens of all the cafés around the arcade of the Palais-Royal and roasted chickens. Then there was bread, cheese, and fruit. That was it."

"I hear there were thousands of people there just to watch," one of the other cooks said.

"That was the best part," Henri said, and he couldn't help giving a proud grin. "Someone said there were two thousand spectators. They all cheered when we came out with platters of the chickens."

"Did you carve them properly?" another asked.

"No, but we didn't leave them whole either so every set of fingers would have to touch them. We cut them apart in chunks and sliced the breast meat. It looked nice," Henri explained.

Etienne nodded approval. "What was difficult about the next day?"

Henri tilted his head. "The rain, but the main difficulty was the location. We made cauldrons full of a white bean ragout. It resembled a cassoulet without any meat in it. There was also mutton. They must have killed hundreds of sheep. The rotisseurs cooked them by the quarter on spits over wood fires that were so low, they were practically coals. They loaded the spits on the thirteenth, at midnight, and covered the fires with tenting when it rained. I didn't sleep at all that night, what with carrying all those beans to the parade grounds from the Palais-Royal. We had to be done in those kitchens by morning because the cafés knew they would be busy on the fourteenth, it being a national holiday. The bakers brought bread over, and we had pears and grapes all down the middle of the table. Not that it stayed looking nice for long. Those country boys must have marched to Paris without a penny to buy food."

Etienne was satisfied. "Mutton and white beans are a classic combination. At least the new regime will allow us to stick with the principles of cuisine. This is a good sign for us all, children."

There was murmuring among the young cooks around the table. They were all rightfully worried about their jobs. Other people certainly were losing theirs. In February 1790, religious orders had been abolished, and in June, hereditary titles were also abolished.

Etienne continued, "Here are the encouraging signs. This government is using the table and these communal feasts as a tool for reeducation. That is certainly much better than if they had taken the position that cuisine was just the detritus of a decadent society."

"Is that why we have been concentrating on making simple things like stocks?" Fanny asked. "So we won't be accused of being too grand?"

"No, we are making stocks because they are the foundation of all our sauces and soups. They are simple, yet essential. Without a good stock, everything that comes after will be tainted. How did everyone do with their chicken stock?"

The week before, all these eager young cooks had copied the recipe for chicken stock from Etienne's own collection of recipes, with the instructions to make it at their home kitchen sometime during the week and write down the exact steps they took and the results. Now, the head cook of each household brought out his notes about chicken stock and read them aloud. Fanny listened politely. She had participated in the whole stock-making process with Henri. The part she liked best was learning how to clarify the stock with eggshells and the whites. But this time of reviewing last week's assignment always made her restless, as she never got to be the one doing the reporting on the new recipe. She wanted to ask Etienne if those of them around the table who were not in charge of a kitchen yet could some week have the lead, but she hadn't dared. After all, Etienne had worked at Versailles. He still respected rank. The fact that he let mere assistant cooks sit in on these sessions was remarkable. And she had learned a great deal from listening to his philosophy on cooking, as she did from helping Henri with their assignments. So she kept her mouth shut.

Etienne glanced up at the sun moving down in the western sky. "Before I go on to the recipe for the veal stock, I just want to touch on the subject that is on all of our minds, what with the fête yesterday. It is important that Henri participated and that his master asked him to. It is a step forward that M. Monnard, who could be considered an enemy of the citizens for the beautiful hotels he has built for nobility and the very rich merchants, understood that this meal was a crucial part of the festivities and came forward to contribute Henri's talents. And Henri did not dismiss the food that he set out because it was simple. No, it was a rare chance for Parisian chefs to work together. The food they produced was honest. We must all be ready to show that our skills are not just used for the follies of the rich, that sharing a meal can be a significant political event. And remember, they can't do it without us. No one in Paris knows how to cook but the cooks."

The group laughed at that. They needed the reassurance. It was hard not to worry about the fate of their employers. And who was to say they wouldn't be punished or beheaded right along with the people they served?

There were rumors that the National Guard and the police had informants at the markets, riding the water carts, anywhere they could have access to the inner workings of aristocratic households. Even in houses where the staff had worked together for years, people were reticent to share their feelings openly about the current political situation.

Etienne stood up. "Now, I will go get the recipe for veal stock. Take out your paper and pens. And remember what we are doing. We are building up our knowledge. We are learning basic stocks. We are learning spice and herb mixtures and later we will learn sauces. These are tools that can be applied to whatever is seasonally available. That way we will never be defeated by the lack of a certain ingredient, because we will be able to transfer our knowledge to what we do have. I go now."

Fanny always did the copying of the recipes because her writing was better than Henri's. Henri had been illiterate when he arrived in Paris. He'd been born in Brittany and had done his first apprenticeship there. When he came to Paris at twenty, he already had been cooking for seven years. After he got to the city, he found out very quickly that cooks had to be literate in Paris. Everyone knew about the latest cookbooks. Reading and discussing the recipes was essential to proceeding up in the ranks of a kitchen. Henri went to his parish priest and asked for lessons, even if he had to learn with the children. That was five years ago. Now, his reading was very good. He had recently started a book on French history and he read several newspapers every day, in-

cluding the radical *L'Ami du Peuple,* written by the famous
Marat. But his writing was adequate at best. He could print
better than write but he took too long at it. He had explained all this to Fanny and told her he didn't want to be
teased in front of his peers.

Fanny, born a Parisian, was very good at both reading
and writing. She didn't mind a bit being the one to make
their copies of the recipes. She coveted the cookbooks themselves, although most of what Etienne passed on to them
was his own, not from another chef's work. She had one
cookbook of her own, Menon's *La Cuisiniere Bourgeoise.* Her
mother and father had given it to her on her sixteenth birth-
day, just a few weeks after she had proclaimed to them she
was going to be a chef.

As the young people were copying, Etienne would call
out hints for the execution of this veal stock. "It is impera-
tive to roast the bones first. Remember last week when I explained how toasting the walnuts will heat up the essential
oils in the nut and impart the aroma and taste to the surface? The same is true with the bones," or "You cannot skim
enough. Skim and then skim again. The impurities are in
that scum that comes to the top. Get rid of it!"

While those who were writing did so, the rest of the
group drank wine and talked in low tones. There were about
a dozen cooks and chefs who came to these sessions and ten
were present today. Six were now copying.

Even though the printed page was commonplace in
Paris, recipes were still often passed on by this means, one
chef copying another. Etienne encouraged everyone to write
down their own way of doing the recipes, along with keeping a journal of what they served every day of their professional life.

As they finished up, Etienne went around and shook the hand of each and every one of them. "I hope we can meet again this week. I will send word. Now go home, and tomorrow, roast your bones," he ordered as way of a dismissal.

Fanny and Henri walked back across the square with the other chefs, everyone dropping off as they came to their household. Closer to number twenty-three, Fanny saw her father's cart in front of their door, the words M. DELARUE, PÈRE ET FILS painted in gold leaf on the back. When Fanny and Henri stepped inside the courtyard, they heard voices. The door to the carriage house was open, and M. Monnard and Philippe Delarue were standing together, laughing.

Her father had the knack for making men above and below his own rank feel comfortable. The men who worked for him thought of him as a friend, and the men he worked for respected him. She had seen this all her life without knowing exactly what made her father different. It had just been in the last couple of years that she could articulate what it was that made him so popular among men. He trusted them to be honorable and he himself was trustworthy and honorable.

Now Fanny stuck her head in the barn and gave a little curtsey. Henri was behind her and he gave a quick bow of his head to the two men.

"Fanny, darling. And Henri. We were just discussing how to fix the broken ornamentation on this side." Philippe pointed at the carriage. "I think I've figured it out. M. Monnard tells me you go over to the marquis's chef for cooking lessons. He was at Versailles until the court left, yes? He must have tales to tell."

"Today it was Henri who told the stories, Papa," Fanny

boasted. "Henri cooked for the National Assembly on Saturday and the fête yesterday."

Philippe Delarue came over and shook Henri's hand. "That must have been a challenge. I saw the tables at the Champ de Mars. It surely was a big production."

Henri ducked his head. "Yes, well, it was an experience. And I thank M. Monnard for giving me the opportunity. He was the one who arranged it."

M. Monnard looked at Philippe Delarue and shrugged. "Who knows where our next commission will come from, eh, Philippe?"

M. Monnard often used Fanny's father on his jobs. Philippe Delarue brought his woodworking artistry to furnish the elaborate mansions M. Monnard built. They had worked together for years. That was how Fanny got her job: M. Monnard had mentioned to Philippe that he needed a new cook to assist his bright, young chef. Philippe said his daughter was looking for a position, that she had started cooking a year before and that he thought she was very gifted. M. Monnard took his word for it and hired Fanny, sight unseen. Fanny would always be grateful to both of them for that.

"Come say good-bye before you go, Father," Fanny said as she turned to leave the carriage house, Henri by her side.

"Fanny, I have something for you. Maurice, I'll send someone over tomorrow to take a cast from the other side of the carriage," Philippe said as he shook the hand of M. Monnard.

Henri touched Fanny on the hand softly. "Go on with your father. I'll start supper." He walked out and over to the new kitchen, the recipe in his hand.

Philippe Delarue put his arm around his daughter and they walked toward his cart.

"Papa, what happened to you yesterday? I waited at home as long as I could," Fanny said.

"It was madness. The traffic was terrible. It was hot. I drank too much and ate too little. The Champ de Mars was a sea of mud from the rain. But it was a glorious day, a day for Paris to remember, and the rest of France, too."

"The Bastille was fun, too. It was nice of M. Monnard to let us all have the day off."

"I think it was mandatory for anyone who wants to keep his head on his shoulders," Philippe said grimly.

Fanny was startled by her father's comment. Who would know, one way or the other, if a master allowed his household to celebrate the Fête de la Fédération?

They walked to the cart, and her father reached into the back and lifted out a box. He presented it to Fanny. "I got this at the street market this morning. One of the fellows said he bought it off a ship that had just come back from Turkey." He slid the top of the box open sideways. "It's a spice box."

Fanny took the box. "I've never seen anything like it. Look at these carvings," she said, examining the box all around. It was covered with carvings of women and food. On one side there was a woman with a big knife, ready to kill a goat or sheep, the carving making it unclear which animal it was. On the other sides were women bearing fruit, holding a sheaf of wheat, stirring a cauldron very much like the one Fanny stirred. Inside the box there were sticks of cinnamon, cardamom, cumin seeds, a nutmeg, some bay leaves, and some dried herbs. "Oh, Father, it's perfect for me."

Philippe smiled with pride in his eyes. "That's what I thought. Old Jean-Baptiste bargained for it to be thrown in with some pieces of wood he bought for inlay off this ship. He put it out at that market stall he and his men keep to sell wood they don't need or a cabinet that didn't turn out quite right."

Fanny laughed. "Oh, yes. The mistakes. Sounds like the furnishings of our house."

"And we sat in better chairs and slept in better beds than most, didn't we?" her father asked, his question more of a statement.

Fanny hadn't meant to make fun of their household furnishings. They, like the majority of the families in their neighborhood, had magnificent furniture that had gone slightly wrong so it couldn't be sold. The pieces were a mix of styles and periods, but they were all quite grand.

It was only the fathers and mothers who understood that each piece represented a costly mistake. The chairs and tables and armoires in their homes signified lost profit in the shape of a clumsy carving or crooked inlay. Of course, some of these mistakes were sold at the street market to recoup the cost of the materials. But that usually came after the family home was nicely furnished. If a better chair or table came up for grabs, it would take the place of a lesser piece. The lesser chair or table would then be hauled outside and sold at the weekly market. The faubourg St. Antoine, not only because it was a privileged zone but because of the nature of the craftsmen there, was a prosperous place.

"Our house is beautiful and so is this box. I'll treasure it, Papa."

Philippe Delarue blushed. "My pleasure, little one. Just

take care, Fanny. It is a dangerous time to be alive," he said and climbed up on his cart with a graceful movement.

Fanny tried to read her father's face as she watched him pull away. What had made him say that today? The dangerous times had started months ago.

Fanny turned and took her new gift inside number twenty-three.

CHAPTER THREE

"I just wondered, Chef, why you never mention Versailles or the court?"

It was early on an August morning, around six, and Fanny found herself with Etienne de la Porte on a *carrosse à cinq sols,* one of the five-penny carriages that ran preestablished routes throughout Paris. They were the only two passengers.

"I am only too happy to share my knowledge of cuisine with you young people. But we are brought together by geography, not friendship. We work on the same square and are serious about our profession. I do not truly know you, or Henri, or any of the other cooks. It is better to talk less of that time, especially when one does not know the politics of others. You never know when a zealous citizen will misunderstand an innocent remark and turn you in to the National Guard."

Fanny understood that but chose to ignore it. "Were you

there last October when the women of Paris marched on the court?"

Etienne de la Porte seemed to forget the silence he had recommended just a moment ago. His eye sparkled with the excitement of having a story to tell. "Yes, I'm afraid I was. I have never been more frightened for my life. There was a blood lust in the crowd—no, they were a mob—that was unforgettable. Even if you agreed with the basic demand, that the king should stop living in an unnatural environment and accept reality, the method was reprehensible."

Fanny thought about her mother and felt the need to defend her. "I'm proud of the women of Paris for doing what the politicians couldn't."

Etienne did not take offense. He looked at her with good humor in his eyes. "Yes, but those women can't afford a cook, child. We must hope for a compromise that will keep us employed."

Fanny thought of her mother again, as a member of the mob that had so frightened Etienne. She decided to move on to other matters.

"Chef, it's just the two of us here. Can't you tell me just a few little things about Versailles?"

A look of suspicion crossed the chef's eyes and face. What was this little one fishing for? "Like what?"

"How many people did you cook for?"

Relieved that her curiosity was about cooking, Etienne smiled without meaning to. "Three to five thousand on any given day."

The large number shocked Fanny. She knew there were lots of people at court, but she would have guessed one thousand at the most.

The chef looked out the carriage window and his eyes narrowed. Fanny imagined he saw the great kitchen of Versailles in his mind. Etienne solemnly talked as he did when he was teaching. "The Maison-Bouche was responsible for this operation, this herculean endeavor. There were seven departments and a staff of five hundred, and that didn't count the servers."

"What department did you work in?" Fanny asked.

"I started out feeding court officials, then I moved up to Le Gobelet."

"I've never heard of that. What did you do?"

"Le Gobelet has, or I guess you should say had as it is greatly reduced now, two departments. Each one had a chef and twelve assistants. One section dealt with wine, water, liqueurs, coffee, and ices. The other section, the one I worked in, was in charge of bread, salt, linens, and fruit. Then I was promoted to la Cuisine, where we cooked for the royal table. We also were in charge of the tableware."

"So you were in the most important department," Fanny stated.

"They were all important. If the court was not well provisioned, they complained incessantly," Etienne said.

"But you fed the king."

Etienne laughed. "Yes, I did that. And the queen, too."

"Is she as horrible as they say?"

"I have never known any other queen, but I suspect this one is very much like the rest. Difficult."

Who was the most difficult?"

"The king's brother. Everyone at court called him Monsieur. Oh, I could tell you some stories about him."

Fanny waited a minute, hoping Chef *would* tell her some

stories, but none was forthcoming. Etienne just stared out the window, daydreaming, she assumed. She decided to move on.

"So why did you go to work for the marquis instead of moving to the Tuileries with the king?"

Etienne turned slightly in his seat, his eyes assessing Fanny. Then he looked away. "After the march of the women, I realized it wasn't worth losing my head to serve the king and cook at his pleasure. I saw the king's guards torn apart by that mob, most of them women. And because of the sheer chaos that day, things happened, things that normally wouldn't occur. I saw a surprising number of people behave less than honorably. I don't want to be in that position ever again."

Fanny shifted uncomfortably. The idea of her mother as a part of a murderous crowd was not something she liked to picture. But Fanny got the impression that Chef Etienne was not talking only about the women of Paris.

Ever since she was a child, Fanny had imagined all kinds of wild, romantic, scandalous scenarios about the court, especially the court at Versailles. She was replaying some of these imagined scenes in her head when they arrived at their destination. Could Chef Etienne have been carrying on a wild romance with a lady-in-waiting? She glanced across the carriage at him. It would be hard to picture an elegant woman of the noble class locked in an embrace with the portly, balding fellow sitting across from her. She smiled and coughed daintily to prevent from laughing out loud at her own vivid imagination.

The carriage stopped at the entrance to Les Halles.

"Thank you for telling me just a little about your former job, Chef."

"We will meet soon. Then the talk will be of veal stock and sauces," Etienne said as he jumped out and extended his hand to Fanny for her to climb out.

Fanny wanted badly to follow him through the market but she was afraid to presume on their slight friendship. Most chefs established relationships with various vendors whom they depended on for special ingredients or who set aside the best of the lot for them, whether it be a turkey, a new cheese, or tiny young vegetables. This was not information they wanted to share with other cooks. But Fanny was encouraged by their talk in the carriage, and she was about to ask Etienne for his tour of the market.

Just at that moment, they were interrupted by a priest who stepped out of the crowd suddenly and took Etienne by the elbow. He nodded solemnly at Fanny, then whispered in the chef's ear. Whatever he said, it ended any possibility of Etienne spending more time with Fanny. His look at her, while listening to the priest, was a combination of irritation, dismissal, and pleading. He was trying to tell her something but was too frightened or surprised by the man to really communicate. Fanny thought the priest crude and ill-kempt. Her imagination, stirred up now and working overtime, wondered if he really was a priest.

"Thank you, again," Fanny said with a bow of the head that she hoped showed the proper respect as the two men walked off together, ignoring her, and were swallowed up into the whirlwind of activity that was Les Halles.

The central market was a great example of how Paris was timeless, yet always changing. It had been established by Philippe-Auguste in 1181, and since that year, there had been some kind of central market on the spot. But the rules and regulations had changed dozens of times. The types of items that could be sold were changed, were moved, were taxed, were raised or lowered in status.

The traffic leading in and out of the market was always horrible. The smells, made worse by a large common grave at the cemetery next door, were always pungent. And the women of Les Halles, the ones who worked in the stalls, were always independent minded and proud of it. They added to the general cacophony with their calls.

The bulk of the food consumed in Paris every day had to be brought from outside. Oh, a few carp and pike were caught in the Seine and some of the convents that had gardens sold off extra produce. But 650,000 people lived in Paris. There were no wheat fields to harvest to make their bread, no dairies to provide milk and cheese, no cattle or sheep grazing in the city limits to slaughter for meat.

When there was a bad harvest, Paris suffered. When there was bad weather and the farmers couldn't get through on the roads, she suffered as well. Then there was the problem of storage. Wheat could go bad, milk could sour, and meat could rot. The central market was a sign that humans could overcome all these obstacles and then two greater ones: the greed of men and the stupidity of bureaucracy.

Without thinking anything about harvests, transportation, weather, taxes, rules, or regulations, Fanny was simply amazed by the market. She could wander through the aisles, watching and listening, for hours. But not today. She didn't have time to tarry. She had come for the baby lettuces and the cheese. This was Friday, the day that the farm woman from Passy came every week with tiny young lettuces she nursed in a greenhouse. The woman had feathery frisee, the ancient variety deer tongue, and Fanny's personal favorite, red oak. Each variety, and there were many, was brought to market in a shallow box, still in the soil it had been grown in. That kept the lettuce alive and still growing throughout the week, as Henri and Fanny just cut off the amount they needed. Fanny bought two boxes, one of the red oak and one of green leaf, and called for a porter so she wouldn't have to lug them around.

The next stop was the cheese aisle, where she ran into Chef Etienne, without the priest, who gave her a little nod without interrupting his negotiations with the Roquefort cheese monger. She bought a whole large Brie—Madame loved Brie—and some goat cheese, then moved to the butter. She chose a pale yellow block from Brittany, which she knew Henri favored over Normandy as it was his home. She also bought a butter cake and was ready to hand them over to the porter when her concentration was broken.

Down at the end of the aisle, coming toward her, was the man she had seen at the Fête de la Fédération and then later that same day at the Place Royale, the handsome one with the crinkly smile. Fanny was surprised that she was actually glad to see him again. This time he wasn't smiling, rather looking straight ahead with an angry expression on his face. He was striding purposefully toward her, looking left and right into each stall. She fully intended to stop him and ask him how he knew her name. She would put her hand out and she would be touching him, he was going to be that close.

But the handsome stranger stopped at the Roquefort stall, the same one Chef Etienne was standing in. The man said something to her teacher, then grabbed his shoulder. They drew close to each other and were talking rapidly. It was too far away and the market too noisy for Fanny to overhear anything but she could tell they were having an argument of some kind. She tried to read their lips, but her porter, who had loaded up her purchases, was asking her where they were headed next. Reluctantly, she told him "eggs" and moved away, following his cart.

While there was always human intrigue at the market, you could not stop progress or block an aisle to observe it.

Before she was ready to take the *cinq* home, Fanny had added two chickens from Bresse and some quail to her purchases, along with the eggs. She was supervising the loading of her supplies in the carriage when she saw the man again, briefly moving through a cross-aisle, and this time he was with the priest, deep in conversation. Fanny felt her pulse quicken. How were these three men connected?

She wanted to run after them, but that would not be ladylike and she did not have the time for it so she resisted the impulse. She could always ask Chef about him, the next time they met. Then she would at least know his name. She tipped the porter and headed home.

"HENRI, come quickly. There's trouble." It was Jules, the footman, calling into the dark kitchen.

Fanny awoke with a start. She turned toward Henri but he was not there. His side of the bed was empty.

"Henri, I need you," Jules said, and he walked a few steps into the room, calling up the steps. Fanny tried to stay as still as she could so Jules would go away. She should not be here.

When Fanny came to Henri's bed, which she did more often than he came to hers because he had more privacy, she loved to fall asleep beside him, pretending it was their honest right to be together. She so wanted to spend the whole night with him. It was Henri who usually was the responsible man, who woke Fanny up after an hour or so, pushing her out the door with a kiss. And Fanny appreciated that, she truly did. She knew she was the one who would be in trouble if they were caught. She would lose her position if anyone did, not Henri. And if that happened, if she were fired for having sex with her chef, her father would be humiliated in front of a colleague. That worried Fanny most of all; to disappoint her father would be the worst. But none of this could keep Fanny out of Henri's bed. She would walk off a cliff to be with him, and she felt sure he would do the same for her. But now, where was he?

"I'm looking for you, Chef," Jules mumbled as he stomped out of the kitchen, slamming the door behind him. Fanny waited a few seconds to make sure Jules was gone, then jumped up and felt around for her clothes in the dark. As she was dressing, she heard voices outside in the courtyard. She could make out M. Desjardins, Jules, and a child's voice, Nicholas, she thought. Fanny grabbed her boots and hurried down the stairs, just as Henri, rushed in the door, panting.

"Where have you been?" Fanny whispered as loud as she could.

"I just went outside to relieve myself and all of a sudden, the courtyard was full of people so I hid behind the carriage house until I figured out they weren't coming to get you to burn you at the stake," he teased as he pulled Fanny toward him, kissing her neck until she squealed.

"Stop it, they'll hear me," Fanny said as she slipped her arms around his neck and tried to pull him closer for a kiss.

He bounced away and up the stairs. "I have to get some pants on and go see what the devil everyone was yelling about. They went to M. Desjardins's office. You stay here until I tell you it's clear," he called down.

The maître d'hôtel's office was right across the hall from her bedroom so it was impossible for her to go back to bed right now. She sat down on one of the chairs pushed up to a worktable and crossed her arms, putting her head down on the table, trying to remain quiet and be patient. Henri galloped down the stairs, ruffling her hair as he passed. "Stay here, I'll be back soon," he said and was gone.

Fanny was vaguely curious about why Jules needed Henri and what was going on, but mostly she was sleepy. She almost fell asleep again with her head bowed down on the table. She would have if Henri hadn't burst back in the door.

"Fanny," he whispered. "I'm going across the square. Wait a few more minutes then the Monsieur will be out of his office."

Fanny could hear a new tenor in Henri's voice. There was fear and excitement and anger mixed together. "What's the matter, darling?"

"It's Chef Etienne. He's been murdered."

CHAPTER FOUR

So now Fanny was walking by herself toward a scene of violence in the middle of the night, imagining all sorts of terrible things.

About halfway to number six, she realized she should have cut through the middle of the square. Instead, she was walking under the arcade, a shadowy mysterious path on any night, especially when one was on the way to a murder scene. The vaulted arches of the arcade reminded her of a convent or monastery. Soft currents of wind moved the lanterns in random patterns and unexplainable rhythms. Fanny was sure she saw figures passing under the arcade far down the way, but there was never anyone there when she came closer. She was perspiring as she did over the ovens in the heat of day, her heart thumping wildly.

Why didn't she return to her room and hear all about it in the morning, as most young women would have? She had no idea what she would learn by seeing for herself, but because they had shared a ride this morning to the market, she felt an obligation to the man. Etienne de la Porte was no longer just a teacher or fellow cook, an icon because of his knowledge and experience at court. He had become human in her eyes on that ride to Les Halles, and she had seen and heard enough to believe that Chef had some secrets. He was a far more complex person to Fanny today than he had been before. So she wanted to do something more for him than "tut-tut" about his death over coffee tomorrow. She was sure that Henri felt the same way, and probably Etienne's colleagues at number six did as well. Otherwise no one outside of their household would have known of this death until the next day.

The outer doors to number six were open and there was a scene of considerable confusion in the courtyard. Most of the household staff and a dozen of the neighbors, mainly servants like Henri and Jules and M. Desjardins, were milling around in dazed circles, murmuring condolences to each other, or gossiping about why and how this might have happened.

Etienne's body had fallen close to the outer doors that led to the arcade. It looked as though he had answered the door and then been stuck down. A large stone pot was overturned next to his body and there was broken glass on the paving stones.

"So, there was noise," Fanny said.

Besides Henri and Jules, the footman who had fetched them and the four assistant cooks who worked for Etienne, the maître d'hôtel of the house and two of the maids were within earshot. When Fanny made her proclamation, no one was actually paying any attention to her, but the maître d'hôtel heard what she said, being a master at listening to several conversations at once.

"You there, Henri's assistant. What do you mean, so there was noise?"

"Well, you must have heard it. This stone urn must weigh two hundred pounds. It had to make a terrible racket when it went over. And something broke." Fanny leaned down and picked up the stub of a candle. "Maybe a lantern with glass panels, maybe that was what he was carrying. He heard someone at the door or he was waiting out here for someone. They pushed him against the urn and it fell over, or they hit him and knocked the lantern out of his hands. Or both," Fanny said excitedly. She liked putting the pieces of the puzzle together.

The maître d' raised one eyebrow and glanced at the overturned urn and the shattered glass. "Well, aren't you the observant one? Yes, there was considerable noise, but when I didn't hear a human voice cry out, I thought a stray cat had wandered in and knocked something over. I was putting on suitable clothes before I came downstairs. By that time your own M. Desjardins had discovered the body."

At that moment, M. Desjardins stepped over to his peer and Fanny.

"Monseiur, how did you find Chef?" Fanny asked, completely overstepping her status as assistant cook to ask questions of the man who ran her household.

"I was out for my usual midnight stroll," M. Desjardins explained, still too shocked by what he found to tell Fanny it was none of her business. Fanny mentally filed the information about the nightly walk for later. She would have to remember not to go gallivanting where she shouldn't be at midnight. "As I passed number six, the door to the court-yard was ajar. Never before has it been so. This indicated either someone forgot their duties to lock up or someone had made an entry or exit without authorization. Naturally, I pushed the door open and found Chef lying here. I ran to get Paul just as he was on his way to investigate the noise." He gazed down at Etienne sadly.

"Poor man. I wonder if he was killed with one of his own knives?" Fanny asked no one in particular.

"What makes you ask that?" M. Boigne, the maître d'hô-tel of this house, inquired suspiciously.

"You must have already figured out that he was stabbed by all the blood on his chest. I don't see the knife, though, not that that means it's back in the kitchen. I guess he could have been shot, but again, the noise . . ."

Now the man was intrigued. He grabbed a lantern, bent over the body, and squinted, straining to see. Several lanterns had been set out in the courtyard but it was still the dark of night. "I would think there would be a smell of gun-powder if that were the case. And yes, the sound of a gun-shot."

Fanny's bent over near the maître d'hôtel, her face close to his in the lantern light. "It seems there are lots of little rips in his nightshirt, which could have been made with a knife. I would surmise they correspond to wounds in his skin. A gunshot would have made a round hole, wouldn't it?"

The maître d' straightened up. "I do not know. I've never had a murder before in one of my houses. Death, of course. The older members of the family are bound to die. I've even had a master struck down in his prime. His heart just stopped beating and he fell over, dead at forty-one. And it goes without saying that I have lost many small children, and newborn infants. But murder, no. This is a first."

Fanny looked around fearfully. "Do you think the killer is still here inside your compound? What if he wasn't meaning to kill the chef and just did that to get in the house? What if he's waiting in the house somewhere for one of the rest of you, or came to kill your master because he's a noble? Oh, but your master is away, is he not?"

"Yes, thank God. He will not be amused at the inconvenience of having his chef killed. I'm going to have to replace Etienne as fast as I can. As for your theory, I have the carriage driver and the other footman going through the house right now. They are armed with guns and clubs."

Henri walked up. "Are the police coming?"

M. Boigne snorted. "The police and the night watch have many duties that they perform more or less proficiently here in Paris. They patrol the streets, fight fires, maintain the prisons, regulate prices, and even handle passports. They provide wet nurses for the foundlings and ring the bells in the morning when the waste wagon is coming. They do not solve crimes that do not have an obvious solution. I called the priest. Poor Etienne needs to receive whatever blessings are available to him."

Fanny found this little man odious. His chef has just been found stabbed to death inside the doors of the household he manages, and he gives a lecture on the strengths and weaknesses of police in Paris life.

Suddenly the two who had searched the house reappeared in the courtyard, shaking their heads. All the men went over to them, eager to hear what they had found. They swore there were no killers lurking in the shadows or under the beds.

As they were relating the details of the search to the rest of the group, Fanny knelt down by Chef Etienne's body again, alone. This time she noticed his right hand was closed tight, perhaps around something. His left hand was loose by his side, palm up, fingers splayed. She glanced up quickly. No one was paying her any mind, so she took a deep breath and touched his right hand gently. His fist was tightly closed in death. Fanny pried the fingers open with some difficulty and found a metal object. She grasped it quickly, not taking time to examine it, and slipped it into her own pocket. She rationalized this rather dubious act by saying to herself that the maître d'hôtel had proclaimed there would be no police investigation. So if anyone was going to discover what had happened to the chef, it would have to be her. Whatever Etienne had been clutching, and Fanny hoped it would be a clue, would most likely be dropped on the pavement of the courtyard and forgotten if she didn't "rescue" it. She would take it home and examine it. If it was meaningful, she would tell M. Desjardins. After all, he discovered the body, which gave him some authority in the situation. Fanny stood up and joined the rest of the group. A maid was coming toward Etienne's body with a sheet to cover him.

All the household staff was outdoors by now. Those who hadn't come out before had fled their beds when the men started searching in every room for the culprit. A few of the women were crying softly, both out of fear for their home being invaded and for the loss of their colleague.

Fanny put her hand on Henri's arm. "I'm going home now. I'll see you in the morning."

"Don't think about this anymore, love. I'll be along soon. Poor Etienne."

"Poor him and poor us, for losing him," Fanny said and gave Henri's arm a little squeeze. She said her good-byes to the maître d'hôtel and the cooks that she knew. This time she walked across the empty square, looking both ways often. She wasn't sure walking in the open was any better than under the arcade. Now she was convinced someone was watching her from the darkness around the square.

"It's your imagination," she said to herself out loud as she walked, glad to hear her own voice. The square was so silent, as she was sure it always was at this time. A passerby wouldn't know that someone had slipped into one of the houses on this night and stolen a life. Fanny hurried in the door to number twenty-three and then quickly on to her room.

Fanny had two advantages over the other female household staff, although sometimes she wished her bedroom wasn't separated from them. She had a private room, thus making it possible for her to sneak out to meet Henri, and she could light a candle. The women could not have candles on the third floor. M. Monnard felt this was a necessary fire prevention measure, so once they went to bed, they were consigned to the dark. She, down off the kitchen, was able to light a candle or two in her room. This time she lit only one, just to quickly examine what the chef had been clutching in his hand. She dug it out of her pocket and felt a little surge of excitement when she identified it. It was a signet ring of some sort. It would take the daylight and a magnifying glass to really tell what it was.

She slipped the ring into her clothing chest and then blew out the candle. As she took off her dress and adjusted her chemise, she thought she heard footsteps right outside. "It's just the Monsieur, going into his office for something," she told herself and pulled down the covers on her bed. Something fell on the floor from the top of the bed with a loud clatter. Fanny was unpleasantly surprised by the noise and jumped in bed, pulled up the sheet, then felt around on the floor to see what had made such a bang. When she found what it was, she laughed at her frayed nerves. It was the spice box her father had given her the other day.

Fanny had a clear image in her mind of placing that box on top of the chest when she brought it into her room and she didn't remember moving it to her bed. Why had it been there tonight?

"I'M telling you, someone was in my room," Fanny insisted again. She had tried to explain to Henri about the spice box being out of place but he was totally preoccupied and morose. Fanny knew he was thinking about Etienne's death, and she understood, but he was doing more harm than good in the kitchen. She had rescued a veal roast that had almost burned up as Henri moped around. She finally just took over cooking dinner, adding a turnip gratin, baby artichokes, and a rabbit stew to the veal roast. She didn't mind. It gave her a chance to work in the new kitchen alongside Henri even if he was not at his best. It also gave her an opportunity to talk over the events of the last few days.

That was the part that wasn't working so well. Fanny had expected Henri to understand how significant it was that the now dead Etienne had argued just yesterday with the same stranger she'd seen repeatedly in the last few weeks. She'd expected him to throw his arm around her for protection when she said someone had been in her room and riffled her things. What she got instead was a series of grunts, a

few repetitions of "Are you sure?" and a general lack of enthusiasm for anything Fanny said. She decided not to mention the ring right now. He would probably be angry she
had touched the corpse or that she had technically stole
something.

So she tried a different tack. "My poor darling. You lost
your teacher and I'm ranting about how someone is lurking
around in my room," she said and threw her arms around
Henri's neck, pressing her breasts into his chest and kissing
his cheek.

For the first time Henri looked as if he had heard Fanny.
"I'm sorry. I've been in a daze. What spice box are you talking about?"

"The one my father gave me the other day. I don't think
you've seen it. I put it in my room."

"So you have this box and you put it away and then . . ."

"And then when I came home from seeing the chef, or the
body," Fanny looked down in confusion. When did a person
become just a body? "I didn't notice the box when I had the
candle lit, then when I pulled down the covers, something
crashed to the floor. I got in bed, fast, it kind of scared me,
and then I felt around on the floor and I found the box. It
was not on that bed when I left my room, I'm sure."

Henri looked mildly irritated at her scattershot way of
telling things, but she did have his attention at last. "So you
think someone was looking for the box?"

"Could be. They could have heard me coming in,
dropped the box, and ran away. Or maybe they were looking
for something else and they just moved the box in the process. I put it on top of my chest." Fanny had a large chest of
drawers and a mirror that her father had asked M. Monnard's permission to bring to the house for her. Most of the

staff had simple two-drawer chests and one mirror for a whole roomful of people, and they had teased Fanny about her papa moving in furniture for her.

"There's a third option. One of the maids could have come looking for you, picked up the box to examine, and put it down on the bed."

Fanny shook her head. "It was dark before I came to you. After the master's supper. No one in our household would come looking for me at ten or eleven at night. And if they did, it would have been too dark to see the box. I think I know who it was." She hadn't known she was going to say that.

"Who?"

"Do you remember the day after the Fête de la Fédération when I asked you if you had been out in the square talking, no, arguing with someone?"

"Not really," Henri said, his demeanor shifting. He looked as if he wanted to get away.

"That day, when I was with my mother, a man almost tripped over us, or rather his prostitute did, or at least that's what Mother said, that she was a prostitute. Later when I was coming home, he was here in the square, arguing with someone who went in our door, I swear it. And he said my name; he said, 'Good evening, Fanny.'"

Henri walked away and started chopping some fennel. "There were thousands of people. You could have gotten two different men confused."

Fanny flared. She wasn't used to Henri not accepting what she said without question. "No. I know it was him. And I saw him a third time at Les Halles. But let's just stop trying to talk about it. You can't think of anything but Chef right now."

Henri walked over to Fanny with a miserable expression on his face. "I just can't get the picture of his body lying there out of my mind. It's the first time in my life someone I know has died violently. I guess that makes me naïve."

Fanny grabbed his shoulders and clung to him. "No, it was terrible. I saw his body all night long, when I closed my eyes. It was as though it was burned onto the insides of my eyelids. But the other things, the strange man, someone in my room, they're bothering me, too. I don't feel safe. After all, the man was arguing with Etienne. He could have . . ." Fanny's voice trailed off. Even as suspicious as she currently was, she didn't really believe this strange man had come in the dead of night to Place Royale to stab Chef Etienne. But then, someone had.

"The man isn't after you, or Etienne either," Henri said as he sank to a kitchen stool and put a hand on his forehead. "I didn't want to tell you this. I was the one talking to that man in the square that night. I hated lying to you but he swore me to silence. The man is a police inspector. His assignment is to bring the revolutionaries under control. He's after your mother."

CHAPTER FIVE

IT was hours later and Fanny and Henri still hadn't had a chance to talk. Right after Henri's dramatic proclamation about the police inspector, M. Desjardins had arrived at the kitchen with news of the master's schedule for the next few days, plus the fact that four more guests would be at dinner today. Then he related all the rumors about Chef Etienne's murder that he had been able to pick up during the morning.

The Place Royale was like a noisy, confused tangle of carts, mules, horses, carriages, water wagons, waste removal wagons, deliverymen, vendors, repairmen, laundry pickups, messengers, and all the stewards, maids, carriage drivers, footmen, cooks, and maids who attended to them. Although the square looked large when it was empty, when thirty-six households were functioning and the masters were in residence, the space filled up fast with the comings and goings of the necessities of daily life. It was also a great place to get scraps of news and gossip from the other households. If a husband and wife had a loud argument at 10 P.M., by 10 A.M. the next morning the whole neighborhood knew about it.

"They say it had to do with the wife of a viscount he had dealings with in Versailles. But that's rubbish. Etienne was much too old and fat to cuckold a viscount successfully. Maybe he gambled. He could have lost money gambling, perhaps to someone at court. I remember hearing the nobles at Versailles loved to engage the help in cards and take every sou of their hard-earned pay," the maître d'hôtel had suggested cynically.

Fanny had diverted Henri's attention away from the maître d'hôtel after that remark. She wasn't sure Henri wouldn't try to defend Etienne's honor, he had been so emotional concerning the chef this morning. She'd feigned a little spill of a pot of boiling water, slopping some water on the tile floor. Henri had yelled at her to be more careful and they had proceeded with the day, the conversation about the mysterious stranger delayed until sometime in the future. But now, it was after dinner and the master and his family were all going out for the whole evening. Henri and Fanny were pretty much done for the day.

The scullery maid had just finished the dishes and was proceeding to mop the floor. "Let's go outside so she doesn't have to work around us," Fanny suggested, tugging on Henri's arm. The courtyard was still hot but at least there was a tiny breeze. The courtyard was bare dirt but they had an herb garden and some beautiful rosebushes, as well as two twisted cypress trees by the entrance, all in pots. Fanny walked over and pinched the blossoms off the top of the thyme and Henri got them each a drink of water from the well.

Many houses in the neighborhood had their own wells but there was the constant fear that they would turn foul. Then they would have to buy their water again from the water wagons. But for the time being, number twenty-three had a good supply of water, cool and fresh tasting.

Nicolas and Simon were in charge of filling up all the water receptacles. There were large copper containers, lined with tin, with a spigot for pouring, one in each kitchen. There was another big container for water on each floor that the maids used to fill decanters for the bedrooms, and one in each of the salons and dining rooms. The boys also filled the water tanks behind the English-style flush toilets. Sometimes this had to be done dozens of times a day. The convenience of water supplied to various parts of the house kept the boys busy.

Henri liked to remove the cover on the well and draw up a bucket himself. He filled two cups from the bucket, then took his napkin, and Fanny's, and wet them down, and finally with a cupped palm he splashed water on his face. When Fanny had finished her pruning, she joined him, both sitting on stools by the one chestnut tree that had been allowed to remain in the courtyard.

Henri handed Fanny her water, then slipped the wet napkin around her neck and tied it loosely. "That should help cool you down."

"You avoided talking to me all day, Henri," Fanny snapped. "You can't tell someone an absolutely horrible story, then go on about your business without another word about it."

Henri sipped his water. "What do you want to know?"

"Who is the man? What does he want with my mother?"

"He would not tell me his name."

"Then how do you know he is really a police inspector?"

Henri dipped his head. "I'm sure, Fanny. You just have to believe me on this."

Fanny stood up. "And my mother?"

"He came up to me at the market one day, at Les Halles. I was with Etienne. The man asked us who worked with Fanny Delarue."

"And then?"

"And I said I did. He asked if I had ever met Martine Delarue. I said I had not but I had met your father. He asked if I ever discussed the Bastille or the march on Versailles with you."

"And you said my mother had gone to Versailles?" Fanny flared defensively.

"No, Fanny. I said we had no time for politics. And Chef Etienne stood up for us. He said cooks were not political, that we worked for who paid us, that our days were full and we were the ones most affected by the price of bread but the last to complain about it. Then the inspector threatened him."

Fanny wiped a trickle of sweat rolling down her cheek. Even with the water and the wet rag, she was burning up, more now than when she'd been leaning over the fire cooking.

"What did he say to Chef Etienne?"

"He turned to him and said something like, 'I'm going to look into your affairs next, Etienne de la Porte. There is something wrong with the way you left Versailles.'"

"What did Chef do?"

"Etienne shrugged and walked away from him. It was impressive. He wasn't afraid at all. He said, 'You must do your job and I must do mine. We go to buy cheese now.'"

"When did you see the inspector again?"

"Fanny, I never talked to him again but I spotted him all the time, here in the square, or at Les Halles mostly. He followed you sometimes. That's what we were arguing about on the day of the Fête de la Fédération."

Fanny slumped back down on the stool with a whoosh of her skirts. "Tell me."

"I was coming home and I saw him out in the square. He said he'd seen you with your mother, that she was one of the people who he was sure had murdered the king's guards at Versailles and also robbed the place. He said there was valuable property that went missing after that weekend. Especially from the queen's bedroom. He also said it was just a matter of time until he charged her."

"No."

"You said we were arguing, and we were. I said he must leave you alone, that you had nothing to do with whatever your mother might have done."

Fanny hid her face in her hands. "Do you think Chef Etienne's death could be connected to this man?"

Henri reacted defensively, but not with great conviction. "No, of course not. If I believed that, then you and your mother could be in danger. No doubt a thief trying to get in the house killed the chef. It has to be a simple accident."

"Liar," Fanny spat out, more hostile than she had meant for it to sound. "You don't believe that any more than I do."

Henri looked bewildered. "Why are you so angry?"

"A policeman is following me and is convinced my

mother is a killer. The same policeman threatened our teacher, who has been murdered, maybe by him. You should have told me the very first time this man approached you. I have to go warn my mother."

Fanny could see that Henri wanted to tell her not to go. As her immediate superior, he could forbid her to leave. But she knew he knew she would chose her family over her job and, if necessary, over him.

"Hurry back," he said quietly.

Fanny wanted to lash out. This man whom she felt so much for had really disappointed her. He assumed he knew what was best for her, had shielded her from vital information, and in doing so, had perhaps put her mother at risk. And what about Etienne? She slipped her apron off and walked away, hoping M. Desjardins would not see her leaving.

FANNY stood in her mother's shop. Martine stayed open until dark in the summer.

"Oh yes, child, I know about Police Inspector Fournier."

For the first time, the mystery man had a name. "Why didn't you tell me?" Fanny asked indignantly.

"I had hoped that the inspector would find someone else to chase. And I guess I didn't take it too seriously at first. I was one of twenty thousand who marched to Versailles. We were joined by forty thousand more. Fournier works for the city of Paris. What business is it of his what went on in Versailles? I thought it a joke. But now that he's following you, too, it has lost its humor."

Fanny was disappointed her mother hadn't defended herself and professed her innocence. She had expected a different reaction. So she added more. "Our teacher, Chef Etienne, was stabbed and killed last night. Yesterday morning he and I shared a ride to Les Halles together. Later, I saw him talking to this Inspector Fournier. They seemed to be arguing or at least talking about something serious. Fournier didn't look happy." Suddenly Fanny remembered something. "You knew him, didn't you, at the festival when the girl tripped on us?"

"He isn't the kind of fellow you forget, is he now? The police would do better to put a plainer man on this job. Fournier is too pretty."

"And you lied to me, said it was a gent with a prostitute."

Martine shook her head. "I suggested that, just said that it could be the case. What was I going to do, ruin your day by telling you that man smiling down at us is a police inspector trying to find a way to arrest me for murdering a king's guard at Versailles? You would have thought me a lunatic."

Fanny crossed her arms and started pacing. Martine walked over to the door and turned the sign to CLOSED. She didn't want anyone interrupting them.

"Let's go back to the chef," Fanny demanded crossly, unsure of her footing. "Can you think of any reason this inspector would have killed him? I need to figure this out because it is all Henri can think about. He burst into tears this morning while he was putting some veal bones in to roast."

"What makes you think the inspector did it?"

Fanny stomped across the floor again. "I don't really. But when I remember the chef lying there, dead, the next thing

I see is him alive and at the market, his head together with the inspector's."

"Oh, my sweet. Did you see the dead body?" Martine asked, stopping her daughter's pacing and putting her arms around her.

"Yes, the footman from number six came to our house, I guess because he knew what good friends Henri and Chef Etienne were. It wasn't too gruesome, Mama. He had on a nightshirt and a robe, and slippers. There was blood on his nightshirt and on the courtyard. And a big urn was overturned and something glass was broken, I think a lantern." Fanny was going to tell her mother about the ring, but all of a sudden, she didn't want to talk about it, still needing for some reason to keep it to herself.

"Stop," Martine ordered, holding her at arm's length. "You have worried yourself into a state. This inspector is nothing to us, a small inconvenience. And I'm sure he didn't kill your friend the chef, either. The revolution is rolling along whether police inspectors or marquis or kings want it to. More and more people have come to believe that we do not need a king to rule France, not do we need the Pope to rule us from Rome."

"Mama, you shouldn't say things like that."

"It's the truth. Inspector Fournier can't stop it and neither can you, Fanny. And I just want you to know you can come back home anytime, should your employer leave the country or the world suddenly. Working as a servant is beneath a woman of Paris in the first place."

Fanny couldn't believe what her mother was saying. When she had told her family what she wanted to do with her life, not get married to a cabinetmaker and stay in the neighborhood, but seek her own career as a chef, she thought they were supportive. Certainly her father was, finding her employment in an elegant neighborhood. Now, she was finally hearing what her mother really believed.

"My employer is not going anywhere, Mother, and Chef Etienne says, said, no matter who runs the country, they will need chefs," Fanny spat back defensively.

"And look where he is today, child."

That took the wind out of Fanny's sails. Her mother's attitude was downright shocking. And here she had run out on her job to warn her about some menacing policeman. That seemed very unnecessary now. "Dead, Mama. He's dead. Is that what you want for all of us who work for the rich?" She stormed out the door.

Her mother rushed after her and called out from the door of the shop. "Fanny, don't be silly. I only want the best for you."

Fanny heard her but didn't turn around.

THE next evening, after dinner was served, Fanny set out to visit her neighbors. Some of the addresses she had been to before, on little domestic errands that sent servants back and forth to their neighbors. "Can you loan us ice or flour or butter until tomorrow?" "Here is a pudding as a thank-you." "May we borrow your meat grinder again?" Some she had never approached before. Out of the thirty-five residences on the Place Royale, there were only six at which no one answered her knock at the delivery entrance, plus her own. Out of the other thirty, most of the encounters were brief.

She would introduce herself, then tell them she just couldn't rest at night thinking about Chef Etienne being cut down right in his own courtyard like that. Had they seen anyone hanging round in the last few days who might be suspicious? If they knew the chef, was there anything bothering him lately? Had they ever talked to Chef about his time at court? That last question was really mostly for Fanny's own curiosity but it couldn't hurt her general inquiry either.

Out of the thirty houses that answered the door, twenty were answered by the maître d'hôtel. These men were polite but they were not going to waste too much time on an assistant cook. What was she doing asking these impertinent questions anyway? Fanny realized somewhere along the way that she was going to have to tell M. Desjardins what she had done, quickly, before someone else did.

Out of the ten houses where the maître d'hôtel was busy in another part of the household and a maid or footman answered the door, she was treated more as a peer, and they would take a minute to gossip, though usually not about Chef Etienne.

A footman from number eight was the only person who had any interesting information. "He's in my card game, and I can tell you we'll miss him. Must have been the unluckiest man in Paris. Lost every week. If anyone at your house likes a bit of card playing, tell them to see me. We need someone to replace him."

At number six, the chef's own household, Fanny took a different tack. She went in the courtyard door unannounced and went down to the subground kitchen. There she visited with the cooks and maids, asked them about the night Chef died, and tried to lead them into opening up in general about the man who ran their kitchen. "I'm happy for the chance to work with someone with his experience, I truly am," said one of the young men who had assisted Chef Etienne at the classes. "But one of the key things I learned is how bitter you can become about your job. I want to stay excited and open to new ideas. There's so much in cuisine that is changing right now. It's a great time to be a cook. I tried to tell Chef that."

Fanny was surprised. She had never seen a negative side to the chef's personality. "And he didn't agree?"

The cook shook his head, dicing carrots for mirepoix as he talked. "He said, 'Just wait until the first time you create a wonderful new sauce and your chef takes credit for it himself. Or the chef forgets to order the fish for an important dinner party and blames you for his oversight. You'll wish you'd become a footman.'"

"And did he pull those tricks on you?" Fanny asked.

"No, he said he wouldn't be the one who'd break my heart, but someone would. I got the impression working at court was a cutthroat operation."

Fanny wanted to sit there and talk about the chef into the evening. But she could see the pace picking up in this kitchen. The marquis must be back in residence and having guests for supper. Fanny thanked the cook, murmured good-byes to everyone, and took her leave.

When she arrived back at number twenty-three, M. Desjardins was out in the courtyard, supervising the unloading of some wine. She decided to get it over with.

"Could I speak to you, monsieur?"

"What is it, Fanny?"

"I did something. I'm sure you will hear about it soon enough so I'll tell you myself."

"Go in my office. I'll be there shortly," M. Desjardins said.

Fanny went down the short flight of stairs to the subground entrance and slipped into the office, which was situated right by the door so the maître d'hôtel could see all the comings and goings.

Fanny sat there and thought about what she'd just done and she was satisfied. She hadn't offended anyone and it made her feel better. No one else was doing anything. At this rate, Chef would be sent off to the Heavenly Gates without a clue to those left on earth of how he was dispatched.

M. Desjardins came in with a triumphant look on his face. "They were going to short me three bottles of champagne. Can you imagine?" He sat down at his desk and looked over at Fanny with his eyebrows up in an inquiring position. "What did you do?"

"I went all the way around the square and asked every maître d'hôtel if they knew anything about Chef Etienne."

"Like what?"

"If anything was bothering him, if he ever spoke of the court and what happened there, and I also asked if they had seen anyone different or strange around the square."

"And the purpose of this is?"

Fanny was embarrassed. Any answer she might have for that question sounded very self-important. Did she think she would find out who killed the chef? Or if not that, then a motive for the murder other than random bad luck? "Henri has been very affected by Chef's death. I thought if I could find out . . . something, it would help him feel more like himself."

M. Desjardins looked over at her, slightly irritated but more amused. "Well, then, ask me your questions."

This surprised Fanny more than she could say. M. Desjardins had never exhibited any sense of humor or irony in the time she had been in residence. Perhaps she would see another side of him as the months passed. She pulled herself up and stood, as she was sure barristers were required to do in a courtroom.

"Monseiur, have you noticed anyone suspicious in the square lately? Someone who perhaps was looking for a house to rob?"

"No, mademoiselle, I have not."

"Did you have any occasion to talk with Chef Etienne, and if so, how had his disposition been recently?"

"I did not know the man well and had only one personal discussion with him in my life so I do not know what his usual disposition was, and therefore would not know if it were unusual."

"And do you recall what you talked about in that one discussion?" Fanny asked, trying to be a good interrogator. She sensed M. Desjardins was making fun of her, but in a kind way.

"Oh, yes, it was fascinating. We took the *cinq* together one morning to Les Halles and the unsettling political climate came up. He told me about his last days at the court. On the day last October when the women of Paris invaded the palace at Versailles, the chef was busy setting up for a dinner in the queen's bedroom. It was one of her preferred dining locations. As it turned out, the queen had to flee her quarters, and he and his staff also went back to the kitchen in a rush when the trouble started. All this left the bedroom unattended for just a short amount of time. Chef Etienne said that in that time someone went in and broke into some locked jewelry boxes and stole a good amount of the queen's jewels. She had just won a ring from the king's brother, Monsieur himself, and she went into a tantrum that it was gone. Every day she thought of something else that was missing, and by the time the court got to Paris, she wanted to search the belongings of every servant who had access to her quarters that day. But by that time, the court had more pressing issues to deal with and the steward told her that was not possible, that the movement of the court would have given any thief ample time to get rid of stolen goods they might have accumulated. He told Chef Etienne that she no doubt had sold most of the pieces she was claiming were stolen to settle her own gambling debts. It was well known she had been on a losing streak."

Fanny was amazed. "Monseiur, if I had known you were such a fount of information, I would not have bothered to hike around the square. Truly, this is just the kind of thing that could be useful."

M. Desjardins stood up by way of dismissal. "I doubt it, fascinating though it is as a bit of historical footnote. I'm sure most of it was fabricated. There were thousands at the court then, and this random chef expects me to believe I'm sharing a coach with a key household member who was in the queen's bedroom on that day? Please!"

Fanny could see his point. "I'm sure more than one person has stretched the truth a bit about that day, one way or the other." She thought briefly of her mother. "But thank you for sharing the tale with me anyway."

THE footmen from several houses had brought trestles and wood out in the square to make tables. The maîtres d'hôtel contributed tablecloths and service pieces, plates and flatware. The chefs had all made a dish that they were especially proud of. Everyone had appropriated a bottle of wine from their master's supply, and so the chefs of the Place Royale prepared to honor their fallen comrade, Chef Etienne de la Porte. It was quite grand, but not so proper as to be mistaken for an aristocrats' feast.

For one thing, all the food was laid out on the table together, not in the three or four flights of dishes that were the current fashion. For another, there were wineglasses on the table.

In society, when a guest wanted a drink, they signaled to their footman, who then offered them a tray with a glass, a decanter of wine, and one of water for mixing. Wine just wasn't drunk undiluted. After the guest had sipped, that glass was whisked away, washed, and put back in use. A single guest could use twenty or thirty glasses. That service wouldn't do for a dinner to honor someone who was a very high level servant, but still a servant. The assembled mourners would have to use one glass throughout the meal.

But at least there was wine and the dishes had been arranged on the table in the symmetrical pattern that was in favor. The maîtres d'hôtel and footmen took the arrangement of the table as seriously as if Etienne had been a prince of the blood. A chef who had been at court was about as high up the domestic servant ladder as you could get, even though everyone in Paris believed the cooks at Versailles weren't as accomplished as the ones in private houses in Paris. When the table and food were arranged just right, the maîtres d'hôtel and footmen and maids departed and left the chefs to it.

Thirty houses around the square were represented at this memorial, all the ones who were in residence at this time. Fanny had never seen anything like it. Everyone had changed clothes into their best dress whites. Those who had earned it wore a toque. There must have been fifty cooks and chefs sitting at one long table on the south end of the square. As they passed food back and forth, chefs toasted Etienne and told humorous stories about him. The story-teller could rarely be heard by the whole table, but everyone would cheer or clap after each tribute, while still eating and drinking.

Most people were sitting with their own households. Fanny was next to Henri on one side and an assistant cook from number six on the other, a young woman with dark, curly hair cut short and dark eyes. Fanny was in awe of her short hair. She finally said something about it. "I love your haircut. It would be so much easier in the kitchen."

The girl nodded. "It's so much cooler. But for me, this is long. I got my job by pretending to be a boy," she confessed with a wry little laugh.

Fanny was impressed. "You must have really wanted to learn to cook. I'm Fanny, by the way. I've seen you around the square. I'm at number twenty-three."

"Lucy at number twenty-one, the Richelieu house. I'm glad to meet you. Did you bring the turkey?"

"Yes, Henri said we should bring something worthy of a great feast day. It turned out moist for a change. Turkey is hard to cook, I think."

"I agree. The breast is dry and stringy before the thighs are cooked. I'm jealous of you, Fanny. I heard you got to go to Chef Etienne's classes. My chef wouldn't let me take the time to attend, although he certainly went himself," Lucy said, cheerful and cutting at the same time.

"Yes, I learned a great deal. I can't believe he's gone. I

know cooks sometimes die young with the lung disease from breathing the charcoal dust. But to be murdered? You never think someone you know will go that way."

Lucy shrugged. "I hear Etienne was shoeing the mule with all his vendors. Maybe someone was blackmailing him, or the steward got wind of it and they had a falling-out."

"Shoeing the mule" was a Paris slang term that referred to the practice of buying products for one price and charging your employer a higher price for them. The term was used because it was common knowledge that mules didn't need shoes, thus shoeing the mule indicated an unnecessary charge. It was common for maids or assistant cooks like Fanny to take a small markup on goods they bought at the market, but that was minor larceny. On a larger scale, the stewards, the ones who ran several homes or estates, and the maîtres d'hôtel, those who ran individual homes, sometimes contracted for goods to be delivered on a monthly or yearly basis, fixing the price for the whole time period, but charging their employer a higher amount. In that case, shoeing the mule could get into some real money. If some of these contracts were for foodstuffs, the supplier might have to pay a kickback to all three: the steward, the maître d'hôtel, and the chef. Then each of the three added on a little more before the bill was presented to the master of the house. It could make the lowliest pound of flour costly to the lord who ultimately paid the bill, or at least was presented with the bill. The nobility were well known for how long it took them to settle their accounts, perhaps, for one thing, because they suspected they were being stolen blind.

Fanny was shocked. She had heard of shoeing the mule, but neither she nor Henri practiced it. They had discussed it and they both agreed it was dishonest. So to hear that Chef

Etienne, hero to Henri and to some extent to her, too, was a thief, even if it was thievery that was widely practiced, was unsettling.

She thought again of the inspector and the chef and their seemingly grim conversation at the market the day of the chef's death. Was the inspector warning Etienne to clean up his act? Maybe Fanny had cast the wrong man as the villain. Now what was she going to tell Henri?

CHAPTER SIX

SUMMER slowly turned into autumn. It was November. Cold air was rising from the Seine and spreading out through the city. Maids and footmen hurried through the streets hugging their parcels for warmth. They stayed close to the sides of buildings on their path, not venturing out where the wind could lash at them.

Fanny had made her usual morning trip to the boulangerie and had come to the new kitchen after making coffee for everyone in the old. She was stuffing a leg of lamb that Henri had boned. Although mutton was still preferred in Paris, many of the chefs had started buying baby sheep and experimenting with cooking various cuts. Henri had split the cost of a lamb with the chef next door. Personally, Fanny liked the mild taste of the lamb better.

She had made some stuffing out of toasted day-old bread, chestnuts, fried onions, and shallots, and diced up a big pile of spinach leaves that she had soaked and rinsed first to get

out the sand. She moistened the whole thing with some of
the veal stock that Henri made religiously now. Fanny
thought it was his way of honoring Chef Etienne. They always tried to have chicken and veal stock on hand since those
last lessons with the chef in August. It certainly made sauces
and soups easier when you had the stock to start with.

As Fanny tied up her roast, Henri worked at the
fourneau. This was another modern amenity the new
kitchen had. The fourneau was a table-like counter made of
tiles and brick. It was a sheath for a series of charcoal braziers that were set down low on brick floors. On the top of
the counter were openings, chimneys, through which the
heat from the braziers rose. Cooks could then put copper
pots over these openings and cook with the heat.

The fourneau was standard equipment in a confectioner's
workroom. But M. Monnard believed they could be useful
to a regular household because they controlled the heat
more efficiently then an open hearth. Also, cooks did not
have to bend over in a torturous position all day. The
counter was built so that a Frenchman of average height
could work at it and not stoop. While most masters barely
knew where the kitchen was in their home, the egalitarian
political climate indicated that a nod to the comforts of the
household staff was smart. The fourneau had been popular
when M. Monnard still had clients.

Business had dried up in the last two months as the
weather cooled off and the political climate heated up.

Henri was totally involved with what was happening in
politics, reading all his newspapers every day and reporting
to Fanny. He was melting some chocolate now, stirring it in
a copper bowl over a brazier and talking over his shoulder.
"Last November they seized all the church property. This

summer they passed the Civil Constitution of the Clergy. Now, the National Assembly appoints even the archbishop. Not the pope, not the king, but the National Assembly. I hear the pope is going to issue a denunciation. He might even raise an army. Wouldn't that be something, if the pope sent an army to Paris to get all his churches back."

Fanny grunted. She'd learned a real reply wasn't necessary when Henri was on one of his tirades. Henri had moved inside his own head since Chef Etienne's death. He let Fanny in only occasionally. Politics had become his favorite topic. Fanny was bothered by it but still hopeful it was just a phase.

"I know you don't go to mass much now. But when you were growing up, was your family more religious?" Henri asked.

Fanny looked up from her lamb. "Well, the nuns taught the school so I guess that counts. We went a few times a year, on holy days. Usually we went on Christmas Eve, Good Friday, and Easter. You know how our neighborhood is, full of independent folks who don't really want anyone running their business, whether it's the church or the king or some Parliament, handing down judgments from on high. The only priests my father respected were the ones who worked at the hospitals, and with the poor out by Château de Vincennes. What about you?"

"We went all the time," he said shortly, as if he was embarrassed by his country-style devotion.

M. Desjardins came into the kitchen, looking paler than usual. His ordinary complexion was a gray pallor. Everyone teased him about being one of the "undead" that were supposed to live in the catacombs. Now the little color he usually had was drained from his face. "There's a crowd down at

St. Paul–St. Louis. They don't look happy," he said with a frown. M. Desjardins hated all the confusion the revolution had caused.

"Do you know why?" Henri asked.

M. Desjardins nodded. "I'm afraid so. The National Assembly has just demanded all public officials and all clergy must sign an oath of loyalty. One of the priests at St. Paul came out on the steps with the papers that the Assembly delivered to every church. The priest said his only loyalty was to God, first, the pope, second. He tore up the documents. Then he went in and locked the church doors. You can imagine how that went over with the citizens. No one was paying any attention one way or the other to this new demand for an oath. Why couldn't the priest just stay in his safe, comfortable asylum? But he had to stir things up by coming out on the steps and defying the Assembly. Now over a hundred people have gathered in front of the church. They are intent on getting those doors open again."

St. Paul–St. Louis was only a short distance from the Place Royale.

"What should we do?" Fanny asked.

"I have talked to the master and he wants to just close the porte cochere and wait it out. We can get by with what we have in the house as far as supplies go. We might not have fresh bread in the morning but that wouldn't be the end of the world now, would it?"

Both Henri and Fanny stopped what they were doing and stared at the maître d'hôtel as if he had just grown wings. To close the door in fear was unheard of. Not to have fresh bread was a true crisis!

"Have you talked to the other houses?" Henri asked, meaning to the other maîtres d'hôtel on the square.

"Yes, and we all hope it will blow over in a few hours. Since Chef Etienne was killed, everyone here has been expecting trouble of some kind. We all have been keeping more candles than usual, we have plenty of firewood and charcoal. Henri, you know I've been encouraging you to keep a large supply of flour and sugar and such. We may just have to make our own bread," M. Desjardins said with a little chuckle, trying for a little levity. When neither Fanny nor Henri responded, he abruptly walked out of the kitchen.

Fanny wanted to rebuke this assumption about Chef Etienne's death, that it was the first of an inevitable string of violent events. The whole neighborhood had decided that the chef was killed as a political statement toward his employer, a true noble. In fact, the marquis had not stayed in Paris long after that unfortunate incident. He had gone to Spain, to visit his cousins there, or so the story was told. Since the murder, his staff at the Place Royale had been released or reassigned to the country estate in the south. Only a caretaker and his wife resided at number six.

While Fanny admitted this could be how it went, a revolutionary trying to carry his message into the very home of an aristocrat, she believed it was more personal. After all, wouldn't a revolutionary have let the world know who he was and what he was doing? No, she just couldn't shake her bad feelings about the chef's death. And she kept thinking about that conversation M. Desjardins had shared with her, the one he had with the chef on the way to Les Halles. She wasn't as sure as he had been that the chef had been exaggerating. Also, there was the matter of shoeing the mule. Neither story had she mentioned to Henri. When you look up to someone, you never appreciate the person who points out his weaknesses.

The mysterious Inspector Fournier had remained just that. Although Fanny watched for him in the market, the faubourg St. Antoine near her parents' house, and even along the arcade at the Place Royale, she hadn't seen him since last August. Was that because, with the murder of Chef Etienne, his work was done? And what about her mother? Was he finished pursuing Martine?

Fanny was not satisfied that they had seen the last of Inspector Fournier, but she put that away in the back of her mind for now. Henri was talking to her rapidly so she had better pay attention. They were starting to prepare for a potential siege.

CRASH. Another rock went through a window somewhere near. Crash again. Fanny could hear them now, laughing and cursing. It was two or three in the morning. The crowd had been in the Place Royale since midnight. Fanny wished for once that she were on the top floor with the rest of the girls. Then she could see the whole square, could see if any home had been damaged or, worse, set on fire.

Fanny knew the crowd had turned the night guard away. M. Desjardins had told her so when he came round and gave her further instructions. Everyone was to stay in his or her room, he said, and get under the bed if necessary. He would move the whole family and the staff to the carriage house if it got completely out of hand outside. M. Desjardins said they could harness up the horses and pile into the closed carriage and make a break for it, but both he and Fanny knew it would be the family they served who escaped if escaping was to be needed this night.

The sheer size of the rowdy group and their drunkenness compelled the night guards go for the National Guard, although the night guard wasn't sure on whose side the National Guard would end up. M. Desjardins told Fanny not to light a candle and so now she sat in the dark, which made everything more frightening, wishing she could scamper up the stairs and look out the windows.

The side of the subground floor, the storage and pantries, facing the street, had no windows so she couldn't go to that side and sneak a peek. The section of the subground floor her room and the kitchen were on had half windows at the top of the room but they were all facing the courtyard.

Fanny's room was the closest to the door, which was four steps down from ground level. There was a wide stone entry and a curved stone overhang to protect it from the rain. The tradesmen made deliveries there during the day under the watchful eye of the maître d'hôtel. M. Desjardins had moved his bedroom but not his office, which was a tiny room only big enough for a desk and a chair on the opposite side of the entrance door from Fanny's bedroom. It was there the maître d' inventoried deliveries, and kept his papers. It was to this room Fanny came now as it had an unrestricted view of the courtyard. She opened the wooden shutters that were installed inside the room. When M. Desjardins was not in attendance, he closed these shutters to indicate as much. Then the delivery person had to find the footman or Henri to accept goods. Now Fanny sat looking out at the dark "new" kitchen where Henri was most likely wide awake worrying, just as she was. She could hear noises from out on the square. It sounded as if there was still a crowd out there. Raucous laughter was punctuated with more breaking glass.

As her eyes grew accustomed to the dark, her imagination started working overtime. She saw all kinds of shadows that she was sure were humans sneaking toward the carriage house and the kitchen where Henri was. She tried closing her eyes, but when she opened them again, the shadows still seemed to be there. Trying to be logical, she looked at the location of the objects in the courtyard. But she had no idea where the moon was in the sky so she couldn't tell what might be casting shadows. She hadn't even realized until now that the moon was full tonight.

There was only one way to solve this, Fanny told herself. She refused to sit there in terror. Fanny opened the door and stepped out in the courtyard.

It was like a different place from the one she had seen through the window. It seemed an ordinary space, without secrets. She turned quickly around 360 degrees and concluded she was alone. The moonlight was bright. No one was hiding in the corners or behind the well. She felt her pulse slow. Her breathing, she realized, had been shallow and jagged. She took several deep breaths and prepared to go back in the house.

Two things happened next, both very suddenly.

Henri must have spotted her out the second-story windows of the kitchen. All at once he was running across the courtyard, calling out in a loud whisper, "Fanny, what in the hell are you doing out here? Monsieur told us to stay in our rooms."

Fanny was about to answer when the big porte cochere doors to the square began to shake and buckle. It sounded like groups of people were throwing their weight at them, trying to force them open. Sooner or later, no matter how drunk they were, someone would figure out they could jigger the lock on the small door, the entrance for pedestrians sans carriage. Fanny herself had slipped that lock loose with her comb rather than ring the bell a few times.

"Get in the house," Henri commanded, grabbing her hand and pulling her along with him. They ran down the stairs and hurried in the door Fanny had left open, throwing the bolt behind them. Fanny quickly closed the shutters in the office and she and Henri took refuge in the kitchen, hiding under a big worktable on the opposite wall from the windows. That way they could at least see the boots and shoes of those who were intent on gaining entrance if the crowd made it into the courtyard.

"What were you doing out there? You could have been killed," Henri whispered, holding her face in his hands and kissing her.

"We don't have to whisper, Henri. No one else is on this floor and I wager no one in the whole household is asleep. I'd bet M. Desjardins is moving the master and mistress to the carriage house right now," Fanny replied.

"You didn't answer me. Don't you ever follow orders?"

Fanny rearranged herself under the table. "I looked out on the courtyard and then I thought I saw something, people hiding in the corners. So I went out and there was nothing there, nothing but the full moon and the shadows it casts. Then you came running after me and the crowd started banging on our door, all at the same time. It scared me."

Henri put his arm around Fanny's shoulders. "Me, too. When I looked down and saw you out there, I realized my life wasn't worth a sou without you. Please be careful."

"Well, at least now we'll die together," Fanny said half in jest, half seriously.

Crash. A stone came flying through one of the kitchen windows. It came to rest only a few inches from Fanny and Henri.

They held each other tighter.

Two pairs of scuffed boots were visible in the moonlight outside. The crowd must have breeched the outer doors. A big fellow bent down unsteadily and peered in. "Push some more glass out so's we can get in here," he ordered his companion.

Henri crawled down to the end of the table and tried to reach his hand up to the table's edge, where he hoped there was a knife.

The second man kicked at the broken window with his boot, causing a few more pieces of glass to fall inward.

Then a torch flared up and Fanny could see the faces of Jules and M. Desjardins behind the crowd, standing back from the windows far enough they were recognizable. Jules was holding the torch and M. Desjardins was holding a gun. In back of them the carriage driver was holding his whip and a club. M. Desjardins pointed his pistol at the two men who were getting ready to enter the house. Fanny remembered his speech about hiding or fleeing. It was obvious that applied to others, not him.

"I have to go out there. My place is with the others," Henri whispered.

The two embraced, then Fanny ran into the dish room to get away from the windows and Henri ran out to join the men, taking a long chef's knife with him. M. Desjardins shot his gun up in the air, after which there was a great deal of yelling and shouting outside. Fanny peeked around the corner, wanting to stay safe but needing to see just as much. The boots had moved away from the broken window, and from what she could tell, the whole group, the aggressors and the defenders of their turf, had moved out of her line of sight.

She heard M. Desjardins raise his voice and threaten to shoot again, this time into the crowd. She heard the crack of the carriage whip. Each time the crowd reacted with bravado but no action. There was a call of, "Give us your silver and we'll leave," but that was all Fanny could really make out. She came tiptoeing out of the dish room and went over to the broken window. The light of the torch was coming toward the window. M. Desjardins was holding it in one hand and the pistol down at his side.

"Fanny, can you hear me?" he called.

"I'm right here," Fanny replied.

"Are you all right?"

"Yes, sir, I'm fine, just a bit shaken up."

"The whole mob never came in, just a few boys with larceny on their minds. They were persuaded to leave, mainly by the arrival of the National Guard in the square, also some policemen, and the night guard. I think it's over. We're lighting all the lanterns we can find out here and Jules will stay by the front. I won't be going to sleep tonight either. And the master is out at the door boarding it up for the rest of the night. He came outside quite bravely with his own pistol, not saying a word, just falling in behind Jules as if he were another footman. Now if you'll come with me."

Fanny peered out at M. Desjardins. The torchlight made him look even more colorless. "Why, yes, sir, where to?"

M. Desjardins looked surprised, then he realized he hadn't told Fanny. "Oh, I'm sorry. I should have reported this first. Henri was hurt with his knife. One of those louts pushed him down and it, well, penetrated his arm."

"He was stabbed?" Fanny was already moving toward the door.

"Just a little," M. Desjardins replied.

FANNY opened her eyes and remembered where she was. Henri was in his bed above the kitchen and she was on a very uncomfortable chair beside him. She'd dressed his wound and made him drink brandy, taking a good swig herself. When he'd fallen asleep, she told herself she was going to stay awake all night, that she would stay alert to returning marauders, but that had lasted about five minutes. Now it was fully light out and she had duties to perform. She might even be late to make the morning coffee.

She got up, put her cap back on, and bent over to kiss Henri on the forehead. He mumbled something in his sleep and turned over. Henri wouldn't be cooking today so she would have to.

As she walked across the courtyard to the main house, she realized by the condition of things that they had been very lucky last night. The fact that the maître d'hôtel and the master, and all the rest of the men, had actually defended their household with arms was hard to believe. The courtyard was full of broken wine bottles, a shirt and two caps left behind, and a discolored spot on the paving stones that made Fanny stop short. That must be Henri's blood, poor love. She hurried on, wondering if this was the beginning or the end of troubles here on the Place Royale.

Then she thought about her mother and the march on Versailles. It was so different when she was the one whose house was being entered, when she was hiding in fear for her life, or when Henri was stabbed with his own knife, even though it was technically an accident. Would her mother be sympathetic to Fanny and her master and the rest of the staff who were just trying to do their jobs? Or would she be sympathetic to the crowds that had terrorized them last night?

When Fanny opened the door to the kitchen, the boys had already started a roaring fire and the scullery maid was cleaning up all the broken glass. It was still freezing in there with the window gone but she could at least make coffee.

"So, Henriette, I'll make coffee and run to the boulangerie, then I'll move over to the new kitchen for the rest of the day. It is too cold in here for us. Hopefully the glaziers can come replace the glass," Fanny said calmly. She was happy to know she wouldn't fall apart in a bad situation, even though she had overslept. When one is eighteen, one is just learning these things about oneself.

"So, Chef Fanny"—Henriette knew how to flatter her betters—"I heard Chef Henri was stabbed. Is it true?"

"Well, he was fighting with a knife in his hand and he was pushed down on the blade and it punctured his left arm. I guess that qualifies as being stabbed. It wasn't just a kitchen accident, that's for sure. But we are still a household that has to be fed, so boys, will you come with me, please, to do the marketing? I'll need you to carry things. I'm going to be a true Parisian today and buy most of our food premade."

AND so the hours flew by, everyone in shock over the events of the night, but everyone pitching in to put things back to normal. Two of the chefs on the square sent food over because they heard Henri had been stabbed and was lying on his deathbed. Fanny took the food, gave a sweet thank-you, and assured everyone that Henri's wound was not going to be fatal. Not that she was sure that was true.

In her heart, Fanny was worried about Henri. Infection was always a danger. Louis XIV, of all people, had died of gangrene in his leg from some common accident, he who could afford the best medical care in the world. And she had seen Henri's wound up close. It went deep. Jules said the knife blade had gone all the way through the flesh of the arm. Luckily, it was Henri's left arm that was wounded and he was right-handed with his knives. He shouldn't have permanent damage to his arm but it was bound to be sore for a while and the motion of using the knives would have to aggravate it. But a sore arm was better than no arm at all. They had to avoid infection.

Henri had seemed very disoriented last night, even before she made him drink all that brandy. She remembered her brother getting hit on the head by a board and knocked out. He and Henri had acted the same. Her papa had called it a concussion and he had been worried sick about his son for several days, sleeping by his side as Fanny as had spent the night by Henri.

M. Desjardins interrupted Fanny's worrying. He looked stricken. "Please come over to the house," he directed tersely, and without waiting for a response, turned and left.

Fanny took her saucepan of mushrooms off the heat, wiped her face, and called up the stairs. "Henri, are you awake?"

There was no response.

"Monsieur has asked me to go to the house. Are you all right up there?"

"Fanny?"

Fanny ran up the winding stairs. "I'm right here, love. What can I get you?" She took one of Henri's handkerchiefs, poured some water from a pitcher into a basin, wet the handkerchief, then went over to the bed and wiped Henri's face.

"Water," Henri said, sounding winded and out of breath. She poured water in a cup and held it to his lips. He lifted his head and drank. For someone whose only wound was in his arm, he seemed greatly debilitated. "Fanny, the man who pushed me, when I went down, he kicked me in the head. Yesterday, I was having double vision. But I'm better now, seeing clearly. I just have to rest a little more," he said and his voice trailed off, eyes closed.

"I'll be back, darling," Fanny said, trying to sound cheerful and bright.

THE arrangement of rooms in M. Monnard's home was like the rest of the household, traditional with some new twists. In the old style, there were no central halls; each room led to the next. The reception or main room led to the dining room, which led to the salon, although the salon hadn't been a room one hundred and eighty-five years ago. Neither had the dining room.

Before, the dinner table had been set up in any room at the master's whim, many times in one of the bedrooms. Tables were trestles and boards, covered with heavy damask linen to the floor. Then the trend toward dining turned to dedicating a room for it, one that could have special marble sideboards to facilitate serving, and gradually, a permanent table was left in place for eating.

Then came the salon. When Paris society started the fashion of having evenings at home discussing current events or philosophy or music, the smart hostess wanted a room dedicated to that purpose. It just made sense that this room would be positioned behind the dining room so it could be used for after-dinner entertainment as well as for the popular salon of ideas, where one generally didn't serve dinner.

Number twenty-three had both of these new-fashioned rooms. As well, M. Monnard had moved the bedrooms upstairs and the salle, the reception room, down to the ground floor. It was in this room that the whole household was now gathered.

M. Desjardins began, "Just so you all know, Chef Henri was wounded in the arm and is recuperating. But that's not why we are here. This is a sad occasion. Monsieur has some news for us all," he said and turned to the master.

M. Monnard was a well-spoken man who could tell a client that his mansion was going to cost twice as much as the estimate, but now he was having trouble finding the right words. He stared at the staff; turned toward his wife, son, and daughter-in-law; then swallowed and gulped for air several times before he could speak.

"I know you are all aware of what happened yesterday. The demand to take the oath of loyalty has not been received so well at some of the churches, especially our neighborhood St. Paul–St. Louis. There was a bit of a riot and part of the crowd from the church spilled over to our beautiful Place Royale. A few from that group broke into our courtyard. Thanks to our maître d'hôtel and the rest of the male staff, we were saved from real destruction. Only Henri was wounded. I spent the rest of the night talking to my family and the morning discussing my decision with M. Desjardins. My family and I are going to England. My son and I are hoping we can find work around London. I will not lose my head for the king. When this madness is over we will come home."

"What about us?" Josee-Marie asked boldly. The rest of the staff was just staring at the master, in shock.

"The maître d' hôtel will give you all a month's extra wages. I have asked M. Desjardins to go with our family but he has declined, saying he does not speak English well enough to be of service. I do not believe that; however, I respect his decision. I then asked him to stay with the house until he finds a caretaker. We will leave tomorrow. I know this is a poor time to be out of work, what with so many households closing down and going out of the country. I am sorry. This house had been in my family almost two hundred years. I hate this as much as you do, but no piece of property is worth our lives."

It took a few moments after the master went upstairs with his family for the staff to react. Then they started talking to each other in low tones. Both of the maids and the scullery maid were crying. Fanny, because she didn't stay up with the rest of the women, wasn't as close to them so she went over to the maître d' hôtel instead.

"Are we to keep regular eating hours, sir?"

"I asked the master about that. A light meal at dinner-time please, Fanny. Don't go to all the trouble of serving numerous flights. Do you have food?"

Fanny was insulted. She had more than food. She had everything she bought, everything she made herself, and everything the neighbors had brought.

"I certainly do, sir. Would you like another supper at ten?" Fanny asked.

"A supper for the family at five, a supper for us after that, and some cold dishes for the family at ten. That should clean out the supplies of fresh food. I'll decide about what to do with the staples by tomorrow."

"Yes, sir."

"Fanny, you are lucky, you know. You have plenty to do for the next few hours. You can't worry and fret about the fact that all our lives have been ruined."

"But we're still alive and kicking, sir," Fanny said as she left the room.

CHAPTER SEVEN

I T was down to just M. Desjardins, Henri and Fanny, and the boys.

The morning had been gloomy and funereal. Women were weeping; men were angry. The shock of yesterday had worn off and the whole staff was faced with the reality of being out of a job. Worry for the future hung in the air like fog off the Seine. And it spread over the entire square. All morning, a maid from one house, a footman from another, would drop by to see if it was true, if their master had indeed gone out of the country. M. Monnard was the first bourgeois on Place Royale to leave the country. It wasn't a good sign.

The family had already left town, as early as they could. Fanny had seen candlelight on the first and second floors well after midnight from her post in the new kitchen, nursing Henri. Madame must have been up half the night packing.

It was better that the family was gone, if they must, because the mood of the domestic household had turned black. One by one they filed into that little office, got their pay from M. Desjardins, and let out a litany of woes about being turned out without any notice, about the shortage of money for Christmas next month, about the lack of opportunity in Paris right now, about their sick mother who needed money from them to buy food. It was all M. Desjardins could do to stay polite, even though he respected them, one and all.

"I believe the master was quite generous. You have already been paid for this month that is not quite over and you are receiving your wages for all of December," he would say in a steady voice. "I have taken the liberty of writing you a glowing letter of recommendation." Then he would hand them their money in a small leather pouch that he had hurriedly bought for the occasion, and the letter. After a suitable time of listening to the quite legitimate complaints, he ushered them out, and before he had time to compose himself, the next staff member would come in and sit down and it would start again.

M. Desjardins had developed a terrible headache in the last twelve hours. He himself had no idea what he would do when he had turned down the offer to go to England. Luckily the master asked him to stay with the house until he found a caretaker. Actually, the master had asked him to be the caretaker, but for a professional maître d' hôtel, being the caretaker of an empty house was hardly a fitting job.

When the office was empty for a moment, he went to the kitchen for a drink of water. He found Fanny on the floor on her hands and knees there, with her rear up in the air as she looked under a table. "Fanny, what are you doing? Is there more broken glass?"

Fanny straightened up. "No, sir, it's all cleaned up very nice and tidy. I was just looking for something I've misplaced. Sir, I wanted to tell you I sent one of the boys for a doctor. I know you wanted everyone to leave as soon as possible, but Henri is not in any shape to go anywhere. His fever is up."

"That will be fine. I have already asked Nicolas and Simon to stay until this afternoon, to help me put some things away. The maître d' at number eleven is taking them. He needed another boy and he said he'd take the pair, which is fortunate. So what about Henri? Do you think he'll soon recover enough to go back home to Brittany?"

Fanny hadn't thought of that as an option. Perhaps it would be better for Henri, Paris not having a great many opportunities right now. But then, what would she do without him? As grumpy as he had become over the last few months, he clung to her more in their private time, and their lovemaking had grown more intense and passionate.

M. Desjardins had decided he would ask other maîtres d'hôtel on the square into the pantries and sell them the staples: the flour and sugar and lentils and such. Fanny had spent the morning organizing it all so the men could come shopping. She alternated this with running out to the new kitchen and checking on Henri often. That was how she came to the conclusion that he was getting worse, instead of better.

So, she had sent for the doctor, and after the kitchen was organized for the sale, she then proceeded to her own room to pack up her things. That was when she noticed the spice box was missing, went into the kitchen to look for it, and got down on her knees to do so, which is where M. Desjardins had found her a few minutes later.

She didn't remember moving the box to the kitchen but the last three days were the kind that made you lose track of things and of time. Was it just yesterday that the master had announced he was leaving? And when had Henri been wounded? Was it two days ago, or three? It was little wonder she couldn't keep track of her personal things.

Fanny had thought about the future last night before she fell asleep, again in the chair by Henri's bed. She and Henri would move to her parents' home. Henri could take up residence in the room for employees, on the third floor above her brother's. She could help her mother in the shop while Henri regained his strength, not that she liked sewing, then they would find a new position. Together. Not every bourgeois was as closely aligned with nobility as M. Monnard so it stood to reason they wouldn't all be so nervous about their heads. And plenty of them were rich enough to want their own cooks. She had fallen asleep with these thoughts. Now, as she moped around the old kitchen, she realized she hadn't sent word to her parents. Her father would have to come and pick her and Henri up, along with her furnishings. She hated to go home under these circumstances. Even though it wasn't her fault, Fanny felt defeated.

"Fanny?" M. Desjardins called sharply. "You didn't answer."

"Oh, sorry, sir. Your question made me think. I hope Henri will stay here in Paris. I'm going to ask my parents if he can stay in the rooms they have for extra employees. He's been here in Paris five years, he surely won't want to leave now," Fanny said with the assurance a Parisian has that any thinking person would not want to live elsewhere. "Someone will need a good chef, and his assistant, too, I hope."

The maître d' nodded. "In the meantime he must get

better. I have a certain amount of money that M. Monnard gave me to close up the house and access to more monthly. He especially mentioned attending to Henri, since he was wounded defending our home. I will pay the doctor and pay for the medicine out of this money, and any surgery that might be needed."

Fanny blanched. "Thank you, sir. Surgery won't be necessary, I'm sure."

With that, M. Desjardins went back to his office and Fanny wandered over to the new kitchen, feeling dislocated and anxious. She was surprised to find the doctor already inside and coming down the stairs.

"Are you the Fanny this young man keeps talking about?" the doctor asked.

"Yes, and how is Henri?"

"Well, no worse than you would expect. You must send the boy who came for me to the apothecary for a salve. I will write it down. And also, I'll give you the 'recipe,' if you will, for a poultice. It is a certain tea and some herbs. You need to put all the ingredients in some muslin or cheese-cloth and tie it on the wound, as well as the salve, of course. This will act to pull out the poison."

"And then he'll be all right?"

"We hope so. Keep his arm above his heart. And pay special attention to the area above the wound. If any red streaks appear, running up the arm, send for me immediately. Amputation will still save him if we have to. But you must watch for the red streaks."

Fanny could hardly speak. She was stunned. Red streaks. Amputation. "Thank you, Doctor. The maître d'hôtel will pay you. He's in the office by the delivery entrance to the main house," she said, turning to go upstairs to check on Henri. As she did, she saw her spice box on a shelf by the ovens. She went over and snatched it up, shaking her head at her own forgetfulness, then headed up the corkscrew stairs.

HENRI was still awake. He was even sitting up in bed, his two pillows arranged behind him and his arm on the bolster. Fanny went over to him and gave him a peck on the cheek.

"What's that you have in your hands?" he asked.

"This is the spice box that my father gave me. I was packing over at the house. I couldn't find it, but when I came over here, there it was. I guess I'm not thinking straight, what with all the confusion. I must have brought it to this kitchen."

"What confusion, and what did you mean you were packing?" Henri asked innocently.

It wasn't until that moment that Fanny realized no one had bothered to tell Henri they didn't have a job anymore. He had slept most of yesterday. She had served him broth and bread, wiped his forehead, but they hadn't talked, more than Fanny murmuring words of encouragement to her patient.

"First, what did the doctor say?" Fanny asked brightly.

"The salve, the poultice, watching for red streaks. The only thing he didn't mention to me that he mentioned to you was the amputation."

"Oh, so you heard?"

"Yes, but don't worry, Fanny," Henri said and gave her a little smile. "I will stay here in bed for a few days with my arm above my heart so I can still be a great chef someday. I will not have my arm hacked off. Now, what about this packing?"

Fanny sat down on the same uncomfortable chair she'd been sleeping on. "There is no good way to tell you this. The very next day after the riot, after you got hurt, M. Monnard said he was moving to London and that everyone has a month's wages. He and his family are already gone."

Henri looked out the window for the first time in forty-eight hours. What was out there now? A different world, it sounded like.

"You mean, the master, the staff, they're all gone?"

"They're starting to leave, but don't worry, M. Desjardins will allow us to stay as long as you need to. He'll be taking care of the place until he finds something else."

Henri broke into a big smile. "Fanny, this could be the best thing that ever happened to us."

"Please explain that to me. We're both without a job or a place to live. How is that the best thing that ever happened?"

Henri reached out his good arm to Fanny and clasped her hand. "I've been dreaming about this moment. Now we can do what we are meant to do: start a restaurant."

Fanny laughed. "You've never mentioned this restaurant business before. I think we better try to find a job first. If we can't find a house where we can work together, maybe we can be in the same quarter of town."

Henri shook his head. "This is a sign. As soon as I can move around, I'll take you over to Palais-Royal and you'll see. I've been thinking about this since I worked over there for the Fête de la Fédération. Fanny, you and I can do this."

"Fanny, Fanny, are you in here?" The call came from downstairs. It was her father.

Fanny got up and held Henri's hand for a minute more. "You have gone mad with the fever. We'll talk about this when you're better," she said sweetly, then turned and went down the stairs. "Here I am, Papa."

Philippe Delarue looked worried. "I had no idea. We didn't buy the papers yesterday. I had a deadline on some cabinets. Your mother, too, she had a ball gown for today. Then I heard about the loyalty oath and your mother read there was some trouble over here that night. You should have sent a messenger."

"Did Mama come, too?"

"She certainly did," Martine called as she entered. "We spoke to M. Desjardins as we came in the door. So Monnard ran away to the Channel this morning, eh? No matter, love. We'll just take you home with us."

"Oh, I can't go with you, at least not yet. Henri was wounded the night of the riots. Stuck with a knife. Some of the folks from the church broke into the courtyard and were trying to get into the house. Henri can't move yet. He has infection in his arm. I'm staying to take care of him."

"I don't like it, daughter," Philippe Delarue said. "We'll put Henri in the back of the cart, take you both home with us, and come back for your things later. I'm sure he'll be fine."

"It's his arm. The doctor was just here and gave me instructions on how to treat it. He said the arm could need to be amputated. How would either one of you feel if you were to lose an arm? You both make your living with your hands just like Henri and I do."

Fanny's father was getting ready to protest until Martine came over to him and put her hand on his sleeve. She squeezed gently and he kept quiet. "So, are you sure you don't want one of us to stay here with you?"

"No, we'll be fine. We have plenty of supplies still left, candles and food and such. M. Desjardin is here and he just paid the doctor and most likely has sent for the salve by now. In a few days, I'll send for you, Papa, I promise. And I thank you both for coming to check on me. It was just awful how the master left in such haste. He was truly afraid for his safety," Fanny said, puzzling over it as she spoke about it.

Martine threw her arm around her daughter's waist as they walked toward the door. "It's just the beginning, love. If the priests don't sign the oath, there will be churches aflame all over Paris."

Fanny wanted to yell at her mother, tell her the stupid mob didn't have the right to burn a church or, for that matter, break into a fine house either. But this was not the time to argue over such things. She had been so glad to see her parents. She felt much more confident now; even if it had started as an act so they wouldn't make her go home, she had convinced herself a small bit.

She would nurse Henri back to health, then they would move to the faubourg St. Antoine and find another job or start a restaurant—if Henri even remembered saying he wanted to open a restaurant.

"I'm just going to check on the patient myself," Philippe Delarue said and went up the stairs.

"Yes, I'll come along," Martine said.

Fanny didn't follow her parents or make a comment. She wanted to give them a minute to spend with Henri alone.

She was thrilled she didn't even have to beg them to bring Henri home with her. They had been very supportive and understanding. Maybe things would turn out better than it seemed they would when M. Monnard was making his surprise speech yesterday.

The Delarues barely tolerated Fanny's sweetheart, but that was not because they suspected the sexual nature of the relationship. They expected Fanny to have experiences.

The reason they didn't approve of the match was because Henri was not a Parisian, born and bred. Of course, Paris was full of immigrants from the farms, from the ships. But Philippe and Martine had always imagined their children would both marry someone from the faubourg St. Antoine and live out their lives near home. What if Fanny married this man and then he got the urge to return to Brittany with her in tow? They had talked about this in the cart on the way to Place Royale, and even before they realized Henri had been injured, they were going to offer their worker's quarters to him. If they could help get both Fanny and Henri positions quickly, in Paris, so much the better.

Fanny climbed the steps only to see her parents both holding the spice box. Henri was fast asleep with his arm still propped up.

"Philippe didn't show me your present before he brought it over. It's beautiful," Martine said and put the box down on Henri's side table. "I put one of his pillows under his arm, just to get it up higher. He didn't make a sound. I think he still has a bit of a fever."

"That's why we can't move right now. We will be fine. No one is going to come in here again. There is absolutely no danger," Fanny said bravely.

Fanny's father patted her cheek. "I understand that you

don't want to leave your sweetheart, who is also your colleague, alone in ill health. But when you are a parent yourself, you will see how we only care about your safety."

"It will be three or four days. Then Henri can travel,"
Fanny said, and the stubbornness could be heard in her
voice.

Martine took her husband's arm. "We'll speak to M. Desjardins on the way out and make sure he has our address.
That way he can contact us should you need us sooner. Take
care, Fanny."

"Thank you both for coming. I feel so much better now,"
Fanny said and she honestly meant it. "I'll see you soon," she
added, kissing both parents on the cheeks.

After they left, she felt so tired she couldn't keep her
head up anymore. She knew she should go downstairs and
scrape together a meal for M. Desjardins. But for all she
knew, he had bought a chicken from the rotisseurs hours
ago. She wasn't his cook anymore.

Fanny lay down beside Henri and was fast asleep in a
minute.

FANNY awoke with a start. It was dark, inside and out.
Henri must have moved and that woke her. He moaned.
Fanny got up and adjusted her clothes. She was slightly dis-
oriented in that way that a nap can muddle one's thinking.

"I need to get the salve. I need to make the poultice," she
mumbled to herself, feeling around for the candlestick. She
found it with an unused stub on the table beside the bed.

M. Desjardins kept all the half-burned candles from the
master's quarters. The staff then used the half-burned stubs
in their candlesticks. Now Fanny inserted the stub in the

candlestick, lit it, and hurried down the stairs. She lit the lanterns hanging from the walls of the new kitchen. Then she lit an oil lantern to take with her and headed for the house, glancing across the courtyard to make sure the maître d'hôtel was not already in his bedroom in the carriage house. It was dark. But as Fanny neared the house, she saw it was dark as well. The clock in the kitchen had read seven o'clock. Surely M. Desjardins hadn't gone to bed so early.

Fanny remembered how she had completely passed out for two hours at the drop of a hat. Perhaps the maître d' had done the same.

Fanny went down the stairs to the delivery entrance. The door to the office was closed. She stepped in the kitchen and looked around. "Monsieur?" she called, then turned and knocked on the door of the office. "Monsieur?"

Fanny listened and waited. It was so still that she quickly became uncomfortable. She opened the door of the office, or at least partially opened it. One lit lantern hanging on the wall cast shadows that moved with a cold breeze from the open window that led to the courtyard. The shutters were closed but the shutters themselves had been pushed back, as though M. Desjardins had been out of the office, and by habit closed the shutters, then came back in the office and pushed the shutters aside, or opened them to speak with someone out in the courtyard, perhaps Fanny's parents when they left. The door was blocked by the desk, which had slid over. The desk had slid over because of the weight of the body that slumped onto it. It was the body formerly inhabited by M. Desjardins, whose first name Fanny realized at that moment she didn't know. It filled her with sadness that there was no one around who would know his first name.

He seemed to be dead.

CHAPTER EIGHT

ANNY reached across the desk and pulled at the limp arm. The head flopped forward. "Hello! Sir, it's Fanny. Please wake up."

She pushed the desk back as hard as she could. Then she went around to M. Desjardins, set her lantern down, and put her fingers on his neck, moving them around frantically looking for a pulse. In the lantern light the man already looked ghoulish. Fanny leaned down and saw the blood on his vest but listened near his heart, hoping that he had just been wounded. There was nothing.

Fanny sobbed. She found herself shaking this shell of a person, shaking him like a rag doll. "Wake up!" she cried.

Then she stopped. Calm now, or in shock, she grabbed both his hands, afraid of what might be there, yet curious enough to examine them. One of them, the right hand, was clenched, just as Chef Etienne's had been. She took the time to identify what he was holding, twisting it out of the dead man's grasp and into hers. It was an earring with some kind of blue stone. Fanny thought sapphires. She thrust it into her skirt pocket, and picking up her lantern, she gently pushed M. Desjardins back in his chair and closed the one eye that had popped open in her manhandling of the body.

"You stay right here, sir, while I figure out what to do," she said solemnly.

As she moved back around to the door, she saw Henri's salve right there on the desk along with the instructions for the poultice. That started the tears again. She picked up the salve and closed the door, wishing she had picked M. Desjardins's pockets for his ring of keys. She didn't want the boys to come in here and get a fright. Of course, Nicholas and Simon might have already gone to their new home, for all she knew.

She cursed herself for falling asleep. Now the last two hours were lost to her, the maître d'hôtel was dead, Henri was in a feverish stupor, and the boys had disappeared, hopefully to their new place of employment down the street. She was on her own.

Fanny rushed back to the new kitchen, irrationally anxious that Henri might have disappeared in her absence. She was glad she had taken the time to light the lanterns on the ground floor. "Henri?" she called as she came in the door.

"Fanny? Where have you been?" Henri called weakly.

She smiled with relief at the sound of his voice. At least he was still alive. "Right here, darling." Fanny held the instructions for the poultice up by the light. She had to get this on Henri's arm tonight.

She rushed around and prayed that she had all the ingredients she needed. There was no way she was going back to the big house tonight. After she had fed the fire, she made herself a cup of tea. She realized she was starving, but she couldn't stop working to find something to eat. Wrapping the herbs in a piece of cheesecloth, she wet the cloth down, then climbed the stairs.

"Here's your salve and the poultice, dear. I fell asleep right beside you for a while," Fanny said and busied herself rubbing the salve on the wound and then tying the poultice on Henri's arm with the ends of the cheesecloth.

"I know. Just having you there made me sleep better than I have since my arm was hurt," Henri said, reaching up his good arm and touching Fanny's hair. "You took your cap off," he said.

Fanny was surprised. She hadn't realized her cap was gone. It must have come off when she was maneuvering around the dead body in the tiny office. For some reason this made Fanny feel more vulnerable than before. Tears just started streaming down her cheeks again, dripping down onto the bare skin of Henri's arm.

"What is it, love?"

Fanny plopped down on her chair. "I have something terrible to tell you. I guess it happened after my parents left, when I fell asleep."

"Fanny, what are you talking about?"

"M. Desjardins. He is dead. It looks as though he was stabbed just as Chef Etienne was. He was in his office slumped over his desk. He didn't have a chance to fight back because his desk is not disturbed like it would be if there had been a fight. The invoices were in a neat pile, just like always. The decanter with water and a glass were there, unbroken. Someone came in and stabbed him in the heart, I think. But there was no knife again." Fanny surprised herself with the details she had absorbed, even though she thought herself dumb with shock.

Henri pulled the covers off and slowly sat up on the side of the bed. "Do you think the killer is in the house?"

"Well, let them be. We can't search through the house in the dark. And if we lit lanterns, a person wanting to hide from us would just keep moving into a room where it was still dark. If a thief killed our maître d' to steal something, let them steal it."

Henri stood up and grabbed his shoes. Fanny pulled on his shirttail. "What are you doing?" she asked.

"We have to hide the body," Henri said as he pulled away from her and walked over to the chamber pot to relieve himself.

"Why? Your arm is supposed to stay elevated. We can't move him with only three hands. But why don't we just call for the night guard?"

Henri was rummaging for his trousers. He found them and sat down on the side of the bed to slip them on. "I have an idea. And I'll tell you but first we need to put the body in the carriage house. We can just lay him in where the big carriage was and cover him with a tarp."

"Henri, you still haven't told me why."

"Because then we can stay here. We pretend that M. Desjardins is still here for a while. Then after a time we can say he went to another post, or decided to join the master in London. You and I took over as the caretakers. Whatever. It will be of no interest soon."

"And why would we want to stay here?"

Henri slipped his clogs on. "So we can start our restaurant, right here," he said proudly. "We are going to have the first restaurant on Place Royale!"

Reluctantly Fanny got up and followed Henri down the stairs. He was in a state from the fever and obviously it was not the time to argue with him. It wouldn't hurt poor M. Desjardins more than he was already hurt if they hid his body for a day. The two stepped outside.

The full moon of two nights ago was now waning but still cast a glow. The rest of the buildings were dark and silent. In contrast, the new kitchen was alight, top to bottom, the windows full of friendly light. Fanny wanted nothing more than to run back in there.

"Go get the wheelbarrow," Henri ordered as he headed for the office. Fanny walked to the room in the back of the carriage house that held all the garden equipment, filled with dread. She had no desire to walk into a dark shed. Little bits and pieces of the other night—the boots, the shadows, an image of M. Desjardins standing with a pistol held high—all played through her mind.

Henri had certainly recuperated rapidly. One minute he was totally incoherent, thrashing and moaning, the next up and ready to move a dead body. Fanny was also curious about where this full-blown plan about a restaurant had come from. The only thing she could conclude was that Henri wasn't rational right now and the restaurant was something he'd been thinking about that had come to the front of his mind during his fever. He certainly wasn't taking care of his arm. She remembered the doctor saying amputation was a possibility. She told herself that all these inconsistencies were part of Henri's fever, that he would be his old, rational self if she got his infection under control. This was some relief but she still felt the weight of the world on her shoulders.

She was uneasy about her parents as well. Why had they

both come over to check on her? It certainly wasn't typical of them, to go together as a couple to visit their daughter, even if they were concerned over her welfare. Had they been the last to see M. Desjardins alive? Had they argued with M. Desjardins for some reason and accidentally killed him? Fanny shook her head, appalled that she was thinking such thoughts.

She opened the door to the storage shed and spotted the wheelbarrow near the front. She only had to move some hoes and rakes to get to it. Quickly, she pulled the wheelbarrow out and started pushing it toward the house, trying not to think about what would be placed in it.

When she entered the house, progress had already been made. She found the desk in the kitchen and M. Desjardins halfway out the door. Henri was pulling him by one leg with his good arm.

"Don't bring the cart down the stairs. Just help me get him up to the courtyard," Henri said practically. He showed no emotions about a person who had hired him for the best job of his career. He also hadn't speculated why the maître d'hôtel had been killed or who killed him.

Silently, Fanny went down the stairs and grabbed one of the dead man's legs, trying not to think about what she was handling. Together they pulled him up the four steps. Fanny tipped the wheelbarrow on its side, and they gave one last heave to place M. Desjardins inside. Then Fanny righted the wheelbarrow, and side by side she and Henri pushed the cart slowly into the carriage house. It was a bumpy ride for the body. Henri held one handle with his good hand and Fanny held the other with both of hers, which created an uneven gait. They made it, though, and Fanny pulled open the doors of the part of the shed where the big enclosed carriage usually was kept, the one M. Monnard and his family had taken to the coast.

Again, Henri took his side of the cart and they pushed it inside. Fanny saw the canvas tarp the carriage driver used to protect the open carriage folded on a worktable filled with bridles and bits and cinches. She went and got the tarp, unfolded it a little, and threw it over the body. "There," she said dully, by now immune to the horror of it all. "I hope you're happy."

Henri did seem pleased and absolutely undeterred by Fanny's sarcasm. "You'll see, Fanny. This is for the best. Now come help me move the desk back. I had a hell of a time moving it out of that little room."

The couple walked back to the house, and Fanny could hear Henri panting. He was nearing the end of this surge of manic energy. But he was cheerful as they walked side by side. "We can put tables out here in the spring. In the meantime, we can use the reception room and dining room and salon. There are always people who don't want to dine outside. Tomorrow we should count the trestles, to see how many tables we can rig."

Now Fanny was afraid he really had gone mad with the fever. At this moment Henri truly believed they could appropriate this grand mansion for their own business. What a fantasy, that they could allow anyone with money to come into number twenty-three and pay for a meal? But she knew there was no way to reason with him now. He would recover and they would laugh about his ravings.

Fanny and Henri grunted and groaned and wiggled to get the office put back together. "I don't think M. Desjardins has had time to tell everyone that the master has left town. When a delivery man comes tomorrow, and you know they will, at least the office will look like it always looks," Henri said proudly.

Fanny didn't even know what to say. Henri had not shown the slightest regret or sadness or apprehension over another murder here on the square, this one in their own house. A reasonable person would show some concern. And he had no idea that everyone in the square did, in fact, know that M. Monnard and his family had left the country.

Just as Fanny was going to suggest they go back to their kitchen and Henri to bed, a pounding came on the door. "M. Desjardins, hello!" an unfamiliar voice said. Like a madman, Henri grabbed the first knife he could get his hands on.

"What day is it?" Fanny asked, then realized Henri had been out of consciousness for two days and wouldn't have the answer to that question. Thinking frantically, she said, "I know. It's Thursday. It's the waste removal. They come Monday and Thursday at night to all the houses here on the Place."

Henri nodded, put down the knife, and went to answer the door.

In the meantime, Fanny lit some lanterns in the kitchen so the men could see their way to the waste tanks. The workers had their own lanterns but she and the maître d'hôtel usually tried to facilitate this ugly job. After she had complained about the waste disposal men dragging the filth through the kitchen, M. Desjardins had purchased two closed metal containers on wheels so the waste wasn't open and sloshing through Fanny's workspace. The visits from the waste disposal were a chore she had shared with M. Desjardins, twice a week. Tears sprang in her eyes as she thought about the maître d'hôtel. She was losing her own control. She turned her head away from the door and tried to breathe deeply, something her mother had always counseled when she had cried too much as a child.

Henri and the men came in laughing and talking together. The workers bowed respectfully to Fanny and went on about their business.

"Just think what would have happened if we hadn't got the office cleaned up," Henri said, as if a child had spilled milk in there, instead of a man losing his life. "I told them M. Desjardins went off with the master out of town. They never see anyone else in the household but you and him." Then he turned and went into the office again. Fanny followed him to the door and watched. He was looking through the drawers as though it were the most natural thing in the world. "I know there's money in here somewhere," he said, continuing his search.

With that, Fanny closed the door to the office and went into her own bedroom for a moment. She couldn't watch such casual pillaging. The structure of the world as she knew it had been removed. Everything was tilted and scrambled and upside down. She sat on the bed, rigid, hands clasped, and closed her eyes tight. When she heard the waste removal men leave and Henri see them to the outer door, she got up and went into the kitchen, and blew out the candles.

She met Henri outside. Neither of them spoke of what they had just done. Henri was walking slowly, his elation of a few minutes ago replaced by silence. She could tell he was having trouble putting one foot in front of the other. "Let's get you back in bed, love. I still don't want you to lose that arm. I'll make you a fresh poultice," she said automatically and to her own ears the words sounded insincere and forced.

But Henri seemed to take solace in them. He leaned on her the last bit of the walk. He was trembling.

FANNY refused to put the lanterns out. She wanted light, maybe all night. The kitchen was bathed in warmth. Fanny herself was cold to the bone. She had built a fire in the small open hearth and pulled up a chair. She had also done something she had never done before in her life: opened a bottle of wine just for herself.

Henri had retreated to bed as soon as they made it back to the new kitchen. Fanny made him another poultice and changed the dirty one. The wound looked pulled and angry but neither of them could detect any red streaks. Fanny gave Henri the bottle of cognac they kept downstairs for cooking. He took a long pull out of it and was asleep in a moment.

Then Fanny had gone back downstairs, where she still was. It was almost one in the morning but Fanny knew she wouldn't sleep. She paced the floor and peered out the windows but it was quiet out there. It was then she opened the bottle of wine and fed the fire. She drank the first glass fast, finishing it nearly in one gulp. Soon, numbing warmth started to spread over her and she poured herself another glass and went to sit by the fire.

Loneliness was not something Fanny was accustomed to feeling. She'd grown up in a home and a neighborhood where there were always people she knew; her own family's business meant people were in and out of the Delarues' quarters often. Then she had moved to a large house as a member of the staff; she was used to living with people.

At first, Fanny had felt proud of her room alone in the

basement by the kitchen. It set her apart from the rest of the servants. But she knew she had missed a lot of companionship in that dormitory room on the third floor with the other girls. She hadn't developed any close friendships.

Now they were all gone. Henri was ill. M. Desjardins had been killed. She was alone, felt alone in her spirit, even if Henri was sleeping upstairs. Not only was she feeling alone but she had lots of decisions to make about her life, things that she thought she wouldn't have to face so soon.

Fanny was brooding over them. Lonely, confused, fearful of a murderer on the loose, worried about Henri's health and his state of mind, upset about M. Desjardins, she sat and drank wine and brooded. Until Henri broke the mood.

"Fanny, where are you?" he called out. He sounded disoriented. "Fanny?"

Reluctantly, Fanny put out the lanterns and poked at the fire. Then she climbed upstairs with the candlestick in her hand.

"Fanny, come to bed, love. Keep me warm. I'm so cold," Henri mumbled.

"I'm right here," Fanny said and felt Henri's forehead. It was hot. She gently rearranged the pillows under his arm, then turned to blow out the candle and put it down on the table, which was really a discarded sideboard from the main house. But before she could do that, the candlelight caught the glimmer of something unfamiliar on the floor near the chest.

It was her spice box, looking as though it had toppled off the chest. When it fell on the floor, another drawer had opened, one that Fanny hadn't realized was even in the box. She reached down to pick it up, then sat down on the floor beside it with a thud. She was shocked by what she saw and slid the candlestick close to the box for more light. Papers with writing on them peeked out from the bottom of the drawer but they were obscured by a layer of money on top of them. Stacks of livres were crammed into this drawer, but that still wasn't what caught Fanny's attention.

The spice box held more diamonds and other precious jewels than Fanny had ever seen before.

CHAPTER NINE

I⊤ was early in the morning and Fanny was trying to revive a cold fire. She finally gave up and went outside for some kindling, then built a proper new one. At the same time she brought in enough charcoal to rev up the oven and also make a fire in one of the charcoal braizers. She had no idea what she was going to cook, only that she needed to cook something.

Cooking was still the realest thing in her life. It had crept up on her when she wasn't actually looking for a "purpose" for her life and gave her one anyway.

But even before cooking insinuated itself into her plans, she had discovered a difference between her and her schoolmates. She kept it to herself, of course, not wanting to be thought strange, but she wondered why her dreams weren't the same as the other girls she grew up with. The other girls dreamed of the day they could be married, have children of their own.

Fanny dreamed about what she would be when she grew up, and it wasn't a wife and mother. She just assumed that would happened, that eventually she would marry and have children. It wasn't even worth speculating about that, worth wasting those precious moments on, the ones when you can lie in bed and daydream about your life. She wanted to *be* something first.

When she was nine, she thought being a nun the most desirable job and the one that she would hold when she grew up. The girls at school would talk about how the nuns actually were married to Christ and wore a wedding ring and they speculated whether Christ appeared to the nuns and wanted sex, like a real husband. This was a source of much risqué discussion. Fanny found herself repulsed by even the whiff of the sexual nature of this career choice and abandoned the idea by age ten.

Then, for a month or so, she wanted to be a laundress.

No one in Paris did there own laundry. They sent their dirty clothes to the laundresses, of whom there were always at least a thousand working at a bend in the Seine. Fanny was very taken with this profession for a while, no doubt because all the little boys she went to school with loved to go down and watch the laundresses work, each having a crush on one or more, each pointing out the superior rear ends or breasts of their favorite. The laundress phase ended when Fanny actually watched the women one day, not the boys watching the women. It was torturous, backbreaking work and it did not seem to Fanny that it could possibly be worth the jeering adoration of twelve-year-old boys to bend over constantly and lift hundreds of pounds of wet clothes every day for twelve hours.

Fanny's attraction to cooking had developed gradually,

and certainly not through her own family's hurried, thrown-together meals, although they had a charm of their own for the lively conversations her parents would have over their mostly purchased food. There was a neighborhood café in faubourg St. Antoine where occasionally she and her family would go to have some wine and a stew. The couple who ran the café worked together so closely. It was a thing to behold. The husband ran the bar; his wife cooked in the back. They fussed and laughed and hugged each other often. To Fanny, it looked like the ideal situation for life.

Then there was the additional bonus: The other people who came into the café loved the wife's cooking. Fanny couldn't for the life of her think of this couple's name. But she remembered her parents and others complimenting the woman on her food, and the woman's face breaking into a big smile. It was the same smile Philippe Delarue smiled when a builder or house owner gave him compliments for his cabinets and he reported it back home. It was the same smile Martine smiled when she finished a dress and the client tipped her extra and commended her.

Fanny herself wasn't the least interested in making cabinets or dresses, had never thought her parents work personally appealing. But she wanted to have that smile, the smile that came when other people recognized that you did something well. And she was sure her way to that smile was through cooking.

It was truly a shame that now, when the man she loved seemed to be offering her a similar situation, to open a restaurant together, she couldn't even consider it because it was all wrong.

Last night she had closed the secret drawer in the spice box, but not before she figured out how it opened and closed. Then she set the closed box back on Henri's side table, where she could keep an eye on it. It was still there, looking innocent and benign, this morning. As much as she wanted to examine the diamonds again in the morning light to make sure they were the real thing, she also didn't want to share her finding with Henri quite yet, not while he was acting so, so unwell. She could just see him grabbing them and running around the arcade, showing them off. She also had to admit, looking at them in the day or night, by candlelight or magnifying glass, she wouldn't know a real diamond from a fake. But who would go to such trouble to hide fakes?

Many of the confusing events of the last few months seemed less daunting to Fanny now that she knew about the jewels, and although she actually had little more real information than she had before, she was sure the jewels were the root of the problems. She hoped that upon reflection she would be able to tie all the strange and unpleasant happenings to the spice box and its contents. But the spice box had come to her from her father, the one person she trusted implicitly. She just could not believe he was involved in stealing jewels or killing anyone. And he hadn't even known Chef Etienne.

Fanny shook her head, trying to clear out all the doubt and confusion. Now was not the time. She had a sick boyfriend who had a serious injury to his arm and was, she had to admit, delusional. And because of those delusions, she now had a dead maître d'hôtel to bury, or should she fight Henri over this? What would be the best thing to do?

One of the possibilities that had occurred to her as she lay awake beside Henri last night was that there was a true maniac out there, choosing one household on the Place

Royale at random, then another, and killing whoever opened the door. If that was so, then she needed to put M. Desjardins back in the office so she could call the authorities and then warn all the other houses. But in her heart she didn't believe that. The spice box was the key. So, was it worth arguing with Henri over the disposition of M. Desjardins's body if his death didn't pose a threat to anyone else? And since she didn't know anything about his family, she couldn't inform them of his death so he could be taken to a family burial plot. Would he want to be buried here, on the beautiful Place Royale, or in a common grave over by Les Halles? She knew he would rather be here, even if his final resting place would be a secret to most of the world.

Fanny poured a cup of coffee and added hot milk. She felt better. That was decided then. M. Desjardins would be buried here, at number twenty-three, where he belonged. But how?

She knew that digging a grave was out of the question for Henri, even with her help. Then she thought of it. Fanny would send for her brother.

Now she could wake Henri.

ALBERT Delarue looked as if he were going to explode. His face was red and his pulse was jumping in his neck. He was standing in the door of the carriage house with Fanny by his side, staring at the body of M. Desjardins, still in the wheelbarrow.

Fanny had had a frantic morning. The maîtres d'hôtel from all over the square had arrived to purchase foodstuffs from their friend M. Desjardins shortly after nine. Fanny had remembered about the sale just in time to go over to the big house and light a fire in the kitchen, check the office once more for any sign of a problem, and think up a lie good enough to convince these men everything was as it should be. She told them M. Desjardins had been called by messenger to the office of the master's lawyer, to sign some papers relating to M. Monnard's departure and had instructed Fanny to conduct the sale. Fanny was in no mood to haggle so the neighboring households got some good bargains on groceries. It also gave Fanny the chance to hint that she and Henri might stay as caretakers. "M. Desjardin is already getting offers," she said proudly, as if her superior were too good at his job to waste time on managing an empty house. When the last maître d'hôtel left, she just had time to check on Henri, still asleep but thrashing and moaning, before her brother showed up.

"Fanny, explain to me again why you hid this man out here in the shed instead of calling the night guard like you should?"

"Well, Henri has this idea about us staying here and turning it into a restaurant while M. Monnard is out of the country. It would just be for a year or so. That way we could save the money we made so we could rent space at the Palais-Royal or someplace proper. Even rue Vieille du Temple is getting a nice row of places to eat; some are just cafés and some serve a whole meal." Fanny knew she was babbling without making a bit of sense.

"And so he kills the maître d'hôtel?" Albert asked with a sneer.

Fanny looked at her brother with impatience and sisterly disgust. He was being stubborn and thick at just the wrong time. "I don't know who killed the maître d'hôtel. I was asleep and so was Henri, and then I went to M. Desjardins's office and there he was, dead. But I also don't know where his family is and I don't want him buried in one of those dumps, where they just sprinkle lime on everyone. And I know I should have called the night guard but I had a lot on my hands. Perhaps in the future I can locate his family and then he can be dug up and given a proper burial. Can you just please help me here?"

Earlier, while the neighbors were shopping through her pantry, Fanny had gone out in the busy Place and called for a messenger. There were always a dozen or so congregated around the statue in the center of the square. All she had to do was point at one and gesture for him to come near. She'd written her brother a letter and sealed it with sealing wax from M. Desjardins's desk so it couldn't be read by anyone but him.

On a normal day her brother was in charge of the workshop and stayed there. Her father went out with deliveries to the grand houses and dealt with the architects and the owners. She hoped today was a normal day, because she didn't want her father to know anything about this, and she had said as much in the note. *"Don't tell Father but you must come to the Place Royale. Try to be here at eleven. I need you. Fanny."*

When her brother had arrived at the house, reality reared its ugly head. Albert Delarue did not have a fanciful side. He was the most practical one in the family.

"I'm here, aren't I? I'm not about to let you get in trouble over this because I know you could not have possibly had anything to do with this man's death. But Fanny, you must understand what is and what is not possible. You and Henri are just going to pretend to everyone that the maître d'hôtel is still alive? How long can you keep that up? And take over the house for a restaurant? What about M. Monnard?"

"He's going to be gone until this revolution settles down. It could be years before he returns. If he starts building projects in England, he'll have to see them through."

Albert shook his head as if the idea wasn't even worth considering. "You really think our mother and father will let you live here with your boyfriend, the chef in there"—he jerked his head toward the kitchen, where Henri was fast asleep again—"and start a restaurant in the house of a man Papa has known for more than twenty years? Papa won't believe your lies!"

"Albert, I don't think anyone, even Papa, would be the least suspicious if we said that we took the job of caretakers. Every house where the master has left has a couple watching over it. We could say M. Desjardins took another position. No one would think that strange. And Henri and I are going to start a restaurant somewhere and we are going to be together, but right now he is very ill so you and I have to give this man a burial." Fanny stamped her foot in frustration.

Albert ignored her outburst. "So your boyfriend was sick in bed and you took a nap. After that you just found this fellow with a stab wound in his heart. Doesn't that worry you in the least? The murderer could still be here!"

Fanny slipped her arm through her brother's. "That's why you and I are going to go through the house together, just to make sure."

Albert started to protest, then thought better of it. "I'm going home and getting two of the lads. Then I'll come back and tell them one of your master's dogs was poisoned by some bad food. You have to bury it before the master comes back. You're going to tell the master it ran off. They are going to dig a big hole. It's a big dog. You and I will search the house while they dig. But then we will leave and you will have to actually bury the poor fellow. Get the one-armed chef to help you. I'll come tamp the dirt down tomorrow."

"What are you going to tell Papa?" Fanny asked.

"I have no idea but I'll figure out something by the time I get back to the shop. I'm a married man so I have experience lying," Albert said, with a tiny little smile on his face.

"Just let me know so we can keep our stories straight," Fanny said as they walked toward the outer door.

Her brother took his rough hands and ruffled her hair. Fanny hadn't worn her cap for days. The discipline of domestic service was already fading. "I won't mention you, don't worry. But this is insane, you know. You can't pretend your maître d' hôtel is still alive and that M. Monnard gave you permission to open his house to strangers who just want a hot meal." Then he left.

Fanny, totally humiliated at having to go so in debt to her brother, took this moment to walk down the arcade to check on the boys, Nicholas and Simon. Had they seen anything suspicious at number twenty-three before they left for their new household? She knocked on the door of number eleven. Simon answered the door and his face broke into a welcoming smile. Fanny felt tears forming. She shook her head quickly to regain control and smiled back. "I just wanted to make sure you two got down here. I guess I missed you leaving."

Simon nodded. "Oh, yes. We came over here early afternoon yesterday. We have to sleep in the kitchen, on a blanket by the fireplace, and tend the fire during the night, but it's not so bad. How is Henri? And the Monsieur?"

Fanny gulped. In a terrible fever and dead, thank you for asking. "Henri is getting better and the Monsieur is busy, of course. I am, too, but Henri and I aren't leaving anytime soon, so I'll check on you now and again," she said and touched Simon on the tip of his nose. He giggled and closed the door.

Fanny walked back home, relieved and also disappointed Simon seemed unaware of his former superior's death. The boys didn't know anything.

"HENRI, before we bury him, we need to retrieve his keys," Fanny said reluctantly. She had thought of that earlier, when she and her brother had gone through the house. There were locked rooms and lots of locked cabinets. It wasn't that Fanny wanted to steal anything; she just wanted to be able to lock and unlock when and if she might need to. They certainly needed to keep the doors out to the square locked now that there wasn't a staff around.

"You're right," Henri said. He was feeling better after sleeping all day. The poultice was drawing the infection out. Now they were going to threaten all the progress he'd made by using his wounded arm. But he was positive and cheerful. When Fanny had explained what her brother had been willing to do for them, and also what part they had to play themselves, Henri got out of bed and started dressing. "Well, it's lucky it's November. I'm sure M. Desjardins is cool as a cucumber in the carriage house. All we have to do is tip the wheelbarrow in the hole and fill it up with dirt."

They were standing in the carriage house now. It was dark, the only safe time to move M. Desjardins to his final resting place, if there was a safe time for such doings.

Henri was holding a lantern in his good hand so Fanny took the lead. Gingerly, she tugged at the watch chain dangling from the body of M. Desjardins. Instead of a watch, a wad of keys was on the end of that chain. She had seen him pull them out of his pocket a hundred times. After several attempts, she finally put her hand on the body and pushed in on his chest, while pulling up on the chain. The keys came out. Quickly she unhooked them from the watch chain and put them in her apron pocket, then looked up at Henri. "Well, let's do it," she said flatly.

It went just about as planned. The body wasn't as easy to dislodge from its seat in the wheelbarrow as Henri had imagined. While he tipped the cart, Fanny had to pull on M. Desjardins's legs until he toppled into the grave. The pile of earth made by digging the hole was cold and not as pliable as they would have liked, but they took turns and had their colleague sufficiently covered with soil in an hour.

Henri was having trouble breathing and his face, illuminated in the lantern light, was covered with a thin sheen of sweat. "It's not as packed as it should be, but I can't do any more."

Fanny took his shovel and hers and started toward the shed. "My brother will fix that tomorrow. We did as much as we can do. Now I have something to say to you. Let's have a glass of wine and I'll change your bandage."

When they were back in the kitchen with the fire going strong and the wine poured, Fanny sat Henri down and put his feet up on a footstool while she worked on his arm. This afternoon, she and her brother had moved two armchairs with upholstery over to the kitchen from the house, along with two footstools. As long as they were alone with a houseful of furniture, they might as well be comfortable.

"Henri, I do not blame you, and in the long run I agreed with you in our course of action regarding Monsieur. I think he would be happier here than in some hideous common grave. But you weren't considering that. Your motives for hiding him were entirely selfish."

Henri looked crestfallen at Fanny's stern tone of voice. He said nothing in defense of their actions.

"Secondly, we didn't even try to find out who killed him. For all we know, we are in danger. I can't believe I've become so careless about my own well-being and so callous about others. When Chef Etienne was killed, I at least tried a little to find out who might have killed him. This time I was only too willing to throw poor M. Desjardins in a wheelbarrow and bury him myself. What if he was religious? We didn't give him the benefit of a priest. Is this revolution making us so uncaring about our fellow citizens? Or is it something the matter with us?"

Henri fidgeted in his chair, his cheeks turning a deep red. It was obvious Fanny was disappointed in him. "And I was the one who talked you into hiding the Monsieur's body. I guess I wasn't thinking straight."

Fanny wrapped cheesecloth around Henri's arm as a bandage and to keep his poultice in place. "The worst thing is if anyone should find him, buried back there, they could think we killed him. The boys, Nicolas and Simon, could tell the police we were the only ones left here when they moved down the street. Just him and us."

Henri was silent, shamefaced. Finished with her work, Fanny sat in the other upholstered chair and put her feet up on the other footstool. "This is a good chair. I could get used to it, I could."

Henri was looking worse by the minute, pale and shivering. She wanted to lead him upstairs and kiss him all over his face. But she wasn't finished. "And another thing, Henri, we can't open a restaurant here. Think of all the neighbors. There are at least five judges on this square. Everyone is in the government in some way. If the revolution has its way, they probably won't have a job long, and this square will be an unpopular place. If the king gets to stay on in all his glory, all these old fogies are not going to want a business here. How many times have you heard them brag about how Place Royale has an arcade but doesn't have a bunch of common shops."

Henri looked crestfallen. "I thought it would be so wonderful, you and I starting a business together. I know it would be popular, Fanny. I don't want to just work for someone else my whole life."

"And I can understand that. My parents were very upset I went to work for wages in the first place. Our family works for themselves. I'm not saying we can't start a restaurant. It just can't be here."

"That's good enough for me. Tomorrow, or maybe the next, when I feel up to it, we'll go to the Palais-Royal, to look around. Now can we go to bed?" Henri asked, no longer able to pretend he wasn't in discomfort.

"You go on, love, I'll be up soon. Go to sleep. Your arm must be sore."

"Throbbing," Henri said as he went upstairs. "Fanny, I love you."

Fanny didn't answer. She waited until she heard Henri softly snoring, then she put a lid on the pot of lamb stew she made earlier with her nervous energy. Albert and his workers had eaten some when they finished their duties. Fanny realized she had not eaten all day but she put the stew outside in the cold. Cooking had not stimulated her own appetite. She went into the pantry, where they kept the pots and pans on shelves. When she had checked on Henri earlier, she had hidden the spice box in there, in a big stockpot. There were too many people going in and out of the courtyard today.

She retrieved the box, opened the drawer, and dove her hand into strings of sapphires, diamonds, and emeralds. Then she recalled the earring she'd found in M. Desjardins's hand and pulled it out of her pocket, dropping it in with the rest. She couldn't help smiling as she stuck her hand down in the tangle of precious stones again and held as much as she could, pulling her hand out of the box and up in the air, pearls a-dangling. As she sat there with her hand held high, full of jewels, moving it slowly so the firelight caught the glimmer of the stones, she tried to remember when her father had first given her this box.

It had been right after the Fête de la Fédération. The next thing she knew, Chef Etienne had been killed and the box had showed up on her bed when she hadn't put it there. Were the jewels in it when her father brought it over to her, or did someone hide them in the box while she was across the square that night? She tried to remember its weight when she had first held it. Then, recently, when all the trouble started, did someone move the box to the new kitchen from her room or did she do that herself? And what were her parents doing with it the other day? The biggest question: What was the point? Was someone trying to put the jewels in the box for safekeeping, or to get them out?

Fanny carefully untangled all the bracelets, brooches, earrings, and necklaces. The sapphires were her favorite and she quickly found the match to the earring M. Desjardin had had in his hand when she found him, a drop pendant of sapphires surrounded by diamonds. Then she found the necklace that matched them. She put them carefully in a corner of the drawer. Was M Desjardins the person who hid the jewels in her box, and was killed when he was removing them, or did he grab that earring out of someone else's hand as he tried to take them? And if that was the case, why didn't the thief and murderer complete the job, taking the box and all the jewels? And what of Chef Etienne? He had been holding a ring in his hand when he was found, a ring that Fanny had put in her drawer. Number six was situated on a corner of the Place, just as number twenty-three was. They were diagonally across the square from each other. What if Chef Etienne had caught the culprit as he tried to break into the wrong house to retrieve the box? A box that was clear across the square at the time? The chef could have been killed in vain, the murderer no closer to his prize than before the death.

Fanny's head hurt. She put the box back in the empty stockpot and fell back in the chair, reluctant to climb the stairs and join Henri on his narrow bed, the bed that had given her so much pleasure before. Soon she dozed off in the chair, exhausted and troubled.

CHAPTER TEN

HENRI had insisted they dress up for this occasion. He had nothing but knee breeches to wear and they were fast going out of style for men as they indicated the aristocratic lifestyle. But for years they had been the kind of pants a man wore when he dressed up, and so today that was what Henri had on, with a nice linen shirt and a dark brown linen vest. He had an overcoat of dark gray. His hair was pulled back with a silk ribbon. He looked very fashionable, like a lord from one of the Eastern European countries, not in in the Parisian style, but stylish nonetheless.

Fanny had pretty clothes when she wasn't wearing her work uniform. Her daily garb was a soft gray dress with the standard servants' white collar that crossed over her breasts in an X design. Most of the women on the square who were in service wore the same thing. But her mother was always sewing her something with leftover pieces of material that a rich woman had already paid for. Since mother and daughter were the same size, she didn't even need Fanny for fittings. Today Fanny was wearing a black-and-tan-striped suit of bouclé wool of a very fine quality. Her chemise, which peeked out the top of the suit jacket, was tan embroidery on black. The skirt was narrow as was the new style. She was a fashion plate.

"They used to have guards posted here, to keep out the riffraff. You had to look like a gentleman to get in. Of course, now that we have the revolution, that's changed. The gardens are always open to the public. But we want to look like we belong, don't we?" Henri asked, not expecting an answer. They were headed to the Palais-Royal, to look at all the cafés and restaurants. It was the first time Fanny had actually been inside the arcade.

Just a few years before, in 1781, Louis-Philippe, duc de Chartres, who was later named duc d'Orleans, was once again almost broke. So he remodeled his Paris estate, building houses that he sold around his great garden. An arcade, like the one at the Place Royale, connected these houses. But unlike the Place Royale, which boasted no commercial businesses around the arcade, the Palais-Royal was full of rental storefronts. And many of these storefronts housed cafés and restaurants. There were also lots of other attractions: a wax museum, puppet shows, vaudeville theaters, billiard salons, even a medicinal bath. In the houses behind, other kinds of commerce transpired. Prostitutes plied their trade and looked down on the scene from the house windows. When they were done with one customer, they had only to go shopping out the window for the next.

"Lots of chefs who worked for royalty opened cafés or restaurants here. Antoine Beauvillers and Jean-Babtiste Barriere," Henri pronounced, pointing at various cafés. Henri hero-worshiped these aristocratic chefs and followed their careers from private households of royal blood to public restaurants. It was one of the reasons he wanted to do the same. "This is Galerie de Montpensier, where the Café Glacier Corazza is. The Jacobins meet there," he said as they walked. He loved being the tour guide.

"And that's the Café de Foy over there, and to the right, the Grand Vefour. All the famous soldiers and explorers go there."

"What is that, where all those people are crowded around the window?" Fanny asked. She was in a daze of excitement. So many people seemed to be able to afford to go to cafés. Perhaps there were enough customers for her and Henri, too.

"That's the Café Mechanique. All the food comes up from the kitchen in the basement through a lift in the middle of the table. The middle of the table, Fanny. Can you imagine?"

They watched for a minute, then Henri pulled her away. "But we're not going there. Proper ladies don't go to cafés. They go to restaurants. We're going to Restaurant de Beauvilliers. Remember, I mentioned him a minute ago? He used to be the majordomo of the Comte de Provence." As they walked toward the door, Henri bowed low. "I 'borrowed' a bit of the maître d's household money. Will you join me to honor M. Desjardins, God rest his soul?"

THEY had artichokes drizzled with an olive oil dressing, fresh grilled sardines, pigeon with tiny peas, a vol-au-vent pastry filled with turbot and salmon, and strawberries in a sugar syrup, all washed down with a carafe of Chablis. Fanny had never felt so grown-up, so in love, so excited about the future. All her doubts of the last few days, her suspicions of others, were gone, or at least were tucked away in the back of her mind.

Henri had insisted they take a carriage home. He seemed totally recuperated. His arm was still bandaged but he was moving it more freely. Fanny felt this "little trip" had given her more insight into Henri. It was obvious he had spent a great deal of any free time he had in Paris at the Palais-Royal.

"In the spring and summer, there's a sundial with a burning glass attached to it and the glass is attached to a shell filled with gunpowder. At noon the heat of the sun causes the gunpowder to go off. It makes a big boom. Everyone watches and claps," he said,

"Henri, I have an idea. Even though I don't feel right about setting up shop at M. Monnard's house, I don't think it would be bad at all to borrow some things, the fourneau and some other things. It would be nice to have beautiful silver to serve with, like they do at Beauvilliers," Fanny said.

"We could leave an inventory list and return things a little at a time, as we could afford replacements," Henri said excitedly. "I know plenty of chefs have been paid off with equipment when their masters left the country. No one would think a thing about it. And M. Monnard would help us if he were here."

The carriage turned into the Place Royale and pulled up in front of number twenty-three. Henri helped Fanny out of the coach and turned to pay the driver. It was then that she saw him. In the doorway of their house, Inspector Fournier was waiting.

* * *

FANNY felt weak. She looked around for Henri but he was still busy with the driver and didn't seem to notice the inspector. This time, the handsome man was wearing an official police uniform. He was blowing on his hands to keep them warm. When he saw Fanny, he smiled, doffed his hat, and bowed his head slightly.

"I haven't seen you for months, Fanny. You're looking well," he said.

Fanny thrust her chin forward in what she hoped was a brave pose. "What makes you think you can be so familiar toward me? You act as if you know me but I don't know you," Fanny said.

She could feel Henri walk up by her side. "What do you want?" he said curtly.

"Just a minute, Henri. Mademoiselle Delarue reminded me we have never actually met, although we saw each other quite a bit last summer, didn't we?" the inspector said, teasing in his voice. "I am Police Inspector Fournier. And you are Fanny Delarue, daughter of famed cabinetmaker Philippe Delarue and Martine Delarue, one of the determined women of Paris who marched to Versailles to bring the king home." Inspector Fournier's voice changed when he mentioned Fanny's mother. Was it menace? A threat?

"What do you want, Inspector?" Henri asked.

"I've been out of the city, working on a rather complicated case. I just returned. And I heard there was trouble here the day the oath was required."

"A Paris police inspector, working out of town? That's unusual," Fanny said sarcastically.

Inspector Fournier smiled. "This is an unusual time in

our country. The case involves some missing jewels from Versailles. I've been working on it for more than a year. Now, would you please tell me what happened the night St. Paul–St. Louis was attacked."

Fanny's knees started wobbling under her pretty suit but she didn't flinch. Henri held her arm protectively.

"That night a crowd gathered around St. Paul–St. Louis. The priest there tore up the requirement, then locked the church. The crowd wasn't happy. They came over to the Place when they got drunk enough," Henri explained.

"And I hear they broke into this house, number twenty-three," the inspector offered.

"No," Fanny replied. "They got in the courtyard and broke a few windows. But they didn't get in the house. Henri and the other men in the household, even the master, came out with arms. They scared the crowd away. The National Guard came to the square. Henri's arm was wounded but it's better now. That's all."

"I wish to talk with the master. I'd like to hear what he thinks about all this."

Henri and Fanny looked at each other. "The master decided to take his family to London," Henri said.

"And he's already gone?"

"Yes, we're staying with the house right now," Henri replied.

Inspector Fournier looked surprised. "Will you let me know if you two stop attending the house? I wouldn't want to leave M. Monnard's house vulnerable. I would make sure the night guard watched it closely."

"Oh, the house will be attended," said Fanny. "Someone will always be here."

Henri took Fanny's arm and unlocked the door to the courtyard. Inspector Fournier stared at the keys.

Henri followed his gaze. "The maître d'hôtel lent me these," he said confidently and opened the door.

"I'm happy we finally met, Fanny," the inspector said as a farewell.

"Thank you," Fanny said softly, and followed Henri into the empty courtyard. Her heart was pounding.

Henri was quiet as they walked to the new kitchen. "Damn him for ruining our special day," he grumbled.

Fanny was thinking about what the inspector said about jewels stolen from Versailles. "No one could ruin our day, love. We had a wonderful meal and saw all those beautiful restaurants. I can hardly wait to plan ours. But now, let's head for bed."

IT was time. Fanny had thought about it through another sleepless night. It was time to tell Henri about the jewels. It wouldn't be right to keep something so important from him another day. Now that he was getting back to his old self, feeling healthier, Fanny's confidence in him and their future was renewed.

He was going through the storage rooms in the house, making lists of what he wanted to borrow for their restaurant. She went over to fetch him.

She found him in the wine cave.

Henri was ecstatic, happy to have a purpose. "Oh, Fanny, there are some good things here, especially from the south. The master loved Hermitage."

"Yes, well, we can't tell ourselves we are borrowing wine

to sell. It's stealing plain and simple. But in two years, I'm sure M. Monnard won't remember what was in this dusty old place," Fanny said, "and most likely it would disappear anyway."

Although there were terrible penalties in the old regime for being caught with even one bottle of the master's wine, the rules were applied only when the steward or maître d'hôtel needed them to be. Now that the revolution had started, those rules were forgotten most of the time. And Henri was right. All over Paris, employees were carting off the possessions of their masters who had abandoned them.

"Henri, I went up to get bread and some meat pies. Come have a break. I made coffee, or I could make you some chocolate."

Henri nodded. "Coffee is fine, love. I'll be right there."

As Fanny walked back to the new kitchen, she went over her speech again. She could honestly say she hadn't known about the jewels until the other night and that Henri was too ill to tell at the time.

She busied herself for the few minutes it took Henri to break away from his work and come in where it was warm. They hadn't built a fire in the main house kitchen and one's breath could be seen in the wine cave even in the summer, let alone in November. When he did come into the new kitchen, he chattered happily as he washed his hands. Fanny was sure the threat of losing his arm had bothered him more than he would ever admit. But she was wrong. It was the first thing he brought up.

"I just want you to know I can never repay you for what you've done for me the last few days," Henri said when he was settled in front of the fire with a cup of coffee and a meat pie. "I know I was half out of my mind. But you supported me, even with poor M. Desjardins. And you healed my arm. I could have been a one-armed cripple. It's one of the reasons I love you so much."

Fanny stepped into the storage room and pulled out the spice box, talking over her shoulder. "The main thing is you are improving. I think you are going to be just fine. Just don't try to do too much today." She sat down, serious and a little frightened; why she wasn't sure. "I have something to show you."

Henri must have noticed the change in Fanny. He looked at her seriously. "What is it?"

Fanny opened the drawer without comment. Neither she nor Henri spoke for a long time. Then Henri looked up at her. "Do you think this is what the inspector was talking about?"

Fanny nodded. "Yes, I do. My father gave this box to me last summer. In the last months someone must have hid the jewels in the box."

Henri's eyes were big. "We know two people who were at Versailles. The late Chef Etienne de la Porte and your mother."

"But anyone could have obtained the jewels from the one who actually stole them, and put them in my box. That's possible, isn't it?"

"Do you think this is what Chef and M. Desjardins were killed for?"

"It's a good bet," Fanny said.

"Then it is dangerous for us to have them."

"I didn't know they were in there until a few days ago. The box fell, I guess, and the drawer came open. I didn't even know the drawer was there."

"So they could have been in there all this time, from the day your father gave you the box."

Fanny went on the defensive. "What are you saying, that my mother stole the diamonds when she was at Versailles and then she and my father put them in a box that he then gave to me so I'd be the one in danger?"

Henri tried to sooth Fanny. "No, darling. But perhaps they were in there when he bought the box. By accident or unknowingly, perhaps."

Fanny let it go. She closed the box and quickly put it away in the other room. "Now that you're feeling better, I just wanted you to know about the jewels. I thought that perhaps they belonged to our mistress, that for some reason she hid them in my box the night of the problems and forgot to get them when the family left so quickly. But after what the inspector said last night, I doubt that's true."

"Fanny, what are you going to do with them? What are *we* going to do with them?" Henri corrected himself.

"We can spend the cash money, I suppose, on things to help us start a restaurant. But we have to figure out a way to give the jewels back without getting ourselves killed or thrown in jail forever. We can't just go up to the inspector and hand them over."

"No, that would be disastrous," Henri agreed.

Fanny could see Henri going over the angles in his mind. She'd already done that, for days. So she changed the subject. "We would have to sell the queen's best necklace to afford a restaurant on the Palais-Royal. So where else do you think we might put a restaurant that would be successful?" Fanny asked.

Henri still had the light of those gems in his eyes. "Why

don't we take out that box and you can try on everything? You'd be beautiful in diamonds. Let's just do it once."

Fanny remembered her time the other night by the fire with the jewels, then quickly dismissed it. They were alluring. She liked the idea of playing with all those jewels and nothing else on, not a stitch. "No, because they're not mine. I don't want to get used to them. Think locations, Henri. Locations. What do you think of the Latin Quarter? Somewhere over by the Sorbonne?"

Henri started to argue, then thought better of it, and allowed Fanny to change the subject. "Students don't have money."

"But teachers do."

"If we're talking about the left side of the river, St. Germain is the place."

Fanny had to agree. "Lots of aristos have moved there. I hear my father mention that neighborhood often."

Henri responded with a shake of the head. "If the aristos have moved there, it won't be safe for long. Look what happened here the other night. This was the first place the citizens thought of when they wanted to do some damage. And we have more robes than blue bloods," Henri observed, speaking of all the judges who lived on Place Royale.

"We don't want our café destroyed by the mobs. What about on this side? St. Antoine is all artisans. We need a place where merchants live, where there are people who have money but aren't snobbish about eating in the company of strangers. The bourgeois love restaurants."

Henri got up. "I know what I'll do. I'll go up to the Temple to the meetinghouse for domestic chefs. Someone is always there, especially now that so many people are out of jobs. I'll ask around. Someone may even know of an empty storefront."

The Temple was another guild-free privileged zone north of the Place Royale. Many professions that didn't have guilds but wanted to have some relationship with others in their field had meeting houses there. Domestic chefs were one of these. Although there were twenty-five food guilds in Paris, not one of them was for those who cooked in the homes of the wealthy. Fanny wanted to go along. But she could tell that Henri needed to do this on his own, to be with other chefs, who were all male. She kissed Henri on the top of the head. He pulled her down on his lap and gave her a real kiss.

"Well, you're feeling better, now aren't you? Off to the Temple with you. Go find out what the news is from your colleagues," she said softly, flirting with him. Henri put his hand under her skirt.

The next thing she knew she was sitting on top of him, stuck together in a heat that didn't generate from the fireplace. As they both sat panting, waiting for their heart rates to slow down, Henri took her hand. "Let's get married soon, before we open the restaurant. We'll have to get a place to live so we should be married. Your parents will feel better if we are. I will, too."

Fanny kissed his knuckles. She had known since the beginning that she and Henri would be together forever. It just seemed natural for them to get married. "But that doesn't mean I want a baby right away. I'm going to be much too busy making food," she said. "Now go."

"Wait. Fanny Delarue, will you marry me?"

"Yes, I will, Henri Brusli. Now get out of here."

* * *

IT was dark and Fanny fussed with the fire once again. She had carefully lit the lanterns in the courtyard, so Henri wouldn't have to walk through darkness. She had also opened and closed the little door that led out to the square at least a dozen times in the last two hours. Henri had left well before noon and he wasn't back yet, and of course, that worried her. What if his fever had come back with a vengence and he was helpless somewhere? She held out hope that he was just out getting drunk with the other men of his trade, letting off steam after an ordeal that left him with a good story.

She could just hear him. "The mob was breaking the windows to the kitchen, but I stopped them. Got a knife through my arm for my trouble," he would say and another chef would buy him a drink.

She went marketing after Henri left for the Temple, planning to make them a nice dinner. Now she was poking at a piece of overcooked sole that had been reheated one too many times.

The clock said it was after eleven and it was then that Fanny remembered the box. She ran into the storage room and jerked it out of its hiding place and opened the drawer. Everything was still there, as far as she could tell. Money was still tucked under the jewels, the sapphires were still in the corner. She let out a big breath and sat down again by the fire with the box on her lap.

She hadn't for a minute thought that Henri would take the box or any of its contents without telling her, no, not at all. But when the unexpected happens, the imagination can start conjuring up strange scenarios. She could see Henri taking a piece of the jewelry to Inspector Fournier to see if it was what he was looking for and the inspector throwing him in jail. She could imagine Henri taking one piece to a jeweler, just to see if it was real, and the jeweler calling the police. But none of that had happened. It was Henri who was missing, not the jewels.

Fanny thought back to the other night, when she sat in this very place and felt so alone. It was nothing compared to now. Now she felt lonely and vulnerable and worried. She felt ashamed for any doubts she'd had about Henri during his recuperation and full of a whole new set of worries. Where was he? She went to check the street one last time.

CHAPTER ELEVEN

FANNY found Henri's lists in the old kitchen and tried half-heartedly to add to them. She lit a fire in the hearth and then made giant piles of copper pots and pans, whisks and spoons, mixing bowls and platters, writing them down as she went.

She went upstairs and made another fire in the dining room fireplace and looked through the sideboard, putting everything she thought a restaurant could need on the top. Then she went to the salon, made a fire, put a collection of porcelain artificial flowers in a chair by the door, went back to the main reception room, and looked around, but her heart wasn't in it.

By this time Henri had been gone from the house on Place Royale for twenty-four hours. There was no way she could convince herself it was a simple case of getting too drunk to make it home last night. Something had happened to Henri. What should she do? Wait here? Go to her parents and leave Henri a note?

Fanny sank under the weight of all this. She stopped pretending, stopped organizing, stopped working. For a time she wandered through the house, exploring the ground-floor rooms in a way she never had been able to when the household was up and running. She examined the silver, really looked at the paintings, sat in all the chairs. Then she thought of something that she was sure would make her feel better. She would take a bath.

The bathing room was M. Monnard's pride and joy. The heated water for the bathtub depended on heat from the chimney, and Fanny had certainly contributed to that today by lighting fires in every fireplace on the ground floor. She was unconcerned with being conservative with the firewood. She would pay for the regular delivery when it came next week, even though there was no one living here to use it up. There was still a considerable amount of money locked up in M. Desjardins's desk, and more in the spice box.

Before she went to the second floor, where the bathing room was located, she went down to her own bedroom and retrieved her bathing sheet of heavy linen. Then she went up the stairs, glanced in the bedrooms as she went, and entered the master bath.

There were two marble tubs, each with its own tank of water. They were connected to the cistern near the chimney on the roof. Fanny started filling them both, adding some dried lavender and rose petals to the bathing tub. Soon the familiar odor of lavender and roses filled the room. Fanny took her clothes off and slipped her cloth in the water, then stepped into the marble tub. It was luxury, pure and simple.

The women domestics had their bath in the kitchen in a cramped tin tub, each putting down their bath sheets in turn and dipping in the same water that had been heated in a pot over the hearth fire. Baths in her childhood at the Delarue house had been essentially the same procedure. Now she was in a marble tub long enough for her to stretch out her legs.

Fanny washed her hair, then lay there until the water had cooled off. She tried to clear her mind, breath deeply and slowly, appreciate the experience and not fret over Henri. But it did not work. She loved the bath experience but it didn't eliminate the big knot of tension at the back of her neck. She scrubbed herself with the olive oil soap that the Monnards favored. It made her skin feel soft.

She got out of the first tub, heaved her cloth up, and wrung it out. Then she slipped the cloth in the second tub and poured in some scented oil that was sitting by that tub. This was the rinsing tub and she didn't tarry long in it as the water was getting chilly.

When Fanny was drying her body with a long, thick towel, she started crying. She had just wasted two tubs of water for one person's bath. It was sinful. She thought about leaving the tubs filled, just in case Henri came back in the next few minutes. But the water was already cold. She pulled the plugs on the tubs with angry jerks and hurriedly dressed. As much as she had enjoyed the bath in this beautiful room with the two tubs, her mood hadn't improved.

The only thing she knew to do now was make a plan to find Henri. She couldn't just sit here another day waiting in an empty house. She walked purposefully out of the house, right into the arms of her father.

"Oh!" She jumped in surprise. "Papa. What are you doing here?"

"I came to check on Henri, to make sure his arm was healing up."

Fanny knew she probably wasn't making the right decision but her first instinct was to conceal the truth from her father, like any teenager.

She turned right around and pulled her father into the house and the old kitchen. There was still a flicker of a fire in the hearth. She rebuilt it with care, so she could talk to her father without looking him in the eye.

"Henri went up to the Temple to the chefs' meeting-house. We're looking for a place to have a restaurant." She realized the implication was that Henri had done this today, not yesterday.

"How is his arm?" Philippe Delarue asked.

"It's much better. I did everything the doctor told me to, the poultices, the salve, we kept it elevated. The wound looks good and his fever is gone."

"Where is M. Desjardins?"

"He went to visit a friend in faubourg St. Germain yesterday. As long as we're here, he might as well take some time to do some things he hasn't been able to."

Her father sat on a stool by the fireplace she was fiddling with. "I think it's time to come home, Fanny."

Fanny turned toward her father and smiled brightly. "We will, I promise. Just a few more days and we'll come over with our clothes. Then you and Henri can come back for our things. By the way, M. Desjardins has given us permission to borrow some equipment from the house, if and when we get a restaurant. After all, no one will be cooking here for a couple of years."

Philippe Delarue looked skeptically at his daughter. "I don't really think he has the authority to do that."

"Oh, now, don't be a stick-in-the-mud. It would save us so much money and we'll return it all as we can afford to. Henri says lots of chefs are getting paid in equipment as their masters flee the country."

Philippe Delarue looked around with concern. Something was wrong but he couldn't put his finger on it. It wasn't the "borrowing" of M. Monnard's kitchen that Fanny was planning. He would see that they didn't abuse that privilege and would clear it with M. Monnard when he returned to Paris if need be. It was the stillness of the house that bothered him. He had been in enough building sites to know when they were merely buildings and when they were homes. This one felt abandoned.

Fanny was wound as tight as she could go. She wanted to tell her father about M. Desjardins and especially about Henri. She would like nothing better than for her father to take over the search for Henri in his organized manner. M. Desjardins, well, it was a burden on her soul, one that she would rather confess to her father than to a priest. But if she did tell him any of these things that bore so heavily on her, he would take her home to faubourg St. Antoine immediately. And she still had a hope that Henri would come in that door any minute. She wanted to be here if that happened. She didn't want him to return to a note that said, "I've gone home to my parents."

She made coffee. "I didn't get bread today but we can go up to the boulangerie on rue Vieille du Temple if you like," she chirped as she gracefully poured both coffee and hot milk into their cups at once.

Philippe Delarue knew something was wrong. A Parisian bought bread every day, even during the worst personal crisis. "So, what's it like here without a household to serve?"

"I don't really know yet. Having Henri's arm to tend to has been a full-time job. But to celebrate his recuperating and not losing use of his hand, we went to the Palais-Royal. Oh, Father, it is very fashionable. We ate at a fancy restaurant, I can't remember the name, and had wine and took a carriage home. It was wonderful," Fanny gushed. She knew she was pouring it on too heavily but she couldn't seem to stop her mouth from babbling or her hands from fussing. She must look like a wind-up toy, she thought.

Philippe Delarue's eyebrows shot up. "My, my. You both just lost your jobs and Henri takes you for an expensive dinner at the Palais-Royal. And next you want to start your own restaurant, is that what I hear? Who died and left you two wealthy?"

Fanny could feel all the color drain out of her face and no amount of acting and lying was going to hide that from her father. "Oh, Henri had saved a little money and we needed a treat, for our attitudes. It was a shock, having M. Monnard leave town so quickly. The restaurant is Henri's dream, it is nothing new. We've been talking about it for months. Now that we don't have jobs, Henri says to look at it as an opportunity, instead of a disaster."

Fanny's father had noticed her go pale, but she certainly seemed upbeat and cheerful otherwise. Perhaps the ripples in the undercurrent he sensed was nothing more than a lover's spat and Henri had left to go cool his temper. Whatever it was, he was going to keep a closer watch on Fanny in the next days. He would be glad when she was back home, with Henri in tow, of course. He could do worse for a son-in-law than Henri Brusli, even if he wasn't from Paris. Philippe got to his feet. "Tell Henri I'll see him in a couple of days. I'll come by again and check on you."

Fanny was relieved and saddened at the same time. She was relieved to have her father depart so she wouldn't have to lie to him anymore. She was sad she couldn't just dump all her woes in his lap. "Thank you for your concern. We'll be ready soon."

Her father drew her close and embraced her. "You smell good," he said with a smile.

"Don't tell M. Monnard but I took a bath up in the bathing room, the one with two tubs. There was lavender and roses dried for the tub."

Her father laughed. "We'll have trouble getting you in the tin tub after that. Don't get too spoiled, Fanny." He glanced around, then put on his cap and waved good-bye.

She waved back bravely as long as he was looking, going to the door and stepping out in the November cold to see her father slip through the small door in the porte cochere, each of them giving a final acknowledgment of the other.

Then she hurried inside and found the cognac bottle. It was nearly dusk, the sun itself far enough on its daily journey to be hidden behind the buildings of government to the west. As she spiked her coffee, she realized it was going to be another long night. But first thing in the morning, she was heading to the Temple.

FANNY had a beautiful, long cape her mother had made with scraps. It was dark blue wool with a lighter blue moiré lining. She was all set to put it on, walking toward the porte cochere in the frosty morning. She had slept in the house, in her own bedroom last night, not wanting to face Henri's bed alone again. But after her father left, she had gone out to the new kitchen, retrieved her spice box, and slept with it under the covers next to her.

When she woke up, she was full of resolve. Henri was not dead. She was sure of that. There was something or someone keeping him from coming home, yes, but today she was going to find him.

She hid the box again, up in the bathing room, then ran down to the neighbors at number eleven and hired Nicholas and Simon to come back to number twenty-three for the morning. This request had included a generous tip for the maître d'hôtel of that house and felicitations to him from M. Desjardins, who had gone to the Latin Quarter to see his niece, according to Fanny's story. She locked as many doors as she could, asked the boys to let in any deliveries, and tell them to come back for their money tomorrow. Of course, she didn't mention M. Desjardins or Henri. And she gave them more money than they made in a month to do this, along with hot chocolate, a baguette, and some cheese. They were installed in the house kitchen in front of the fire.

Fanny's moral questions of the last few days about M. Desjardins and the jewels, the ambiguous ethical waters she'd been treading, all that clutter in her mind, was gone, at least temporarily. Finding Henri safe and sound was all that mattered. With that single purpose in mind, she stepped through the small door onto the square and right into the arms of Inspector Fournier.

For a moment she thought she was still in bed and dreaming, having something akin to a nightmare, the kind where you are trying to go someplace but you can't get there, you get lost, search through crowds of people, someone is pursuing you, your anxiety builds. Then she felt that all-too-awake response she had to the inspector. Her cheeks were on fire.

"Ah, Fanny Delarue. What a beautiful cape. The lining almost matches your eyes. I say almost, because the color of your eyes is matchless. Totally unique, although I guess that's the wrong word because your mother has those same color eyes." As he said this, Inspector Fournier peeled back an edge of the cape to reveal the lining, as one would peel an orange. He then very formally helped her on with the cape, straightening it and patting her shoulder, as if she were a child.

Fanny wanted to be able to appear as confident as the inspector. His demeanor really was impressive. "What may I do for you, Inspector?" she said coolly, not really in his league but good nonetheless. She hoped she could pass for an indifferent servant.

"I thought I would stop by and visit with Henri this morning."

"Henri is not here."

"Then perhaps your maître d'hôtel?"

"M. Desjardins is not here either. They are running errands. Our duties are rather inconsistent now that the master and his family are gone."

Inspector Fournier started to enter the small door in the porte cochere. "I'll just wait for them."

Fanny held his arm to detain him from entering. All she could think about was the turned earth up close to the carriage house in the back. "I don't know how long they'll be gone. It would be a waste of your time."

In one swift movement, which reminded Fanny of how he'd handled that girl last summer, Fanny went from being in control to being pinned against the side of the building. The inspector held both of her arms tightly. "Fanny, I am almost out of patience with you and all those around you. Someone has made a terrible mistake and it must be put right or disaster will follow. I am warning you," he hissed in her ear. Then he kissed it, taking her earlobe in his mouth softly, flicking his tongue inside the cupped part of her ear.

Fanny realized that to all those bustling around them on the Place Royale, they looked like lovers. She also realized she should shove him away, dispel that image, in her own mind as well as what the world saw. But she couldn't, physically because her arms were pinned, and for some other reason, too.

The whole encounter was over in seconds: the whispered warning, the physical restraint, the violation, and her love of it. He released her with a slight tip of his head.

"I will take your warning to heart, Inspector," Fanny said as evenly as she could, staring straight into his eyes. "But could I ask you to come back later, when one of the men you asked for will be home? It does not suit me for you to wait about."

"Until then," Inspector Fournier said and walked away toward the middle of the square. Fanny headed north.

THE Temple, besides being a privileged zone of Paris, was also full of history. The Templar Knights were founded in 1112 A.D. to assist pilgrims traveling from Europe to Jerusalem. The pope loved the order and gave them exemption from all authority except his own. This included paying taxes either to the church or the state. And so the

Knights Templar grew in status and power, even though they took vows of personal poverty. Rich pilgrims awarded the order with land and goods. They built castles, not only in the Holy Land, but in European states as well. In Paris, they had a walled community of their own. This enclave, and a similar one in London, was the repository of vast riches. And because of their facilitating of travelers, the Templars became skilled at handling money, becoming bankers.

It was then that rivalry with other military orders, mostly the Order of Hospitallers, flared. Because all of their rituals took place in secret, their enemies could use rumor and innuendo against them effectively. As secular governments became stronger, they, too, opposed the power and wealth of the Templars.

It was one of these secular rulers, Phillip the Fair, who was able to bring charges against the Templars horrifying enough to convince the pope, Clement V, to dismantle them as an order. On a single day, October 13, 1307, Phillip arrested all members of the secret society in France. They were accused of idol worship, spitting on the cross, and having sex man with man.

After torture and confessions questionable in their truthfulness, many Templars were burned at the stake, including the Grand Master, Jacques de Molay. The Temple castle in Paris was given to the Order of Hospitallers, who had control of the area from 1307 until the revolution took over the keep and other buildings held by the religious order. The wall had been dismantled and the stones used to pave streets a long time ago. But the dungeon remained and the eerie look and feel of the whole area exuded danger and mystery.

The fact that people could come to the Temple to avoid debtor's jail added a layer of desperate people to the whole mix.

Fanny had been there only once. She had been eight or nine, and her father had gone to see a glazier who had his workshop there. Fanny remembered two things, and both had made an impression on her: the dungeon keep, hulking and dark, and how eager her father had been to leave the area. What was it he said? Something about how amassing power and riches always compels others to take it away from you. Could that be what was happening with the king? And the church?

Once Fanny got in the Temple area, it was easy to find the chefs' meetinghouse. It was in a one-story building, consisting of a long row of workshops. Each served as meetinghouses for various artisans and craftsmen who didn't have guilds. It was possible to post a request for a worker there, or to request a job oneself. Across the street was another low row of businesses, mostly taverns, coffee-houses, and cafés.

Fanny went right into the storefront with a painted sign of a toque hanging from the front. She found several young men and a couple of old ones, sitting around a table, playing dominos and drinking Burgundy Marc. Someone was pulling on a pipe and the smoke in the air had a nice, sweet aroma. The camaraderie quieted down when Fanny walked in the door. All eyes turned toward her, not hostile, not lecherous, just coolly interested. "Yes, mademoiselle?" a voice called.

"I am Fanny Delarue. I cook at M. Monnard's in the Place Royale. My chef, Henri Brusli, came here two days ago, looking for some information. I am sorry to say he has not returned home. I am, no, we are afraid something unto-ward has happened to him. I was wondering if any of you saw him and could tell me where he was going?"

"Yes, was he asking about spaces for a restaurant, a lad from Brittany?" one of the other young men asked.

Fanny wanted to say he'd been in Paris long enough not to be tagged with the Brittany label, but she knew a city full of immigrants always identified you by your place of origin. "That's him."

The same young man spoke up again. "He was here for an hour or so. We gave him a few locations we thought were possibilities, where some chefs that we know had moved on. He went across the street with another fellow for a beer at Taverne Templar. That was the last we've seen of him. He must be in some trouble by now." Several of the men agreed. No one could stay gone without letting the maître d' hôtel know and keep his job.

"It's not like him. We just want to make sure he is well. He had a wound on his arm," Fanny said, telling more than she'd meant to.

"You know, now I remember," an older man joined in. "He showed us that wound and we told him the apothecary down the street had an ointment that really worked on knife wounds. They worked it up special for the chefs. 'Couldn't hurt,' he said. "Maybe they would remember him."

Fanny went across the way to the tavern. It was a friendly, boisterous place. Fanny ordered a glass of wine when she saw several women seated at tables, none of them appearing to be prostitutes. In most of Paris, women weren't allowed in taverns, but in the faubourg St. Antoine, and it seemed the Temple as well, women were allowed much more independence. As the barkeep was serving her, she pushed several sous in his direction. He took out the change and she indicated he should keep the remainder. That got his attention. "Would you like a table?" he asked.

"No, but I'm looking for my chef. I'm a cook over on Place Royale. He was here on Tuesday and he had a bandage on his upper arm. Long, brown hair. Do you remember him?"

The bartender lost the small glimmer of interest he had in Fanny. She was just another wife or girlfriend looking for her man. "He got a message, you know, a boy brought it. He left in a fluster," the man stated flatly, moving away as he spoke.

Fanny finished her wine and left quickly. What in the world? How could anyone have known where Henri was, then have a message delivered that would send him out in a "fluster" as the bartender put it? She was heading toward the apothecary when one of the young men she'd spoken to came out of the chefs' meeting house and ran across the street to her.

"Mademoiselle? I forgot. Someone came looking for your Henri yesterday. A big, good-looking fellow. I wouldn't be surprised if he was a flic," he said, using the slang for police.

"Thank you," Fanny said with a grateful smile, and the cook went back to his game of dominos.

It must have been Inspector Fournier who was searching for Henri. But how did he know Henri had come to the Temple in the first place? And why did he ask for him this morning if he knew he was missing?

Fanny didn't fare so well at the apothecary. The shop was crowded, the woman at the cash box was busy, and she hadn't worked on Tuesday. Fanny tried to ask the other two people behind the counter but they shrugged her off.

She went back outside and started to walk aimlessly toward the keep, not really thinking about where she was going. She was grateful her lover had not lied to her. He had indeed come to the Temple to find information about restaurants. He had drunk at the tavern across from the meetinghouse, left when someone sent him a message. That was all she had learned, that and the gut feeling she had that Inspector Fournier knew something. It meant she would have to seek him out, or wait for him to come to her. She knew that wait wouldn't be a long one. Only this morning he had promised to return to the house on the Place Royale.

Fanny had come to the centerpiece of the Temple quartier, the keep. This medieval dungeon was dark and dirty, with six hundred years of pollution caked on its stones. It cast a long shadow on the surrounding streets. Fanny walked along the perimeter, lost in thought. Presently, two men dressed as guards came rushing out of a small door.

"Mademoiselle, you are looking for Henri Brusli?"

Fanny's face tightened. "Yes, is he all right?"

Neither man answered directly. "Come with us," one of the men ordered, and Fanny did just that. They entered the keep through that same small door. It was the room of a concierge, bare but for a table and chair. They led her through it to a hall with doors on both sides.

Halls were unusual in Paris. In most buildings, one room led directly into another. There was usually no way to get from the front to the back without going through the rooms in between. Servants, children, masters and mistresses all had to walk into other people's most intimate spaces. So Fanny felt uneasy walking down a hall. She was tense, a little frightened even. But her feeling of unease wasn't enough. It didn't give her the vision to see that she was in danger.

The next few seconds were a blur for Fanny. She couldn't recount it later, even to herself. Big hands pushed her and another set of hands enveloped her mouth. She strained to bite a finger but she couldn't get her mouth loose from the grip to scream, let alone bite. The next thing she knew she had been pushed or thrown into one of those doors in the hallway. It turned out it didn't open to a meeting room or salon. It was a dungeon cell.

Fanny whirled around as the door slammed shut. She threw her body at the closed door, knowing it wouldn't open. She couldn't understand what would be the point of locking her in a dungeon, then she remembered. The spice box. She could be in here while someone searched number twenty-three and stole the spice box. She only hoped she had done a good job of hiding it. And she also hoped Henri hadn't been harmed because he truly didn't know where it was. Or the boys. Nicolas and Simon could be in danger at home. She leaned up against a corner of the room as there was no bench or chair. Besides standing, sitting on the floor was her only choice, but the limestone blocks that the walls and floor were fashioned out of were shiny with dampness. She wouldn't sit down until she couldn't bear to stand up anymore.

Time passed. Actually it was about an hour, but Fanny had no idea how long it had been. This was not a situation in which thinking clearly was easy. There were no windows, only the bar-covered opening at the top of the door and a tray-sized opening at the bottom of the door that Fanny assumed was for food. For a while, Fanny thought it was dark outside, even though she knew she had left home at nine or nine-thirty in the morning and it couldn't be later than noon.

She worried about the boys, being in change of an empty house that had a hidden treasure in it. Persons unknown—the police or someone else—could invade it at any minute, and all of them would be after that treasure. Someone could break and destroy all of M. Monnard's possessions, everything he had worked a lifetime to accumulate, all because Fanny chose not to relinquish the jewels, jewels that she would never be able to wear or sell. Fanny knew the reason she was afraid to just be forthright with the jewels was because she was afraid her mother had stolen them in the first place.

Rubbing her eyes, Fanny walked to a place closer to the door, then leaned her shoulders against the wall and set her feet apart out from the cell wall a bit.

She started considering the jewels again. First, there was the possibility her mother had stolen them and put them in the box without her father knowing it. The second possibility was that Chef Etienne had brought the jewels with him from Versailles and hidden them in Fanny's spice box because they weren't safe with him anymore. As far-fetched as that possibility seemed, Fanny knew it was much easier for a domestic servant to gain access to another household than one might think. People walked in and out of the courtyard all the time. Chef Etienne was a respected artisan. If he was found unexpectedly in the Monnard kitchen and he said he was borrowing a cake mold, no one would blink.

The third possibility was that the jewels were stolen not by either of the likely suspects, the two who had been at Versailles at the time of the loss, but by a third party who was using the box as a convenient hiding place. If this third possibility was true, the plan must have been interrupted. Surely the jewels had been in Fanny's box longer than she originally thought. The fourth possibility Fanny just could not eliminate was that the jewels were planted to incriminate Fanny or her mother or perhaps someone else.

As she stood thinking about this, the door opened and a man with a black leather mask over his head walked in. It was the mask of the executioner, Fanny knew, even though she had never seen one before. Her pulse jumped in her neck so rapidly she put her hand on it to somehow contain it.

The man grabbed her arm and pulled her close to him. When he spoke, his accent was thick. Fanny thought it that of Marseilles. "The fate of Henri Brusli is in your hands. You must forget about Chef Etienne. You'll be told what to do." he growled, and pushed her roughly through the door to the hallway. Down the hall she could see the open door of the concierge room and daylight. She ran toward it. The room was empty and she stumbled out onto the street, then hurried away from the awful place.

CHAPTER TWELVE

FANNY didn't like waiting. She had been so sure she would come home to a house violated and in a shambles somehow, but instead, Nicolas and Simon had been asleep in front of the fire, thrilled to have such an easy day.

After she went back down the street, Fanny checked and the spice box was still right where she had left it, up in one of the bathtubs under a bathing sheet. She went outside to the new kitchen. Nothing was out of place. She even went behind the carriage house to check on M. Desjardins, rest his soul. The grave looked as it had when her brother had finished with it, down to the bales of hay he had stacked over the mound. Now that the horses were gone, the hay wouldn't have a reason to be moved.

So it didn't appear that anyone had invaded what for the moment was Fanny's domain. But she had been given a message. If Henri's fate was in her hands, what was she to do to keep him safe?

She assumed she would have to trade the jewels for Henri's life and that was fine. She wanted to be rid of them. She was certain now the deaths of Chef Etienne and M. Desjardins were related to the jewels in the spice box. The words of the man in the Temple keep made that clear. But why didn't he mention M. Desjardins also? And what did "forget about Chef Etienne" mean? She hadn't actively asked questions about him for months. And why didn't he just come out and say something about the jewels? Fanny had never felt so confused. Freedom for Henri depended on her interpretting these rather sketchy clues properly.

She settled uneasily in the new kitchen, building a fire and making some coffee. There was no fresh food, so she made crepe batter, went up and straightened Henri's room while the batter sat, then she lit one of the charcoal braziers in the fourneau and found her crepe pan. It was then her mother walked in and Fanny, unexpectedly for both of them, ran to her arms.

"I didn't expect such a warm welcome, daughter," Martine Delarue observed, and gave Fanny a kiss on both cheeks.

"Oh, Mama, I've made a mess out of things."

"Yes, well, that's natural, Fanny. Life is a messy thing. What has happened?" While she talked, she was removing her coat. She went over to the fourneau and started making crepes, taking over as naturally as if she had been working in that kitchen forever. "You sit down and have some wine and tell me what's the matter. We'll have some crepes," she said.

Fanny obeyed. She opened a bottle of wine, poured two

glasses, then sat on a stool and watched as her mother made crepes and, at the same time, made a sauce for their crepes out of butter and sugar and some cognac, plus the juice of an orange. Fanny had observed Martine making crepes so many times as a child, it was a most reassuring thing to watch right now.

She needed to confess and she started with M. Desjardins. "Mother, the other night, the day the master left and you and Father came to check on me, I found the maître d'hôtel dead in his office and then we decided to bury him here but Henri's arm was still bad so Albert . . ."

Her mother nodded and interrupted. "Albert told me. He was concerned."

"He told you we buried M. Desjardins behind the carriage house? He wasn't supposed to tell anyone," Fanny objected.

Martine shrugged. "He also said you didn't kill him, if that makes you feel better."

"Albert has never been able to keep a secret."

"But he didn't mention this to your father. I didn't either. Philippe would haul you home immediately."

"Oh, Mother, there's more," Fanny said softly.

Martine didn't say a word, just raised her eyebrows and looked at Fanny as if she was waiting for her to say what was on her mind.

"The other day Henri went to the Temple and he never came back. I haven't heard a word from him. So, today I went looking for him, and yes, he did go to the domestic chefs' meeting house, but no, they hadn't seen him since. Then I got thrown in the Temple keep, in a dungeon cell. A man with the executioner's mask on came in and told me Henri's fate was in my hands and they will contact me and then he threw me out." Fanny looked pleadingly at her mother, as if Martine would be able to straighten it all out.

Martine found two pewter plates, folded some crepes on them, and then poured the sauce over the crepes. She gestured toward the upholstered chairs, handed Fanny a plate and they both sat down. "Now that's a story. Well, let's eat. You can't think straight on an empty stomach and my guess is you haven't eaten in days."

Fanny was hungry. She realized this when she got a whiff of the crepes. She sat and ate, glad for the interruption. She had had every intention of telling her mother about the jewels in the spice box when she started, but she was still reluctant to share that information with Martine. Did Martine already know about them?

It was a terrible day, one of the worst days of growing up, when one didn't trust one's mother totally.

When their plates were almost clean, Martine smiled across at her daughter. "Those were good crepes, Fanny, very tender. So, who do you think abducted Henri, and why in the world would someone bother? I don't mean to be unkind, but this is a country full of people with riches beyond compare. If you were choosing to kidnap someone, wouldn't you choose one of them? What can you possibly give them in order to get Henri returned?"

This was the perfect time to show her mother the contents of the spice box. Instead she continued her deception. "I agree with you, Mother, Henri doesn't seem a candidate for kidnapping and extortion. I don't know what's behind his disappearance. It could be something we don't know about him. People are so mysterious." Fanny's stomach roiled as she lied to her mother. Why couldn't she talk about the jewels with Martine?

"And the masked man didn't really give you any concrete instructions," Martine observed.

Fanny shrugged. "I'm sure that will come. Mother, Inspector Fournier has been around lately. Henri wasn't too nice to him. Today he came to the door again and I didn't let on that Henri was missing, told him I was leaving and Henri wasn't at home. But I heard in the Temple a handsome flic was asking about Henri yesterday, or that's what they thought. Yet today he comes to the door and asks for Henri. Why would he do that if he already knew Henri was missing?"

"To see what you'd do, child. I'm sure he'd like nothing better than for you to cry on his shoulder."

She remembered the flick of his tongue in her ear. "No, he seems very driven, very caught up in his work."

Martine touched her daughter's face. Fanny was a smart young woman but she didn't understand men yet. "I think Inspector Fournier quite capable of having two agendas."

"He said he was on the trail of some jewels stolen from Versailles. And I think he suspects you, Mother."

"Ah, jewels, is it? That makes sense now. We knew the inspector was watching me. And I couldn't understand it, especially if they thought I'd been in on killing the guards. Not one person has been arrested for killing the king's guards and never will be. Life is cheap to these people. But some jewels, oh my God, we must get them back, back in the big chest with all the other jewels the king and his ancestors tore from the hands of the citizens."

Again Fanny was frustrated by her mother's political polemics. Martine just wasn't going to say "Oh, Fanny, he is so wicked to suspect me of committing a crime. I would never do such a thing" as much as her daughter wanted her to. If Fanny was looking for some assurance from Martine that she was an innocent, that speech wasn't it. Fanny was especially disturbed by the fact that her mother described the big chest all the jewelry was kept in. How did her mother know that? Or was it just a figure of speech?

"I hope that if there's a connection between the jewels and what's happened to Henri, we see it clearly soon," Fanny murmured.

Martine got up, and put both of their plates down in the dry sink. She held her hand out to her daughter and Fanny took it and stood up. Then her mother started gathering up her coat and hat.

"I don't think the inspector has Henri. If he did, then he wouldn't have been asking after him all over the Temple quartier. It won't be long before you find out what is going on, what 'they' want. And when they contact you, I want you to send for me. You've been through so much in the last few days. Don't try to do this all yourself."

Fanny switched the topic back to something that was bothering her. "Do you think I'm horrible for denying M. Desjardins a church burial?"

Martine shook her head. "A more important question is who killed him and why? You treated him with your own brand of dignity. As Albert explained it, you don't know his family, his employer is out of the country and you didn't want the poor fellow to end up in a common grave. Now when you find his family, if that even happens, they will have something to bury. The church burial is for those alive who still care about such things. But why would anyone kill your maître d'hôtel now, after your family is gone? Wasn't someone else on the square, wasn't it the chef you were taking lessons from, wasn't he killed, too?"

"Chef Etienne. Yes, right at the entrance to his court-yard."

"What if a disturbed person is randomly killing people who live on this square, just as they answer the door? There's no one to answer the door at number twenty-three but you. You're very likely in danger, sweetheart, one way or the other. And I would tie you up and take you home but I know you would come right back here as soon as you could because this is where you think they will contact you about Henri."

"I can't leave now. But I want out of here as soon as possible. I can hardly wait to move home. Mother, Henri asked me to marry him." Fanny knew this was entirely the wrong time to tell her mother this, now when Henri was missing, but she was just eighteen and it was her first proposal. She couldn't wait.

Martine held her tongue from any kind of exclamation, good or bad, about this news. She kissed her daughter. "Then we have to rescue the handsome knight from the dungeon where the evil lord is keeping him prisoner so he can marry the princess," she said wryly.

Fanny didn't want her mother to leave. The suspicion and distrust toward Martine had been replaced with warm feelings. It didn't make any difference to her right now what Martine might have done in Versailles or elsewhere. Her mother had walked in the door and made crepes and it had comforted Fanny immensely.

"I will send for you as soon as I know something," Fanny said, and watched as her mother went out on the square. Unlike her father, Martine didn't turn to wave good-bye.

* * *

THE hour or so Fanny had spent with her mother had raised her spirits immensely. They had not solved anything, nor had she been especially truthful with Martine, but it had been months since she had seen evidence of their connection, and today, when she needed her mother, there she was. Martine had treated Fanny like a grown-up, acknowledged she had to make her own mistakes, and she had also given assurance that she would be there if Fanny needed her. So why couldn't Fanny be forthcoming with Martine? She didn't know the answer to that one yet. It was something about the jewels for sure, and the politics. Fanny realized she knew little about the politics her mother was involved in. But when her mother talked about how the government was more concerned about jewels than people, she saw her mother's side of things for the first time. Fanny respected her mother's position more than she had before, even though it still bothered her.

However, it didn't help Fanny decide what side she was on personally. She still didn't know if she was a revolutionary or a royalist.

What if her mother was right and she was assuming all the wrong things? What if it was a disturbed person or a personal vendetta responsible for the deaths, someone who came around the Place Royale, someone who thought Etienne and M. Desjardins had done them wrong. What if it was the waste removal man or the person who sold water or the greengrocer? What if it was someone who hated the numbers twenty-three and six? The thought of the killings as random was soothing to Fanny, in a strange way. Perhaps it was less personal than what she'd been thinking.

Fanny was finally ready to rest. She didn't want to sleep upstairs in Henri's bed but she went up and gathered some of his blankets and pillows. She pulled the two upholstered chairs together and stretched out. As she dozed off, she was resigned to the fact that she would try to do her best for Henri, without really knowing what that was right now.

The next thing Fanny knew, she awoke with a hand across her face.

"Shhh," the voice that came with the hand whispered.

Fanny waited a good ten seconds before she opened her eyes. She wanted it to be Henri, surprising her with a triumphant return home. But she knew without looking that it was the inspector.

She couldn't help herself; she stuck her tongue out and insinuated it between two of his fingers.

Before she knew it, the inspector had gently captured her tongue in his fingers. He leaned across her body to whisper to her, "Don't forget, Fanny, how good it felt this morning when I kissed your ear. Wasn't it the most exciting feeling?" He removed his hand from over her lips and replaced it with his mouth.

Fanny tumbled through space in the next few seconds, losing her body, feeling only her lips and the ones pressed to them. This was a different type of kiss. It was exciting and dangerous and expertly executed.

When the kiss was over, when she had regained her own sense, she started hitting the inspector's shoulder. "How dare you. You broke in!"

"You loved that kiss, didn't you?"

"What are you doing, you bastard? Keeping my boyfriend away from me so you can torture me?"

"I thought your mother would never leave, Fanny."

"Have you been here since my mother left, since I fell asleep?" Fanny hit him again on the shoulder.

"We can't help ourselves. You put your tongue between my fingers, just like I touched your ear this morning with mine. Don't you see, Fanny, how it is between us?"

Fanny was trying to get up but the chairs slid apart and she went to the floor. Inspector Fournier was not tangled in the covers and chairs so he was able to step clear. For a moment he was towering above her. She felt as helpless as she ever had. At the same time she was burning up, sexually aroused in a way she never had been with Henri.

Before she could disentangle herself, he was on top of her on the floor. This was the first time their whole bodies had touched, and even though they were fully clothed, Fanny couldn't help arching up to him. She was surprised that he didn't put his whole weight on her as a show of strength. His hand was reaching under her chemise, searching for her bare body as he turned his lips to her breasts. Fanny had fallen asleep with all her clothes on. So her breasts were pushed up with a corset band that fit around her body right under them. They were presented to the inspector like two ripe apples, half hidden by the neckline of Fanny's dress. He kissed them both softly. Fanny was beside herself with desire and excitement. But she knew she must not do this. She opened her eyes. "Please don't," she said.

The inspector rolled off her slowly, removing his hand from under her dress. He propped up his head with one hand, lying on his side. "How can you ask that? We are meant for this moment," he said wearily but not impatiently.

"I don't know who I'm kissing and I didn't invite you here. Are you the police inspector imposing your will on a little cook, or are you a man with a passion for a women? I have to know who you are. I don't even know your first name. How can I be intimate with someone I must address by his title?"

The inspector sighed deeply, then adjusted his clothing and got to his feet. "I am both, Fanny, the police inspector and the man."

Fanny sat up and arranged her bodice, making sure everything was as covered as possible.

Inspector Fournier laughed. "You look like a little angel down there." He extended a hand to help her up.

"Where is Henri?" Fanny asked, sensing the moment of intimacy was over.

"I'm working on that. In the meantime don't try to tell me anyone else is living here. I'm sure your maître d'hôtel is off to another job by now. And I was able to open the front door easily. How can your parents allow you to stay here when you could be in danger so easily?"

"I refused to leave until Henri is back. If you don't know where he is, then who has him?"

"Poor Fanny. Her chef has run away," the inspector teased. He threw his cape around his shoulders. "I'm alerting the night guard to stand their watch outside this number twenty-three, instead of in the middle of the Place. The rest of the square doesn't have such a precious treasure," he said as he bent over to kiss Fanny one last time.

As her cheeks were heating up one more time, she wondered if he was talking about her, or the spice box.

She remained silent as he walked out. "It's Jean, by the way. But everyone calls me Fournier," he said.

"Farewell, Jean," Fanny called to his silhouette as he disappeared in the darkness.

The remainder of the night was one of restlessness. Fanny would fall asleep, then wake up with a start, afraid someone had entered the kitchen again. Each time she awoke, she would mull over the visit with the inspector.

He could have come to steal the spice box, and when she woke up, he decided not to murder her for it. After all, he did seem to have some tender feelings for her. Then he stole a kiss for his trouble. But what would be the point of his killing anyone for the spice box when he could just arrest the person and take it, and probably dip into the jewels himself without anyone being the wiser and still return them and get a promotion?

If he had come for the jewels, he would have to know specifically where the jewels were, and there was no indication that he was even aware of the spice box or that the jewels were hidden in it.

He might have come for her, after all.

Fanny thought about all the stories of sex in her neighborhood she'd heard as a child. Many times it involved a man taking advantage of a woman or a woman manipulating a man by using sex. Never that she could remember, when the man was the older, more powerful one in the relationship, did it turn out well for the girl. Be it her employer, her uncle, or the man who sold her bread in the morning, the girl was most likely going to end up brokenhearted and out of a job, sometimes pregnant to boot.

She didn't want to have a relationship like that if she didn't have to. The fact that Fournier was good-looking with a powerful job did excite her. The fact that he could take whatever he wanted from her was also somewhat exciting, especially since he hadn't. Fanny had been surprised that he stopped when she asked him to.

She respected Jean Fournier more tonight than she had this morning—that was certain.

*   *   *

FANNY awoke full of resolve again. She went into the house, lit several fires, made coffee, and then had a bath.

She had searched in the Temple quartier and could only say that Henri had been at the chefs' meetinghouse. She had been taken to the Temple keep against her will and still had no idea if Henri was in another of those stone cells. But it had given her an idea.

Now she was going to search for him in another prison, the Conciergerie on the Ile de la Cité. It was the most populous prison in town. At this point, as horrible as it was, she wished him there because the other places he might be—the morgue, the hospitals—were worse.

She had no idea of the rules of the Conciergerie, whether one could see prisoners or not. So she hurried out the door to visit the boulangerie on rue Vieille du Temple. She had heard Violet, the daughter of the owner, talk about delivering bread and meat pies to the Conciergerie.

The boulangerie was a happy place, full of that rich, yeasty aroma that inhabited are buildings where bread was baked or beer was brewed. Because everyone in the neighborhood passed through every day, it was the place to go for news, gossip, and everything in between.

"So, Fanny, I hear your master took off for London. What about your job?" Violet's father, M. Lafarge, asked.

"Henri and I are planning to open a restaurant," Fanny said with a fake confidence that sounded pretty good to her.

"Well, there's a place available right down the street, not more than three or four storefronts. Take a look at it. It was a caterer's so it must have a kitchen."

"Thank you, I will. Is Violet here? I would like just a

minute?" Fanny said sweetly. She knew it was taboo to talk to the help but she also knew everyone bent the rules for their own children.

M. Lafarge motioned to the back room with a father's soft heart. He also gave Fanny a look that said, *Don't stay long*.

The kitchen of the bakery was a bustling mess of a place. Loaves of bread, unbaked and rising, were everywhere, in the baskets with linen linings, the baguettes in the metal cylinders, rolls on flat baking sheets, flour on every surface.

One baker was cutting the tops of the risen, unbaked loaves with an instrument that looked to Fanny like her father's razor. Each shape loaf got a different cut. Another baker was watching the oven carefully, with his peel in hand, ready to take out each loaf when it was ready. A female baker was making cakes of some kind, pouring batter into small molds.

Violet was organizing a delivery, counting out loaves and placing them in baskets.

"Violet, have you been to the Conciergerie yet?" Fanny asked, forgetting to announce herself or say hello first.

"Hello, Fanny, what are you doing back here?" Violet said without paying much attention. She didn't want to lose count.

"I wondered if I could go with you to the Conciergerie to make your delivery," Fanny said.

Violet looked her up and down. "Today?"

"Today, tomorrow, anytime," Fanny said.

"You are in luck. I'm getting ready to go right now. I guess I can ask you why on the way. Now count out fifty of the big round loaves. They go in these flat baskets," Violet ordered.

Fanny helped load the wagon and then the two girls took off. Violet handled the mule team herself and was a very aggressive driver.

As they scooted between two closed carriages, the sign of aristocratic passengers, Violet cracked the whip with a flourish.

Fanny was laughing and hanging on for dear life. "I can't believe your father sends you to the prison by yourself."

Violet smiled proudly. "Not at first. He would send the deliveryman with me. But now we have two wagons, we deliver so many places. Most of the Palais-Royal cafés use our bread."

"And the most famous prison. They don't have their own ovens?"

"Not bread ovens. The kitchens were built when the king was in residence there, at the Palais de la Cité. The palace is mostly for lawyers and judges now. The king hasn't lived there for hundreds of years. The kitchen was never big enough for all those that hung around the king. Mostly it was just for him and his family they cooked. They always bought most of the food they used from caterers and bakers like us. Now, instead of hundreds of court folks, they have hundreds of prisoners. They still buy most everything from outside."

Fanny knew she owed Violet something of an explanation. "Violet, I'm looking for someone." She didn't want word of Henri's disappearance to travel through the neighborhood. "Is there a way to find out who is in the prison?"

Violet nodded. "There is a concierge and everyone has to be signed in. I give him extra bread so it shouldn't be too hard."

Then Fanny realized she would have to tell Violet more

information if she wanted her help. "Henri and I had a little fight and he hasn't been home for a few days."

"Poor dear. First your master runs off, now your boyfriend. Are you two going to get married, if he's not stuck behind bars?"

Fanny smiled and tried to look heartsick, which wasn't too difficult. She batted her eyes. "He asked me. Then we tried to decide where we would live, if we would stay in service. Henri wants to have a restaurant so badly. I guess I wasn't excited enough about it. It's so scary, not to be paid."

"I'm telling you, you should get that space near us. Just think of all the important houses there are in our neighborhood. It is so fashionable to eat out in restaurants now. And all those folks who live around us don't always like to go down to the Palais-Royal," Violet chatted.

"I promise I'll come see it tomorrow. That would please Henri so much if I found a space. Don't tell anyone, please, Violet. It's so embarrassing. I don't want every cook and maid on the Place to know . . ."

Violet laughed. "That your boyfriend is off somewhere with the boys playing cards and drinking? Don't worry, love, I won't tell. Let's go across the Pont Neuf. The Pont du Change is so narrow and crowded," she explained and took the bridge that all Paris called new, even though it wasn't.

They headed back east on the Ile de la Cité, pulling into a small courtyard off the Boulevard du Palais.

"Now usually, they have a spare boy who will help us unload," Violet said as she jumped down. She turned toward Fanny. "Here's the plan. We go in and unload. Then you and I take some loaves to the concierge. And I also brought him a tart. I ask if a Henri—what's Henri's last name?"

"Brusli."

". . . if a Henri Brusli had been brought in the last week. What day did you see him last?"

"Last Tuesday."

"So we ask him if we can look at the sign-in book. Now grab as many baskets as you can. We have a way to go," Violet said.

Fanny wasn't prepared for the grandeur that lay on the other side of the door.

The two young women stepped into the Salle des Gems d'Armes, a room Fanny guessed was the biggest she had ever been in.

The Salle des Gems d'Armes was the underground room that corresponded in size to the Grand Salle on the ground floor. The Grand Salle had been the receiving room for the kings of the Middle Ages. Downstairs, the Salle des Gems d'Armes was the eating and meeting hall for the court, a giant workers' hall, big enough for two thousand people, for those in the employ of the king. When the king moved away from the Palais de la Cité, the grand hall upstairs was transformed to use for court proceedings and the room Fanny and Violet stood in became a series of storage rooms and cellars. But the ceiling still arched gracefully in four high naves across and the room was still more than sixty meters long. It was grand indeed.

Fanny stood there. She had been taught about this place in school. She remembered it was Phillip the Fair who finished it. She remembered that because her own father was a Philippe. Fanny squinted out at the room and tried to imagine it when it was full of courtiers, talking and eating and gossiping, when knights in shining armor walked in this hall and so did women in tall, pointy headdresses with veils floating off the tip.

"Hello, Fanny?" Violet shouted. The kitchen was on the west side of the hall, and that was where Violet was headed. "Stop daydreaming, will you?"

Fanny hurried after her and they made four trips back and forth, along with two boys, from the wagon to the kitchen unloading the bread.

The last trip, Violet slipped a tart out from under the driver's seat, wrapped up in muslin. "They keep saying they're getting a cart for inside here, to carry the food. But they never do. It's truly pitiful when the government of this city, the greatest city on earth, can't afford a cart," she said as they wobbled back inside, trying to balance the baskets of bread without spilling them, and keep going forward.

After their last trip, Violet and the kitchen steward counted the loaves together, then both signed off on that number on an invoice, which they each got a portion of. Violet took four loaves she hadn't charged for in the official count and the wrapped tart, and jerked her head toward the door of the kitchen. There were dozens of cooks organizing the rations, the meager ones that went to the prisoners, the more substantial for Palais employees. They paid no attention to which direction Fanny and Violet turned when they left the kitchen. The two young women headed out to the prison office of the concierge, where Violet was greeted with enthusiasm.

"So, Violet, who's your friend?" the concierge said as he took the loaves and the tart. "And what is this?"

"A musician's tart. It's made with nuts and dried fruit. Supposedly, musicians were paid with these in the old days because they didn't go bad like a fresh fruit tart would. They could carry them about. And this is Fanny."

The concierge's office was in a small, open, wooden cell

with bars on all sides. On the opposite side from where
Fanny and Violet had entered, there was a long corridor
named the Prisoners' Corridor, where prisoners could walk
unfettered from one place to the other.

To further strengthen the concierge's position in this corridor, he commanded a platoon of guard dogs that he sent
out on patrol along with guards. So in a small space, there
were men employed to keep the peace, men who had lost
their freedom, and vicious dogs employed to keep the men
who had lost their freedom in check. This caused a great
deal of noise and confusion. But the concierge seemed above
it all, calling out orders and directions and giving out huge
rings of keys to the guards.

"Fanny here has lost her man. Would you be a love and
see if Henri Brusli is visiting your fair establishment?" Violet asked with cynicism that seemed appropriate to the time
and place.

The concierge laughed heartily. "This Henri must be a
fool to leave a pretty little thing like you. Well, for your
friend Violet I'd do almost anything. She keeps me fed. Let's
just see," he said and stepped out in the corridor, looking
unconcerned about the prisoners walking around him. He
walked into another wooden barred cell next to his own. It
was the Clerk's Office, with several thick ledger books lying
on a table. "When?" he asked, adjusting his glasses and sitting down to examine the book.

"Anytime in the last two weeks," Fanny answered,
widening the search. Just in case.

"Luc, who is in charge here in Paris nowadays? Who ar-
rests people?" Violet asked, making conversation cheerfully.
As they walked by, prisoners whistled and greeted the two
women with enthusiasm. Violet was completely inured to

all this attention. She was used to it. Fanny felt uncomfortable and suspected the men, most of whom were boys really, were undressing them in their minds.

"Three groups. The police, who work for the lieutenant general, he's the head of the city police. He still must obey the king. The night guard, they do a lot of arresting because the worst comes out in people at night. Then there's the National Guard, who work for the National Assembly or whoever's in charge this week. It keeps us full." The man got up with the jingle of keys accompanying his moves. He moved back to his office-cell. "No, Henri Brusli is not one of our guests. That's a Brittany name, isn't it?"

Fanny felt tears running down her cheeks. "Oh, thank God. Thank you, thank you. Yes, Henri is from Brittany."

"Maybe he went back there to Brittany," the jailer commented. "It's going to get worse here in Paris before it gets better."

"No, I know he's here. I'll find him," Fanny said with more confidence than she actually felt.

Where in the hell was Henri?

CHAPTER THIRTEEN

IT was midnight on New Year's Eve. Seventeen ninety-one was born. Fanny had opened the best bottle of champagne she could find in M. Monnard's wine cellar, at least the best label she was able to identify. She had been waiting for tonight, anticipating what her New Year would bring, and even wondering what the night would reveal.

It seemed very appropriate to her that she had decided to celebrate the New Year by counting the money in the spice box. Appropriate because it was that money that would make it possible for her to open her restaurant.

Fanny had not fallen into despair this last month. She had kept up her pretense on the Place Royale: All her friends and acquaintances in the other households were told that Henri was visiting his family in Brittany and would return after the holidays so they could proceed on their new dream, to have a restaurant right here in the neighborhood.

If the gossip that circled the square like wildfire perhaps wasn't that optimistic, was dubious about Henri's returning from his birthplace, no one said an unkind thing to Fanny about it.

And as for M. Desjardins, well, that was a big surprise. Fanny had become a good liar. No one would ever have thought he wouldn't return from his little visit to the Left Bank. But for reasons that Fanny was not no privy to, she explained, M. Desjardins had sent a note from his relatives' house and said that he had a chance to move out of town with his family and was going to take that chance. Fanny did talk about this sudden defection with any other maître d'hôtel or maid who asked, just to make sure the news got passed around. She also bragged that she and Henri had been hired by M. Monnard's lawyer as caretakers, so they had a job until they could get a restaurant up and running. She would say she never thought M. Desjardins the type to desert the house, but then hadn't the master done just that? There was simply no loyalty anymore. And at this stage in the story, everyone agreed with Fanny that one had to think of oneself in these turbulent times. Everyone wanted to stay, well, alive and for some that meant leaving town or the country. The political climate was very touchy, they all agreed.

During December, Fanny stubbornly refused to abandon number twenty-three Place Royale and go home to the faubourg St. Antoine and her parents. She was able to be truthful up to a point with her mother, and her mother was obliged to handle her father.

Christmas was unbearable for everyone. Fanny was worried sick; her father couldn't understand why Henri wasn't with them; her mother watched every encounter between the two of them with bated breath. Fanny had to lie and tell her father the same tale she told the neighbors, that Henri had decided to take this chance to go back to Brittany for the holidays because he didn't anticipate having the chance again for years. Albert, not so silently, held M. Desjardins and his unceremonious burial over Fanny's head. Albert had his own thoughts about the murders on the Place Royale and the ethics of keeping silent about M. Desjardins.

"Little sister, what if someone else is killed in the same way as these other two there on the Place? Someone opens the door and is stabbed. How will you feel if you could have warned the neighborhood and you did nothing?" Albert demanded. Fanny had to admit they were good questions. But she kept her mouth shut and lived alone in the big house or the cozy new kitchen building, pretending everyone was accounted for, if not present.

Fanny had started New Year's Eve in the salon, thinking it fitting for a special occasion. She had the candles lit, had even climbed the ladder to light the candles of the giant chandelier. But from the ladder, she looked around the beautifully appointed room, a room she had never even walked through while the master and his family were in residence. And she knew this wasn't the right place to celebrate the New Year. She got down without lighting the candles, collected the spice box and champagne, and headed for the new kitchen.

There were two reasons Fanny was counting the money tonight. She was ashamed over the holidays when she realized she had no idea what the box actually contained. It just seemed reasonable to know what one's inventory was, whether it be stolen gems or cash or nutmegs. Her early brush with the jewels, the night she covered her hands in them, feeling greedy and covetous, had shamed her into never touching them again. She saw their allure and didn't trust herself with them. But tonight she would put that silliness behind her. She had been aware of the contents of the spice box for several weeks now. She had to be sensible and make a written inventory list of the box's contents.

She needed to count the money for a different reason. She was going to use it for the restaurant, and tomorrow, or today, January 1, she was going to pay a year's rent in advance on the storefront at the corner of rue de Rosiers and rue Vieille du Temple—if she had that much money. It was the empty caterer's shop near Violet's family boulangerie.

Fanny didn't for a minute feel badly about using the money. Unlike the jewels, money wasn't anyone's. It just passed through your hands on the way somewhere else. Even the king was always out of money and did a poorer job of keeping the country in funds than, say, her father did their family.

So, just after midnight, drinking champagne, Fanny took a pen and paper and wrote down a description of every piece of jewelry in the spice box, arranging the pieces on a big worktable as she took them out. It was a blinding display of sparkle. Fanny placed two large candelabras on the worktable to catch the jewels' light. She wanted to take the whole lot, or at least her favorite pieces, into the mistress's boudoir, where there were mirrors all around, and try them on. But she didn't. The risk of something happening to them kept her from playing with them the way a young girl does with her mother's pearls. And it also reminded her of Henri asking her to try them on and the picture she had in her mind of herself, naked and bejeweled.

And pearls there were, so big and lustrous Fanny gasped

when she examined them. The idea of keeping them floated through her mind briefly, but she pushed that thought out and the pearls went on display on this table she normally used to roll out pastry dough.

When the jewelry was all inventoried, Fanny started counting the money. There was unfamiliar paper money and gold coins. Fanny wasn't sure when the government had started issuing paper money, but as she started to count what was there, she saw there was English, Swedish, and German money mixed in with French gold livres. She carefully made separate piles of it all, recording the totals of each currency on a separate piece of paper. Without counting the paper money, and not counting the foreign currency, there were 31,000 French livres. She would be able to pay for a restaurant with that, pay the rent and furnish the place, buy food, and have a little something left to get a room with. Fanny couldn't live in St. Antoine with her parents and work in the Marais. It was too far to go each night after a hard day's work.

With the money and jewelry out of the spice box, Fanny could see what else was in the bottom drawer. It contained pieces of paper, different papers, with what looked liked recipes on them. The writing, the languages, on the papers was all different. Fanny couldn't read any of them but she saw measures that led her to believe they were recipes. It was a cookbook of sorts. This was almost as exciting to her as the other contents of the box. Fanny could hardly wait to get back to cooking again.

Tomorrow she would pay the rent, and then she could start to move some of her borrowed things into the storefront—the kitchen supplies that were here. She had discussed tables and chairs with her father. They had decided on a cast-iron base for the tables that one of Philippe Delarue's friends fabricated. Philippe had argued that Fanny should wait for Henri to choose the tables but she assured her father that Henri wanted her to go ahead with the plans while he was gone. She told these lies with the smooth assurance that came with practice.

Fanny had thought long and hard about what she wanted to do if Henri never came back. Her first responsibility was to save his life if she could. But it had been more than a month since she was thrown into that horrible dungeon room and told his life was in her hands. And still she had not been contacted. She had to admit that something might have gone wrong. She might never hear from Henri again, and so would she want to go back in service at another private house without him? The answer was no. Fanny felt she had learned plenty from Henri and Chef Etienne. Her natural Parisian instinct was to go in business for herself, not to work for others. And the money in the spice box gave her the chance to do so without having to borrow from her family, who no doubt wouldn't lend her the money on her own.

Her father had asked her how she and Henri could afford to go into business and Fanny had lied again, saying Henri had inherited a small amount from his grandparents. Her mother looked at her dubiously when she explained this wonderful coincidence to them. But Fanny had still not told her mother about the contents of the spice box. She tried to several times, but the words just wouldn't come out. So she babbled on about how lucky it was, Henri getting this money just when M. Monnard had left the country and they were out of a job.

Fanny had decided it wasn't safe to keep everything in the spice box. She found two empty jewelry boxes up in the mistress's boudoir, but then put them back. Even a bad thief would check out jewelry boxes, no matter where they were stashed. She then decided on a tea container and a flour tin. She wrapped half the jewels in a piece of muslin and hid them down in the flour, then did the same with the other half and put them in the dried tea leaves, being careful they were covered completely.

She then put the recipes, or what she thought were recipes, and the money back in the spice box, and hid it upstairs under Henri's bed. She had devised this rather elaborate schedule of hiding the box in a different place each night, using the house, the kitchen, and the carriage house in a revolving method. Perhaps next she would separate the foreign currency from the French.

It was two in the morning. Fanny had drunk a whole bottle of champagne, but she wasn't tipsy a bit. The challenge of counting and inventorying both jewels and money had certainly kept her alert.

She fed the fire two more logs. Then she brought out the duvet and pillows she kept in the storage room for when she slept here in the kitchen. She didn't do that as much as she used to. Her old bedroom in the house was still her favorite. She had tried sleeping in the various grand bedchambers on the first and second floors, but besides the warmth from all the curtains and draping around the beds, they just made her uncomfortable. She was perfectly content sleeping in the cellar, as some might call it. She had a beautiful chest with inlay and a mirror as grand as any up in the master's quarters. And these things were hers, given to her with love from her own family.

As she pulled the two upholstered chairs together, she heard a noise outside the kitchen door. Her heart started pounding. What if it was Henri, released to her tonight, in the first hours of the New Year? She hurried to the door, opened it, and found Inspector Fournier cleaning mud off his boots with his hand.

"I didn't want to track mud inside," he explained, then straightened up and smiled.

"It's two in the morning," Fanny scolded, even though she was secretly glad to see him. "What in the world are you doing here?"

Fournier shrugged. "I was passing by and I asked the night guard if you had returned from your parents' house, where you spent the holidays. When he said you had, I thought wishing you a Happy New Year was in order."

So the inspector knew where she was and what she was doing, did he? And he had the night guard reporting to him concerning her whereabouts. This frightened and pleased Fanny, in about equal parts. That was the general effect the inspector seemed to have on her.

She went over to the water cistern and wet a cloth. Then she started wiping the mud off Fournier's hands with this cloth, trying to appear casual, matter-of-fact. She was shaking just slightly.

Fournier caught her hand with his. "Happy New Year, Fanny," he said, then leaned down to kiss her. She had plenty of time to turn away but she welcomed the kiss instead, leaning into it with passion. She knew her response showed a lack of character, but since their sexually charged encounter, her dreams and fantasies had been of Fournier, not Henri.

Now she pulled back slowly. She wondered if he was married, if there was a woman somewhere in Paris spending New Year's Eve alone while her husband was out working.

"And a Happy New Year's to you, Jean," she said shyly. She took both his hands and led him into the big room. "Do you want champagne?"

Fournier swept one of those long arms around Fanny's waist and pulled her in toward him again. "What is it about you? I haven't been able to keep my mind or my eyes off you since the day I first saw you."

"Is that a yes to champagne?" Fanny said as she disentangled herself. She had another bottle of champagne chilled outside. She didn't know why she'd grabbed two bottles, but she had. She quickly went out to retrieve the second bottle, then busied herself getting two clean glasses from the storage room. She didn't know why she'd brought over six champagne glasses to the kitchen the other day either. Did she wish this to happen, without consciously thinking about it?

Inspector Fournier settled into one of the comfortable chairs, watching her bustle around without comment for a minute. Then he said, "I would love to toast the New Year with you, Fanny. There is almost nothing else I would rather be doing." He tried to grab her as she passed near him but she dodged his hands and they both laughed.

Fanny brought the champagne glasses over and gave Fournier the bottle. He twisted it open and poured for them.

"To 1791," Fanny said brightly.

"To us," Fournier murmured. They touched glasses and drank.

Fanny sat down across from him and he put his hand out toward her. She slapped it away and pressed her arm against her breasts, hiding them, her glass in the other hand. "I have to ask."

"I know. I can't find him, Fanny. Henri has fallen off the face of the earth. I think we have to consider foul play."

"So you're saying that whoever that man was who threw me in the dungeon at the Temple, you don't know anything about it and you can't find Henri?"

"Two things are possible. He left town, went back to Brittany without telling you. Or he is dead or so injured that he can't get back here."

"Then why did the man in the mask tell I was the one who held his life in my hands?" Fanny asked, flustered, the words stumbling over each other. She felt hot and dizzy and angry and defensive. The champagne had gone right to her head this time.

"That was more than a month ago, Fanny. Perhaps someone kidnapped Henri, and then before they could tell you what they wanted, he was accidentally killed. Maybe he tried to escape. It's possible, you know. There wouldn't be any reason to wait this long with their demands if they still had a live hostage."

Fanny's chin was quivering. "Yes, I suppose it is possible. And he could have slipped and hit his head and fallen in the Seine and drowned and his body got swept clear downstream and we'll never find him. That's possible, too, isn't it?" She was yelling now, tears streaming down her cheeks, eyes hard as glass. "I know I should just forget about Henri, but I can't. Will you please leave?"

Inspector Fournier looked worn out. He stood up and picked up the champagne bottle, tilting it to his mouth delicately. He drank, then set the bottle down as he headed for the door. "That's hard to do, did you know that, Fanny? You have to be careful or the bubbles go up your nose." He turned and looked at her, a pitiful sight, nose and eyes running, heart right there on her sleeve for the breaking. He wanted to wipe her nose and kiss her tears away. "You know what I think? I think you have something someone wants. And until you let go of it, you will not have Henri." Then he left.

Fanny sat down and pulled the duvet up around her, then grabbed the champagne bottle and drank carefully the way Fournier had done. Was Fournier just making an observation, or making a threat?

"ALBERT, do you know the legal definition of 'bourgeois'?" Fanny asked this bizarre question from her position up on a ladder, painting.

"Some of it," Albert said, his mind still on his work.

Albert and Fanny were painting the storefront that was to be her new restaurant. Albert had come over two other times this week for a few hours to help Fanny.

"What do you remember?" she called across the room.

Albert finished his brush stroke before he answered. "Let's see. You have to have lived in Paris at least a year and a day. You have to own property. You have to pay your taxes in person."

"And you can have no direct involvement in agriculture," Fanny contributed.

Albert chuckled. "I just remember thinking we will never be bourgeois. We make and sell our own goods. You have to sell someone else's goods to be bourgeois."

Fanny climbed down her ladder. "I remember something like 'someone who was not a noble but who lived by investments or rent instead of trade or manual work.' I didn't remember the part about living in Paris a year. Good memory, brother." She went over to get a drink from a copper water container. One of the best features of this location was the well in the basement. Buying water for a restaurant could be expensive.

Albert kept painting. "Why are you asking?"

"Because the bourgeoisie will be my customers in this neighborhood, if they don't get arrested along with the nobility this year. Them and the judges, of course. I've been thinking about what's going on with the government and how it might affect my new business. You know, even if you don't give a fig about politics, what's happening can ruin you. Henri wanted us to open the restaurant at number twenty-three, Place Royale, M. Monnard's house. After all, it's beautiful and empty. But I thought it was too grand. No regular people would come there, especially now. Then when we were broken into, it became impossible. Place Royale will continue to be a target," she said knowingly.

"I'd try to convince you to open back in our neighborhood where the artisans live, but we're all losing work and might not be able to afford a restaurant meal. Papa and I are so slow right now, we were thinking about going to Germany for a while, to study with one of those fancy cabinetmakers. It has to get better. I wish they'd just kick the king out, make him go to London or, better yet, Austria. That's where his sluttish wife is from. I think we should tell them we'd sign a peace treaty if they'll take the king. Let the Austrians support them for a while."

"Albert, I've been reading the newspapers. It was something I promised myself I'd do this year. When you have your own business, you have to be informed."

Albert smiled. His sister had turned into a Parisian after all. "And so?"

"Well, the newspapers seem to be split on the subject of restaurants. Some think the idea of a former chef for the aristocracy, that's not us, of course, cooking for anyone who can pay is a sign of a healthy change in society. Some think it is going to be the ruin of the common man, rich food being a corrupting influence."

"That's such nonsense," Albert observed, still painting. "Fanny, it's a business, for God's sake. You buy the ingredients for one price, then you add the cost of your labor, and don't forget your rent and other costs, and mark up the selling price so you make money. Hopefully someone buys what you have for sale. Otherwise you won't be able to purchase more ingredients the next day. Some people, mostly those who have worked for wages all their lives, see that as being greedy. They don't understand that if you give away the food, or the furniture, you'll be out of business in a week."

"I just have this love of cooking. I didn't realize I was going to have to think about the politics of it all," Fanny said.

"Here's what I'd do," Albert offered. "I'd put a communal table right up near the front window. Anyone can come in and sit down with their fellow citizens. Then I'd have separate tables in the rest of the restaurant, so people can have their privacy if they want. That way, you should satisfy those that think restaurants are a function of the revolution and need to honor the equal citizens stuff, and those that think if they are paying they should be able to talk to and eat with who they want."

Fanny was surprised. Her brother had never talked to her very much as an adult. He still treated her like a child most of the time. But now he gave her a thoughtful commentary on her new business, one that accepted a range of political views and tried to accommodate them. Father and Albert must have talked about this kind of thing a lot concerning their own business. "That's a very good idea, Albert. I'll do that, if Henri agrees."

Now Albert put down his brush. "Sister, do really think Henri is ever coming back? I think you should call this place Chez Fanny and throw a chicken at him if he shows his face again."

"Cooked or raw?"

Albert looked at his sister to see if she was smiling or not. She was.

"I still believe Henri could be alive and in Paris. I still believe he would be back with me if he could," Fanny said defensively, thinking of the spice box and how she still had something someone wanted. "But I accept the fact that he may have just left forever. It was tough, Henri getting stabbed and all. He was distraught."

"He fell on his own knife, sis. That's not exactly some terrible crime."

"He was pushed on his knife. And I was there. That mob meant harm. But let's not discuss it. I still have faith, Albert, that Henri loves me and he will come back."

Albert put his hands on Fanny's shoulders. "We didn't talk about the fact that I told Mother about the maître d'hôtel. I thought you needed your mother to share that load. You're still just a child."

"I did need to talk to Mother. But she's so political right now, she interprets everything through the eyes of the revolution."

"Which isn't bad," Albert asserted. "It's good to have a family member who cares."

Fanny was thoughtful now, thinking of the dead man

who had been her boss. "The part that bothered me the most was his not having a priest. And Mother really helped me with that. She said that religion was for the living and I, we, saved him from that smelly pit over by Les Halles. It made me feel so much better."

"Who do you think killed him?"

"A thief trying to get in the house," she said resolutely. Perhaps a thief looking for the stolen crown jewels from Versailles that, oh, by the way, our mother might have stolen.

Now Albert got a drink of water. "All this, the architect leaving the country, the maître d' hôtel getting killed, and then your boyfriend disappearing, all of it is part of this damn situation with the king. Over in the neighborhood, they want to lop off his head, and hers, too. But the Assembly fights among itself so much, they can't decide on what to do with the king or how to run the country. I am afraid it's going to get worse."

"The world is changing, brother. We have to change with it."

The door of the storefront opened and a boy came in, dressed in the uniform of a fine household. "Fanny Delarue?" he asked.

"Here, boy," Fanny said, feeling in her pocket for a sou. She handed him the tip and opened the sealed envelope he had handed her.

A note inside read: *Come to the Roman baths tomorrow at noon. More will be revealed. Henri is alive.*

Fanny smiled and handed the note to Albert. "See? Henri may be home by this time tomorrow."

"I hope so. I'd also like to know how that boy with the

fancy suit found this place. There's no sign. How would anyone know to find you here?"

"Someone is watching me. It's as simple as that. But it's all right if it brings Henri back," Fanny said.

Finally.

CHAPTER FOURTEEN

FANNY found not a priest but a bureaucrat. She was looking for the door to the frigidarium, but walked into the chapel of the abbots of Cluny instead. Because it had been taken over by the new government when they confiscated church property, a young man in the black suit of a clerk, not a parish priest, was taking inventory.

"How do I get to the Roman thermae, monsieur?" Fanny asked. "I came here with my school once a long time ago, but I guess I don't remember where the entrance is."

The young man smiled. It wasn't often he had company, or at least pretty, female company. "It's around on the southwest side. I came here, too, with my school. The copper workshop was in there. Was it when you came?"

"Well, I don't remember that. But I'll never forget how cool it was in there. It was hot outside that day and here it was, this big room. You'd think it'd be hot as Hades, especially now that you explain it was a metal workshop. But it was cool, very cool," Fanny remembered.

"It's strange to me the abbots of Cluny in Burgundy built their home and chapel in Paris right up against the Roman baths. I wonder what they were thinking?" the clerk mused.

"Maybe they wanted to be near the college across the street." Fanny surmised as she prepared to leave the chapel. "Thank you for directing me," she said and walked out into the garden, curving to the south as she went.

She had been so nervous all day. Her brother had begged to go with her but she insisted on making the trip alone. Any chance that Albert would be hotheaded and ruin her opportunity to get Henri back was not worth risking. She would give them the jewels—that had to be their demand—and Henri would return home and that would be that. But she certainly hadn't been foolish enough to bring the jewels with her. She would make them spell it out before she traipsed around Paris with those.

Fanny stepped into the frigidarium, a vast and impressive room, and the temperature dropped immediately. The workers were scurrying about, pounding metal and shouting back and forth. The height of the groined vault ceiling created a spectacular echo. The ghosts of the Romans who ruled Paris when it was called Lutetia rattled around in this room.

Fanny tried to stay to the perimeter walls so she wouldn't be in the way. She decided that after she had walked completely around once, and if no one approached her, she would find the foreman and ask for help. She didn't have to wait that long. The foreman came to her and squinted into her face, studying her.

"You must be the one," he said.

"The one what?"

"I'm supposed to give you this box. Said you were a pretty little thing with strange, green-blue eyes. That's you, all right," he stated and handed her a plain wooden box.

"Who gave this to you?"

"A boy. Just a regular delivery boy."

"Thank you so much," Fanny said and smiled her best smile. The man hurried away and Fanny turned her back to the room but started to open the box right then and there. She hadn't really expected this. She had envisioned getting to talk to someone in person. Or better yet, that Henri would be here, waiting for her.

But that wasn't what was in store for her today. Instead, there was a note and an object wrapped in tissue paper. The note said: *This is so you will take us seriously. You will hear soon. Don't let the inspector follow you.*

Fanny quickly unwound the tissue. In it rested Henri's little finger. And on that finger was the signet ring Chef Etienne was clasping when Fanny knelt over his dead body. She had thrown it in her own clothing chest the night of his murder and forgotten about it. What did it mean that it was now on this gruesome finger?

Fanny's stomach tightened, then flipped over. Her gag reflex kicked in and she had to shut her mouth to keep from vomiting. She sank to her knees without meaning to, clutching the box, faltering at putting the top back on, her mind racing faster than her hands.

The foreman saw this and rushed over to Fanny's side. "Here, now, let me help you. You're as white as a sheet. Bad news?"

Fanny let him help her to her feet. She wanted to scream at him, demand he tell her who had done this, where this "gift" had come from, where Henri was. Even in her agitated state, she knew none of that would do any good. "Thank you so much. I haven't eaten today and I felt a little faint."

Fanny and the workman made it to the door. She smiled again and thanked him one more time and started walking toward the river, intent on getting home before she really broke down. All night she had allowed her thoughts to be so optimistic. She had actually imagined having a romantic dinner with Henri tonight. What a fool she was.

As Fanny crossed over to the Ile de la Cité, she recalled her visit to the Conciergerie. She had been hopeful that day as well, hopeful she might find her true love in jail, as pathetic as that was. Her whole life now was just a series of arcs, anticipation that something positive was in store, that Henri would be found, then those hopes dashed. But this time was the cruelest of all. This time she was coming home without Henri, but with his little finger.

Fanny knew she was going to have to examine the finger again. She so admired Henri's hands, the hands she declared should play the piano. She was sure she could recognize whether this finger was actually Henri's. Could that be possible, that something about it would be familiar, or had this piece of flesh and bone, so full of personality when attached to the rest of the person, been rendered anonymous by its detachment? Was it now only the sum of its parts: muscles, nerves, and bone, nothing more?

Fanny thought about how M. Desjardins had become a problem to be solved instead of a man in a very short period of time. As she was walking toward the Place de Grève, the city hall, she realized that all of the death she had been around in the past months had convinced her of the existence of what the priests called a soul. That seemed a very profound lesson to be learned, and she supposed that was one good thing that had come out of all this.

She could just hear herself as an old grandmother, tending a pot of soup and filling her grandchildren full of scary tales. "Yes, I know that we have a soul because I see what a shell we become when our life leaves us. Why, back in 1790 and '91, when people were getting killed left and right, and my lover's finger was hacked off by some kidnappers, I sure learned about the soul," she would rave, and the children would tell their parents that grandmother was funny, talking about fingers and kidnappers.

It was about this time that Fanny felt her own life force seeping away, at least the energy she had started the day full of. All of a sudden, she could barely walk. The act of putting one foot in front of the other seemed to be too demanding. She wanted to sit down on the sidewalk and cry. The image of how that would appear to the throngs around her made her laugh, but it was a sharp, barely controlled laugh, nothing that represented joy or happiness. Hysteria was claiming Fanny. She wisely realized she was on the edge and grabbed a *cinq* to take her the rest of the way home. The carriage was crowded, so she sat silently, clutching the box, until she arrived at her stop.

When Fanny arrived on the Place Royale, it took her a short time to realize it was noisier than usual. She had retreated far into herself. When her friend Lucy from number twenty-one ran into her running fast, only then did she realize something was amiss.

"Lucy, I'm sorry. I wasn't paying attention. Where are you running to so fast?"

Lucy looked at her strangely. She gestured with the

bucket in her hand. "You must have been away marketing. There's a fire, Fanny. And I'm afraid it's at number twenty-three. Your house."

The two women turned without another word and ran across the square. Fanny was filled with dread and anguish. Had she foolishly left a pot on the hearth? But she knew the answer to that. She hadn't cooked since she started working on the restaurant, buying something from Violet at the boulangerie and perhaps a piece of cheese. She could tell she had lost weight by the way her uniforms fit, her old uniforms being her work clothes when she painted and cleaned at the storefront.

So, no cooking fires. She also knew she hadn't started any fires for heat in the big house before she left for the Left Bank, only a small fire in the hearth of the new kitchen for warmth as she dressed. She hadn't even made coffee at home this morning, taking a cup at the Tabac on rue St. Antoine.

Fanny knew on such a place as this square, where the houses butted up against one another to form a continuous unbroken whole, fire was feared most of all. That was why Lucy was running to help with her bucket, and so were other servants from all around the square.

The scene at number twenty-three could have been worse. There was a great deal of smoke billowing up, but as Fanny entered the courtyard, she saw an organized line of cooks and servants passing buckets along toward the source of the fire, the new kitchen. A water carrier wagon had moved right into the courtyard to supply water and a whole group of boys, Nicholas and Simon included, were pulling water up from the well as fast as they could. As Fanny got nearer the kitchen building, she saw who was leading the effort in such an organized, efficient manner. It was Inspector Fournier, directing several policemen.

Fanny stood there, stunned, still clutching her box. She looked around for a place to put it, knowing she should take her place in the brigade. But she wasn't thinking clearly or quickly, her mind muddled, and it took her several seconds to work through this. She decided to put her macabre cargo in the carriage house, and started over there as if in slow motion.

"Fanny, we've almost got it," Fournier yelled, spotting her amid the smoke.

She nodded in his direction numbly. She had to put the box holding the finger somewhere safe. When she opened the door to the tack room, she noticed that all the remaining harnesses and bits, the ones not worn by the horses when they left Paris, were strewn on the floor. But she couldn't remember if it had been like that always. She couldn't even remember when she'd been in this room in the daylight last. She put her box on a roughhewn worktable and ran back out to the fire line.

Fournier was coming toward her across the courtyard. "It's out. It wasn't much, but when the police spotted smoke, they rang the fire bell, then it took a while for them to get inside. I was in the neighborhood and came by to check on you. By the time I arrived, there were more than enough helping hands to work like a team. But any fire takes time to put out. And Fanny, there's something else."

Fanny had been standing there, dumbfounded. Lucy came up to her and patted her gently on the back. "Thank God you have this separate kitchen," she said. "If you need anything, come over to twenty-one."

Fanny nodded silently. When Lucy had moved away, she looked up inquiringly.

"Someone has torn the inside apart. By that I mean they tossed pots, pans, dishes, books, everything is out on the floor, upstairs and down. Someone was searching for something, Fanny."

"Yes," Fanny said, then she turned and headed toward the group of workers who had saved M. Monnard's property. She needed to thank each one of them. She spoke to the boys and they started passing around cups of water. Nicholas ran into the house and came out with a stack of linen towels from the kitchen. The boys wet them down and passed them around as well so the men and women could at least wipe their faces. Everything smelled of smoke. After a few minutes of this, Fanny hurried back over to Inspector Fournier. "Please stay, if you can. I need you."

FANNY was walking through the rubble of the new kitchen. She was thankful so little of value was still in there. The spice box, the money, and the jewels were safe in the main house. Much of the kitchen equipment she meant to take to the restaurant was already packed in one of the storage rooms in the original kitchen. There was plenty of room there, so Fanny just put everything she intended to take in one of the rooms out of the way. This included all of the good knives that had been in Henri's kit, as well as the better whisks and copper pots. Dented stockpots and old cast-iron skillets and dutch ovens were about all that was left in the new kitchen and a fire never hurt a cast-iron skillet. It would take days to clean it up, but Fanny had already asked

Nicholas and Simon if they could spare two hours a day for her. She would let them do it at their leisure.

Henri's clothes were a sentimental loss to her. They would have to be burned. The second-floor sleeping loft didn't receive any actual fire damage but Fanny was sure not even the best laundress on the Seine could get out the smell of the smoke.

As she picked up items and examined them, Inspector Fournier stood by the water container and the basin, stripped to his waist, washing up.

Fanny tried not to look at him but it was impossible. He had well-defined muscles on his stomach and arms and back. She thought about the bathtubs in the main house, of Fournier and her in one of them together, then put that image out of her head.

As she went through the debris and he washed, she told him about going to the Roman baths and what had occurred there.

"Fanny, I want you to go get the package with the finger. It may be just a bit of bone and gristle meant to scare you. And I believe that the note sending you to the baths was just a ploy to get you out of the house so someone could take their time and search."

"But I go out of the house every day. It wasn't necessary to send me on a wild-goose chase," Fanny said defensively. "I received the message about Henri and going to the frigidarium not here, but at the new restaurant. If they just wanted to search the house, they could have done it anytime I went over there to paint."

She left the new kitchen, crossed the courtyard, entered the tack room, and went to the table. The box was gone.

Fanny spent a few minutes searching, trying to remember everything as it had happened earlier. But it was all a blur. The only thing she was sure of was that she had put the box containing Henri's finger on this table in this room. Defeated, she went back in the new kitchen.

Fournier was buttoning his shirt. "What's the matter?" he asked cautiously when he saw Fanny's face.

"The box with the finger is gone. And all the bridles and things were strewn around when I went in there the first time today. Maybe someone was in there, saw me leave a package, and took it, thinking it was valuable."

Fournier walked over to Fanny, who seemed to be stuck inside the front door, not moving. "Fanny, in a minute we are taking whatever things you want out of here and leaving this place. We're moving you to the main house. But first, I want to tell you something. I know you won't listen to me, but I have to tell you anyway."

Fanny numbly walked to the two upholstered chairs, chairs that would now have to be redone before they could go back in the house, and sat down. Like a naughty schoolgirl, she was ready to be scolded, gazing blankly out at some focal point in the room, not looking directly at Fournier.

He did not sit down. Fanny was too distracting. When he sat close to her, all he wanted to do was touch her. "The fire, in my expert opinion, was set. There was a stack of kindling and paper and a long piece of cheesecloth or muslin, all things that would catch and burn, right in the middle of the floor. I know you don't keep your kindling in the middle of the floor. I can't for the life of me figure out why he, or they, sent you off on a wild-goose chase so they could search out here, but the house, as far as I could tell, they didn't touch. I went down to the delivery entrance and the door was still locked I looked inside and everything seemed neat and tidy. So, they must have chosen to search the kitchen and carriage house first. Why did they set the fire, instead of continuing to the main house? And what do you suppose they were looking for?"

"It will be over soon," Fanny said woodenly. "The note said the finger, it was a finger, I swear, was just to get my attention."

"You won't give me the jewels and let me handle this, will you? You're going to try to handle it yourself and probably get killed in the process?"

Fanny couldn't let Fournier have the jewels or even admit that she had them. Then she wouldn't have any bargaining power. "I don't know what you're talking about," she said flatly, without any attempt to conceal the lie it was.

"And I don't suppose you are going to send for your parents either?"

Fanny put her hands together as if in prayer. "Please, just give me a few more days." She could see that Fournier wanted to slap some sense into her. She was a suspect, yes. He believed she had the jewels in her possession. And he would try to manipulate her to confess and give them up to him. But he knew whoever had Henri wanted the very same thing.

"One week. It's a Wednesday. Next Wednesday, if you haven't received any more word of Henri, then I'm taking you home myself."

"Thank you, Fournier," Fanny said barely audible. She felt nothing. Except cold. It was frigid in this place; everything had been doused with water, and the January weather was fast turning it into ice.

"I can see your breath," Fournier said with surprise.

With that, Fanny's teeth started rattling. She allowed herself to be taken to the main house and she remembered to bring the keys, handing them over to Fournier without comment. He unlocked the delivery entrance door and set about building a big fire in the kitchen hearth, then asked Fanny if she would make them some tea. While she was doing that, he went outside in the square to make sure the policeman he had posted there was on his job. When he came back in the house, the kitchen was cozy and warm. And Fanny was pouring hot water in a teapot from the water kettle on the hook.

"I hope it's not his," she said.

Fournier looked at Fanny with concern. She was in shock. He hoped a cup of tea and maybe a good shot of cognac would snap her out of it. He should have moved her out of that cold, wet mess of a kitchen sooner. "The finger?" he asked.

"I didn't look at it thoroughly. Henri has such beautiful fingers. I think if I really examined it, I could tell. But wouldn't it be simple to get a finger off a dead person? When I was little, some church here in Paris was supposed to have a relic of a finger of Christ, or maybe it was Peter. We talked about it in our school class. We wanted to see it. Then one of the nuns heard us and told us it was not a real relic. She said there were unscrupulous people who would misrepresent items even to churches, and that the true relics were authenticated by the pope in Rome." Fanny handed Fournier his cup of tea, her hand shaking.

He went looking for the cognac, wondering what else might bring her back to the real world from the edge she was hovering on. He opened the door to the bedroom accidentally, thinking it another storeroom. Immediately he knew it was Fanny's, and even though it was only four in the afternoon, he wanted to put her to bed.

"I'm going to keep this door open for a while so your bedroom can get warm," he said, still searching for the cognac. He went into the pantry and found a bottle of port and one of cognac, so he brought them both out. "What's your pleasure?" he asked.

"My pleasure? That would be ice cream," Fanny said with a giggle. "I love strawberry the most."

Fournier gave up on getting a rational answer from Fanny and poured a good splash of cognac in a glass that he found in the dish room. He poured one for himself, gave Fanny hers, and clinked their glasses together. "This will warm you up," he said with a pat to her head. "Some days, Fanny, you just can't win. I've had many of those days in my life, especially in my career as a police officer. Well, my sweet, this is one of those days for you. You're pulled away to receive the severed finger of your boyfriend, who seems to have been kidnapped. When you come home from that, you discover a fire in your household complex and a crowd of your neighbors fighting it. Then you lose or someone steals the finger you were given as proof that your boyfriend is indeed a hostage. And the building that was set on fire was also torn apart in some sort of desperate search."

"It sounds bad when you put it like that," Fanny was just able to quip.

"I propose, dear Fanny, that you surrender."

"How?"

"I want to put you to bed. I know it's just dusk, but you need to drink the cognac down, and give up for the day. And I'm not going to let you sleep in your clothes. Do you have a warm nightgown?"

"Bottom drawer."

"Good. Now just sit here and drink and I'll be back in a jiffy."

Fanny drank a big gulp of the brandy and sipped some tea. She liked the idea of giving up on this day.

Fournier came back in with a white flannel nightgown with pretty pink ribbons on it, again courtesy of Martine's handiwork. "Put this on. I'm going outside for a piss," Fournier ordered.

Fanny obeyed. She was out of optimism for the time being. The world seemed too complicated and ugly. She took off her clothes and threw them in a heap. They were smoke damaged and she had every intention of burning them tomorrow. She sniffed at her skin and it wasn't much better, but she couldn't go through all the steps to make a bath tonight. She would just have to change her bed linens and clothes tomorrow and send the whole lot to the laundress. Now she walked into her bedroom, naked but for her socks and boots, to get a chemise to slip on before the nightgown.

She dressed and sat down on the bed to remove her boots, leaving the door to the kitchen open so she could catch some of that fireplace heat. This whole procedure of getting up, coming into the bedroom, putting on nightclothes, and taking off her boots, had barely taken five minutes, but when she was finished pulling off her stockings, Fanny realized Fournier hadn't returned from his trip outside. She felt the adrenaline start to pump once again through her body. He should be back by now.

Fanny rushed out the delivery door. It was getting dark but she could still see around the courtyard clearly. The smell of smoke still hung heavy in the air. And there was

Fournier, lying still on the grass, near the back of the carriage house.

For one second, Fanny had a brief worry about whether Fournier had seen the grave under the bales of hay. Then she felt ashamed, running toward him, telling herself that was what happened when one started lying and living with secrets. Instead of worrying about Fournier's health, she was worried about what Fournier had discovered. It was so wrong.

Fanny absolutely expected Fournier to be dead, like the chef and the maître d' before him. At the very least, she expected him to be stabbed, as Henri had been. But he groaned when she touched him and reached for his head. There it was, a nasty blow to the back of his head. It had caused an egg-size lump to form and there was some blood caking around where the skin was broken. Fanny was thrilled.

"Fournier, are you awake? Someone hit you on the back of the head. Do you think you can walk?"

The inspector seemed half in and half out of consciousness. He pushed up on his elbows, but soon sank back to the ground, facedown. "Oh, that hurts," he muttered, out of breath. He lay there breathing heavily.

"Oh, thank God you're alive," Fanny gasped, short of breath herself from the fright and the cold. Now that the sun was down, the temperature was dropping. "Let's try to get you up. I'm going to count to three. I'll lift you around your belly, and you push up."

And with only one false start, Fournier got to his feet. Fanny threw his arm around her neck and walked him slowly into the kitchen of the main house trying to support him as best she could. At first he was so woozy he couldn't walk straight, but in the short trip to the house he seemed to get his bearings.

"That'll teach you to go outside to relieve yourself," Fanny cracked.

"I had my back to the house, clear out by the carriage house. Someone snuck up. They must have had a wooden walking stick. It couldn't have been a fireplace poker or I'd still be out. I'll wager they wanted to get out of the courtyard so they hit me and ran for the outer door. Fanny, go check it."

Fanny helped Fournier to the only armchair in the kitchen. She slipped a stool under his feet to lift them, then quickly wet a towel and put it on his wound. "Hold this. I'll be right back," she said as she put his hand on the towel.

Fanny could see from the doorway that the pedestrian door to the square was open. She ran up the stairs and over to it, closing it and pulling the metal bar over to lock and hold it closed. Then she ran back inside, barefoot with only her chemise and nightgown on.

"Now it's you who needs the cognac," she said. She fed the fire, lit the wall lanterns and a few candles around the room, got a glass, and poured Fournier a stiff drink. Then she cleaned his head, threatening to cut all the hair off around the gash if he didn't be still.

Fournier was quiet. Usually so glib, he hadn't said a whole sentence after his initial explanation of events. He sipped his cognac and Fanny tended to his wound, babbling to make up for his silence.

"Now, I have something important to ask you," she said as she threw the bloody towel in the pile with her clothes. "I want to give you something else to wear. Your shirt smells of smoke and has blood all over it. Would you mind if I went up and got something of the master's? He isn't so muscular but he's tall like you. I'll just get a nightshirt. I'm sure that will fit you."

Fournier looked surprised. "I can't very well wear a nightshirt out on the streets of Paris."

Fanny knelt down in front of him, looking up in his eyes. "That's what I want to ask you. Please stay here with me tonight. I can't stand the idea of being here alone. I'm afraid, and that's the truth."

"Are you sure I need a nightshirt?"

Fanny got up and put her hands on her hips. "Very sure. I wasn't asking you for sex, just for companionship. Understood?"

Fournier didn't think he could have performed tonight if his life depended on it. He was dizzy, his head was throbbing, and he was still worried about Fanny's safety. "Understood," he agreed.

Fanny lit a candle and slipped it in a candlestick, then disappeared.

Fournier fell asleep in front of the fire, his head tilted uncomfortably to one side. It took Fanny a while to find the master's wardrobe full of incidentals. She had never helped put away the laundry so she wasn't familiar with the whereabouts of everything. When she made it downstairs, she shook Fournier awake.

"Come in the bedroom. You have to use the chamber pot tonight. I don't want you out of my sight again. It's behind that screen," she said and indicated one corner of the room. "I'm leaving the door open to the kitchen so the heat can reach us. And I'm sorry my bed is narrow. It's not a mere cot but it's not grand with curtains and such, like the beds upstairs." She said all this as she led him into her room. He looked around with confusion. "I don't get it. Do you want me to sleep with you?"

Fanny jumped under the covers. "I certainly do. I meant it when I said I don't want you out of my sight. Hurry now and change out of those revolting clothes. I promise I won't look. You can go behind the screen if you don't believe me."

Fournier changed into the nightshirt of M. Monnard's. When he climbed into bed with Fanny, her feet almost made him jump back out. "Everything is lovely and warm except those blocks of ice you have on the ends of your legs," he said as he put his arm around Fanny and drew her near.

She snuggled up and threw her arm over his chest. "I'll put them under your legs. They'll warm up."

And that was how they fell asleep, curled up like an old married couple.

CHAPTER FIFTEEN

MORNING was something else. When Fanny woke up, they were sleeping like spoons and she could feel Fournier's body through their nightclothes. She sat up quickly, and Fournier ran his hand down her spine.

"How's your head?" she asked him.

He put his hand on the wound and felt gingerly. "It's closed up. That's good that I didn't get blood on your pillows."

"Not only that, you were a perfect gentleman. What a pleasant surprise, Jean Fournier. Will you answer two questions for me?"

"I'll answer one. Don't be so greedy," Fournier said as he went behind the curtain to relive himself.

"How old are you?" Fanny called.

"Thirty-three. How old are you?"

"Eighteen."

"Eighteen and not married yet? Why, you're almost an old maid."

"What were you arguing with Chef Etienne about last summer at Les Halles?"

Fournier picked his clothes up off the floor and shook them. "Good one. Very sneaky. I told you. Only one question per customer."

Fanny jumped out of bed. "I'm going upstairs to get you some clothes. You can't wear those. They're going to the laundry with mine."

Fanny went upstairs and got clothes for Fournier, wondering why he wouldn't answer her question about Les Halles, then remembered that they both smelled of the fire. So she started filling the bathtub and laid the clean clothes next to the tub. Then she went back downstairs.

"Fournier, please go upstairs and take a bath. The water is running so you can't say no. I'll make coffee," Fanny said in a bossy, I-won't-take-no tone of voice.

"Won't you come, too?" he asked, putting his hand on her buttock through her nightgown.

"No, I won't, and I'll thank you to keep your hands to yourself." Fanny turned around and fiddled with the fire and the water kettle. She could just see them together in that tub. "It's up two floors, on the first floor," she said.

Fournier left the kitchen and Fanny thought about all that had happened yesterday. She had been so upset about Henri's finger. Then there was the fire, then Fournier being hit over the head, not to mention that someone had stolen the finger. She certainly didn't want to stay here on Place Royale anymore, but she had to remain a few more days. She would trade Henri for the jewels. Then there would be nothing to protect, no more jewels to hide, no kidnappers, no murderers. And no more reason for Inspector Fournier to spend time with her. Fanny considered that a loss that she would feel the rest of her life. It wasn't a matter of liking him better than Henri. Henri was her love, the man she was going to marry. But Jean Fournier had taken a special place in Fanny's heart.

As Fanny made coffee, she heard someone pounding on the outer door. And here she was in her nightgown. She hurried into the bedroom and slipped on one of her uniforms, then looked around for a cap or a collar. She didn't spot either one, so she slipped on her boots without socks and ran outside to see who was knocking.

When she opened the door, it was Martine Delarue standing there, not a tradesman. "Oh, Mama. The most horrible things happened yesterday. I'm so glad you're here."

Martine took her daughter's arm and squeezed. "Tell Mother," she said as they made their way back to the house.

As Fanny and her mother drank coffee, Fanny poured out the news of all the events that had happened in the last twenty-four hours. She forgot that Inspector Fournier was upstairs until he walked down the back stairs into the kitchen.

"I know I look a fool but at least it's better than that nightshirt," he said without looking up.

"Oh, Jean, my mama is here," Fanny said with a fake cheeriness.

Inspector Fournier and Martine eyed each other warily.

"Fournier, I just told Mother you got hit on the head. I hadn't got to the part where you spent the night here. It was strictly for protection, I assure you, that and the fact that he had been knocked unconscious."

Fournier regained his composure. "Why else would I allow myself to wear clothes too small?

The two women giggled.

He had on a pair of black velvet knee breeches that barely hit the knee, a natural linen shirt, and a brocade vest. "I will keep my overcoat," he said with wounded pride as he picked it up. "Fanny, try to stay out of trouble today. Martine, you, too." With that he put on his coat, turned up the collar, and left.

Fanny and Martine broke into hysterical laughter.

"It looks like you and the inspector are, what shall I say. . . . ?" Martine waited for Fanny to explain.

"He always seems to show up when I need him, and sometimes when I don't," Fanny mused.

"So the note with the finger didn't say what the kidnappers want?"

It was only then Fanny remembered she hadn't told her mother about the jewels. "No," she said honestly. "The note said I would hear soon, that the finger was to get my attention and not to let Fournier follow me."

"And that last part, do you intend to obey?"

Fanny was shocked. "Of course. I would never do anything to jeopardize Henri. Fournier didn't see the note, or the finger either. And he'll never know when I hear from the kidnappers."

Martine studied her daughter. She was lying about something but Martine couldn't quite pinpoint what it was. Were she and the police inspector lovers? Was Henri already dead in some terrible accident? "I came by to go with you to your new restaurant. Do you feel up to it today?"

Fanny was happy her mother was interested. "Of course. I want as much done as possible when Henri comes home." She hugged her mother. "Let me finish getting dressed. I don't have any socks on."

"I noticed," her mother said dryly.

Yes, something was definitely going on.

"VIOLET, where do you get a team of horses?" Fanny and Violet saw each other every day now that Fanny was moving in on the same street. Violet's father had been very helpful: He had assisted her in contacting the owner of the building, recommended a lawyer right on rue Vieille du Temple who would take care of the lease, and generally was good for advice about the neighborhood. Both Philippe and Albert Delarue had gone into the boulangerie to introduce themselves to M. Lafarge. Thereafter, he took a paternal interest in Fanny. Now, she was allowed to go directly into the kitchen.

"What do you need horses for?" Violet asked. She was icing the tops of some tortes as they talked and Fanny was eating the cake trimmings, the part Violet cut off to make the layers even.

"I have a carriage. I need a pair of horses and a driver, for this Sunday."

"You know we have nothing but mules. But we do have a driver. I'll talk to him when he gets back. He might want to make some extra money. Sunday he only works until two."

Sunday the shop was closed; the guild rules required it to be. But Sunday was a big day at the cafés of Palais-Royal. And Sunday was just another day at the Conciergerie. They all still needed bread. So the family baked the bread on Sunday, getting up at two in the morning and aiming to get done and send the deliveryman out so they could still make the last mass at church.

"Two would be fine. If he could rent some horses and come to number twenty-three, or do you get the carriage before you get the horses? I guess I never paid attention. Anyway, I need to be someplace by four."

Violet grinned slyly and raised her eyebrows. "Is Henri finally coming back, now that you've done the hard work at the restaurant?"

Fanny didn't want to sound too confident. That might queer the deal. "You just wait and see. Let me know what the driver says." She grabbed one last bite of cake and left the bakery.

Yesterday, the day after the fire, she didn't hear a thing from the kidnappers. After her mother's inspection tour, she stayed in the storefront as long as she could, hoping she would receive a message. Then, in the afternoon, she had gone back to the house on Place Royale and directed the boys in the cleanup. During this time she left the porte cochere open, to announce she was home. But it had not done any good. Fanny had spent another restless night, pacing around the kitchen, making cup after cup of tea. She couldn't be satisfied. When a day was full of action: fires, visits to the Roman baths, assaults, she felt that things were out of her control. When nothing happened, Fanny did not take that as a good thing and rest; she felt ineffectual, anxious to move forward.

This morning, as she was walking to the storefront, the minute she turned onto rue Vieille du Temple, the delivery boy spotted her. He was waiting in front of the storefront. He trotted down the street toward her. "Mademoiselle? A letter for you," he said in his high, youthful voice.

Fanny fumbled for a coin for the boy and took the letter. She kept walking as she tore it open. It said: *Four on Sunday afternoon. The gazebo of Parc Bagatelle. Dress up. Bring the jewels. Henri will be there.*

Fanny unlocked the storefront and went in, but she knew she wouldn't be able to work today, maybe not again until Henri was home, safe and sound.

She locked up, went to speak to Violet, then went home and riffled through the mistress's clothes, looking for something to wear on Sunday. She thought about asking her mother to make something for her, but the idea of a rush job to go pay off a kidnapper seemed wrong. She went out and worked with the boys when they came in the afternoon, throwing out anything made of fabric and burning it in a fire pit in the courtyard that she felt safe about using. The boys had brought all the furniture outside and were scrubbing the worktables.

And so another day passed.

On Saturday, Fanny got up, got dressed, and went to the restaurant. She halfheartedly started painting the woodwork and then her father came to visit, saving her from doing work her heart wasn't in.

After they greeted each other and talked of the tables and chairs for a bit, Philippe Delarue got down to the point.

"So, Fanny, I want you to tell me what kind of a restaurant this will be. Or what kind it will be from your point of view. I understand you can't speak for Henri."

Fanny was glad to share her ideas with her father. The restaurant was a topic that represented the future, not the present, which was full of unresolved problems, or the past, when all the problems started.

"Did you know, Papa, that the first restaurants were shops where you went to get a restorative? It was a cup of broth that they made with chickens and gold coins and vegetables. It was a stock, basically. And it was fashionable but also political, to eat at a restaurant because it was the opposite of what people considered 'royal' cuisine, which was service after service of dish after dish. It was one little cup of broth. Well, I don't want to sell restoratives."

Her father was amazed. "Who taught you all this?"

"Chef Etienne," she said. "Now, the tavern or eating house is a place everyone pays the same and then they all sit down at communal tables usually. And everyone eats the same food. I don't want that either. I want to give people a choice of what they have to eat and they pay by what they order."

"I think that's a great idea."

"And I don't want it to be fancy, more like Grandma's cuisine, you know, the stuff you remember that your grandmother cooked that you get hungry for."

"And I suspect even the wealthy bourgeois would rather have a plate of lamb stew than roasted peacock."

Fanny remembered she had a partner. "Of course, Henri might have a different idea. He's thought about it longer."

"But we don't know what Henri thinks since he's deserted you," Philippe said quietly.

"No, that's not true. What did Mother tell you?"

"That I had to ask you about Henri's whereabouts. That she couldn't break a confidence."

"Papa, Henri disappeared. I had no idea where he'd gone. I didn't know if he would ever come back. It was horrible."

Philippe Delarue put his arms around his daughter. "I'm so sorry."

"But it's fine now. I heard from him, and tomorrow he's coming back to me. Then we'll open this restaurant and get married."

"Just know that if, for any reason, he doesn't, I'll try to help you open this place. With the money, I mean."

Fanny looked blankly at her father.

"You know, the money he inherited that you were going to open up this restaurant with."

Fanny broke into a big smile. She'd lost track of the lies she'd told. "Oh, yes, the money Henri inherited. Don't worry, we'll be just fine. Tomorrow it will be all over."

"I hope that's true, precious. I love you no matter what."

"I know you do, Father. I count on it."

As usual, Philippe Delarue turned and waved good-bye to Fanny as he left. Fanny felt terrible for lying to him. To the rest of the world, it had become easy.

CHAPTER SIXTEEN

FANNY looked at her image in the mirror. She had found a suit in Mme Monnard's closet that was made of deep burgundy velvet. Her own mother might have sewn it, for all she knew. Martine had made clothes for the mistress occasionally. It was large on Fanny but not so much that she couldn't wear it. And it didn't have a hoop skirt so it must be fairly new. It would look fine with her cape. She found the hat that seemed to go with the suit. It was navy with a velvet ribbon the same shade of burgundy around the band. It had layers of veiling cut in different lengths so they stuck out in a saucy way. She thought she looked beautiful, if she did say so herself. She dug around for a pair of kid gloves, then down to the kitchen to fetch the jewels.

Fanny exchanged the money for the jewelry, fishing out diamonds from the flour and tea containers, taking the money out of the spice box and replacing it with the jewels. Then she shoved the foreign money in the flour, the French in the tea, and put them far in the back of the pantry shelves. She headed for the carriage house. She wasn't going to be pretentious and allow the driver to pick her up at the front door of the house, which she had never walked through in her life, not even now, when she had the place to herself.

The deliveryman from Lafarge's boulangerie was hitching up the horses he'd rented with money from Fanny. He smiled at her. "This sure is a pretty rig," he said, indicating the carriage.

Fanny was grateful it wasn't raining or snowing. Small, open carriages were very much in fashion right now, mainly because the king always took a big, closed one. But no one who had a choice would use an open carriage if it was raining out.

"Hurry now, I need to be there at four," she said nervously, clutching the spice box.

Soon they were headed west to the Parc Bagatelle. Fanny had only heard of this place. The land had been confiscated from some rich person and now was a garden and park for Parisians to go to spend some time out of doors. That was really all she knew. She thought Marie Antoinette had had something to do with it.

Fanny tried to stay calm. It was going to take an hour to get there, she was sure. And as much as she enjoyed seeing people notice her in a carriage, she really couldn't relax and enjoy much of the moment. She closed her eyes, and the next thing she knew, the driver was calling to her. She was embarrassed. How she must have looked driving through the city, practically from one end to the other, snoozing away.

A set of beautiful iron gates was up ahead, gilded and painted, open with plenty of carriage traffic.

"Where, miss?"

"The gazebo."

Inside the park there were elaborate gardens, a promenade where couples were strolling, and musicians playing. They even passed a carousel with children riding on it. Fanny had never seen anything like it.

The gazebo was off the road up on a small hill. Fanny got out, telling the driver to circle on the carriage path and come back by here every so often. Then she straightened her hat and walked up a gravel path lined with boxwood hedges, trying to look calm and confident in case anyone was watching her.

The gazebo was grand, with an ornate high roof, Greek-style statues placed at intervals, and two benches to sit and watch people walking through the maze, which covered the little hill in front of the gazebo.

Fanny entered the gazebo with her box and sat down on one bench. On the other there was an older woman, who had her eye on two children playing in the maze, most likely her grandchildren. Could this be the kidnapper?

"This is a beautiful place. This is my first time to come out here. I wonder, who did it belong to before?" Fanny asked, not really expecting an answer.

But the old lady was ready and willing to talk. "It recently belonged to the comte d'Artois, the king's brother. That lovely folly over there"—she indicated a small, graceful château with her walking stick—"was the result of a wager between the comte and Marie Antoinette."

"What's a folly?" Fanny asked, more curious than ashamed she didn't know.

The old lady smiled. "A building intended only to be

used for pleasure, to have little dinner parties, or a dance, perhaps. The queen built several of them at Versailles."

"Oh, please tell me more. What did the queen and her brother-in-law wager on?"

"The comte bought this little estate and the château was in total disrepair. The queen bet he couldn't build a new château in sixty-six days. They both love to gamble, you see."

"What happened?" Fanny asked. She was totally entranced.

"On September 21, 1777, they began. Nine hundred men worked here day and night. Day and night, can you imagine? They worked by torchlight. My dear departed husband was one of them, that's how I know the story. The comte hired musicians to play for the workers, to keep them going. It was finished in sixty-five days."

Fanny found the story sad somehow. "He won."

"And they had their fête here as planned." The woman got up and waved at her grandchildren for them to come. "Now the revolutionary government has taken over the lovely Bagatelle, for the enjoyment of the citizens. I'm glad, aren't you?"

That made Fanny laugh. "Yes, I am. And thank you for sharing that story." She looked expectantly at the woman, thinking this was the moment she would ask her for the spice box. Fanny even picked it up from the bench next to her and put it in her lap, so she could hand it off. But instead, the two grandchildren ran up, breathless and begging for a treat, and the three of them walked away.

Fanny sat there for a few minutes, wondering what to do. She got up, paced back and forth looking around, then sat back down.

She didn't have to wait long. Henri walked into the gazebo, seemingly from out of nowhere.

Fanny jumped up and ran to him. She covered his face with kisses, laughing and crying at the same time.

Henri smiled. "I wanted to see you all dressed up. You look so pretty when you're not in your work clothes." He walked over to the spice box. "Are they in here?" he asked.

"Yes, darling," Fanny said, blind to what should have been obvious by now, still looking around for the kidnappers.

"Good. Well, then, Fanny darling, I'll be going."

Fanny couldn't understand the words; they were such a surprise to her. "Where do you have to go to give them the . . ." It finally hit her. Perhaps there were no other kidnappers? She sat down heavily on a bench, suddenly unable to carry her own weight, and bowed her head.

Henri was bundled up in a dark blue overcoat. His hair was loose on his shoulders. He refused to meet her eye, watching the park attentively, as if he were expecting someone else. "Fanny, Fanny. I put them in this box, I merely needed your help to retrieve them."

Fanny looked at him with complete puzzlement. This was the first man to take her to bed in her life. She had trusted in him that much. This monstrous betrayal just couldn't be happening. She blinked rapidly to prevent the tears from starting to pour.

Henri continued, "You know you wouldn't have agreed if I'd told you about them and explained that we should keep them. You are much too good-hearted."

"You killed Chef Etienne? How could you? You were in bed with me at the time," Fanny stammered.

"No, if you remember, I said I'd been outside for a piss.

But I killed him before you came to my bed. He came to the door and I stabbed him and put him in that big urn, the one that was tipped over beside the body. But I guess I didn't distribute the weight correctly. The urn tipped over the first time a cat brushed against it or the wind blew and our teacher fell out. I had hoped he wouldn't be found for a day or two."

"But why did you kill him?"

Just then a young couple walked into the gazebo, holding hands and talking low. When they saw Henri and Fanny, they quickly left.

I'll wager they misunderstood this as a lover's quarrel, Fanny thought bitterly. She wanted to grab the spice box and fling it at them, let diamonds and rubies fly through the air, let them catch as many as they could. But she remembered Henri's skill with a knife. She couldn't let these young lovers be hurt.

"He was the one who started it all, you know. It was Chef Etienne. Well, he didn't actually steal the jewels, someone else did that, someone I never met. His job was to smuggle them out of the palace, and he was successful at that. They were going to sit on them for a time, then sell them and split the profits. He came to me last August, told me about his good fortune, as he called it, and said a police inspector was on his trail and he would feel better if he could store the jewels over at number twenty-three for a short time. That way he could make a grand gesture and insist this police inspector search his quarters, even the house if they wished. For this he offered me the pearls."

Fanny supposed it was Inspector Fournier Henri was referring to. "But when you saw how much there was, you killed him for it," Fanny said dully, staring at the floor. She had stopped trying to get Henri to look in her eyes. It was too painful.

"His partner would never know who had them. I went over that night to pick them up, made a snap decision to cut myself in, killed Etienne, then hid the jewels in your room on my way through. I'd already inspected the spice box, just in case it had anything valuable in it."

"And if it had, would you have killed me for it?"

"Fanny, please, don't be ridiculous. I have nothing but love and warm feelings for you."

"Do go on, Henri. Tell me about M. Desjardins."

"It was those damn evening walks he took. The night Chef died he had just made it to that side of the arcade when I flew out the door of number six. He was still down at the other end of the block so I headed home the opposite direction. But I knew that night he might have seen me. He hurried home, and sure as the king is rich, he caught up with me out in the courtyard. I had a tablecloth full of something. He calmly stuck his hand in the bundle and saw what it was."

Fanny was half listening but it was difficult not to think about her own situation. She was stung. How foolish she must have seemed to Henri, innocently risking her job to sneak over to his bed. Did he ever really regard her with respect? She forced herself to focus on his story, wondering as he spoke if he was lying. "So then you had a partner," she said dully.

Henri smiled, still working her, charming her. "I assured him he could have part of it, went to meet you, and when you fell asleep, I went over to your room and hid the jewels. M. Desjardins took another round of the square and unfortunately discovered Chef where he had tumbled out."

"And months later you killed him, too."

"I discovered him dipping into the inventory, trying to sneak a few pieces. We had a difference of agreement about how long we should wait before liquidating our assets."

"And I bought that whole story and actually got my brother involved in burying him. You must have enjoyed that."

"It was a bonus. I knew after that if you ever became too difficult, I could always threaten to tell the authorities about a certain body buried at number twenty-three Place Royale."

Fanny had to ask. "Why the pretense of a kidnapping? Why not take the box and the jewelry months ago and just disappear?"

"I really thought the revolution would be complete by now. I thought lifting something from Versailles would get you a medal instead of a hangman if I just waited. And I had that uneccessary partner. The night of the riot, I saw a perfect chance to get rid of him but I fell and wounded myself instead. What luck, eh?"

Fanny said nothing.

"Oh, yes, the kidnapping. It offered us both a way to save face. You could always believe your lover was lost to some terrible revolutionaries who needed the jewels to buy arms, or some such tale. I was going to leave you a note saying as much, but you know how poorly I write, Fanny. You would have recognized my spelling in a glance. Then this week, I thought I'd just steal the box away, but I couldn't find it. In the end, I feel you deserve an explanation."

"Where are you headed?"

"Out of Paris, of course. Spain, maybe, or England. I'd like to give you something out of the box, please take your pick. Everything but the sapphires and the pearls. I'm assuming the money is already gone and that's just fine. I have a buyer for the sapphires, and I promised the pearls. I'll take the rest and sell them out of the country."

Could anything be worse than this? Not only had Henri lied and killed, he was now trying to tip her, like some hired worker who had done him a good job. Fanny was so tired. She rubbed her temples. She just wanted him gone.

"If you don't leave now, I'm going to start screaming," she said quietly, still pressing on the sides of her head. "There are plenty of people here in the park. You'll be caught. I don't want your jewels."

Henri got up. "I did enjoy our time together. And by the way, it wasn't my finger," he said, showing his hands. He had the signet ring on his little finger, for effect, Fanny supposed. "I got it off a body at the morgue. Did you know the morgue is right there in the Bastille area? The ring belongs to the king's brother. When they're all dead, some collector will pay a pretty penny for it. Thank you for retrieving it for me from Etienne, but you hid it in your chest, you naughty girl."

"That's me," Fanny said softly. She could hardly get the words out.

And with that Henri was gone. Fanny didn't bother to see what direction he'd headed. It made no difference. But then she remembered the fire. She stood and strained to see him. "When you were looking for the box the other day, why did you start a fire?"

Henri heard her question. "You are good at hiding things, Fanny. I was frustrated. I sent you off to the left bank so I would have plenty of time to search for the box but I didn't find it. I'm sorry about the fire. It was just a fit of pique. But thank you for putting the box with the finger in the carriage house where I was hiding. I was glad to get this ring back."

Fanny could see his form outlined in the dusk. As Henri walked away, she was startled to see a tall figure slip out of the maze toward him. It all happened so quickly. The man, Fanny was sure it was a man, grabbed Henri and pulled him into the maze. From what she could make out in the dim light, Henri's attacker caught him around the neck, cut off his air by pressing on his throat with an arm, and then pulled him from behind, Henri's feet dragging. She didn't see the spice box fall to the ground. Henri must be using his strength to keep it secure, she thought. He must be letting himself be moved, confident he can get away in the maze. And he had been calculating up until now. He was the one who chose this spot. He certainly had plenty of time to learn the maze or plan an escape route.

Fanny didn't think about what she was doing. She would wonder about it later and admit to herself that even after finding out how tremendous Henri's betrayal was, she couldn't help reacting to protect him when he was threatened, when he was in danger.

She ran out of the gazebo down the hill to the entrance to the maze. When she got there, she realized she couldn't see an overview the way she'd been able to from the gazebo, but she could hear the rustling of the hedges and the grunts of a struggle. She started walking toward the sounds but got turned around twice. Sounds bounced or were somehow deflected off the hedges. "Henri!" she called, realizing that for all she knew, Henri believed her to be behind the attacker. And she should have hired someone to protect her, she realized now. But she had believed in Henri so completely. As she heard someone running toward her, she had flashes of past moments when the pieces hadn't exactly fit together.

When Chef was killed, Henri wasn't in bed when she awoke.

She pushed through the hedge to get to the place she thought the sound was coming from, but when she got there, her face burning from the scratchy hedge, the path was empty.

When M. Desjardins was killed, Fanny awoke from a sound sleep because Henri had moved. He no doubt was getting back in bed, pretending to be delirious.

"Henri! Are you all right?" she called. This time two sets of footsteps were running, louder now. Fanny walked cautiously toward where the sound was coming from. There was a gasp of surprise from someplace very near.

Fanny stopped and tried to get her bearings. She didn't know if she should go farther into the maze or make her way outward, toward what she thought was the entrance. And it was getting dark now, so she didn't have much time to figure it out. If she could escape the maze and get up to the gazebo again, perhaps she would still be able to see them. She closed her eyes for a moment, trying to picture how the maze had looked from up above, then started walking in what she thought was the correct direction. Henri appeared from around a corner. There was a dark stain on his overcoat in the chest area. He staggered, and then fell to his knees. He looked at her and Fanny saw his expression change to a glimmer of recognition.

"Henri," Fanny said firmly, her voice catching. She wanted to run to him but she stayed far enough away so he couldn't grab her if this was a trick. "The last thing you will see on earth is my face, Henri Brusli. I loved you."

As if her words had been a wind he couldn't withstand, Henri toppled over and the spice box fell out of the inside of his overcoat, too bulky to stay in place without Henri's grip holding it. Fanny gathered her courage, then walked quickly over to him and took the box. She didn't try to revive him or determine if he was breathing. She knew he was gone.

In the few minutes it took for her to find her way out of the maze, Fanny changed her mind about what she should do next dozens of times. Eventually she decided not to make a run for the carriage, knowing it might not be there when she needed it to be. Whoever had killed Henri was after these diamonds, and she had to make sure they got them. She wanted the jewels out of her life. She headed back to the gazebo.

Fanny sat in silence, not calling out for help or weeping and carrying on like a woman should do who had just lost her first love. Every time she would feel the devastation try to overtake her, she would push it away, push all thoughts away. She couldn't fall apart now. Eventually, it could have been twenty minutes or two, a man walked into the gazebo with a lantern in his hand, his face in the shadow. At first, Fanny thought he was a lantern carrier, one of the thousands in Paris who, for a few pennies, would accompany one home along dark passages. "I know, the Parc is closing," she said. When she got up and turned to leave, clutching the spice box, to her amazement, it was Inspector Fournier. She should have been thrilled to see him, but instead, she realized who had killed Henri.

"Jean, I guess you followed me."

The inspector walked over to her and held out his hand. Fanny handed him the spice box. "No, I followed Henri."

"So that was you in the maze?"

"Your Henri had some courage, I must say! More than he had brains. I was certainly not going to allow him, some nobody from Brittany, to run off with the queen's jewels. Or, I should say, my jewels."

Now this was a twist that Fanny hadn't seen coming—not that she had suspected Henri to be a killer either. She obviously could not be allowed to choose her own husband because she had no taste in men. The two she had feelings for were both crooks and worse.

"So you were Etienne's partner? That's what you were talking about at Les Halles. I should have known."

"It seems like a big theft to you, doesn't it, Fanny? But it was nothing compared to what others took and are still taking. Etienne and I became friends when I was a member of the King's Guard. We only took a little something to remember our time at Versailles. Henri had to pay for Etienne's death with his own life. Sorry."

"Honor among thieves. And you're the last man standing. Congratulations."

Fournier walked over to Fanny and put his hand on her cheek. "You are the loveliest young woman I've had the pleasure to spend time with. I'm sorry we won't be able to continue that. You and your family should consider leaving the country, too, Fanny. The king is going to lose his head soon, and then things will really turn bad. Oh, and following your mother, that was just a ploy to keep my employers off the real criminal. Me." He leaned down and kissed her on the cheek.

"Would you mind walking me to the carriage? I hear there are unsavory characters in Paris these days," Fanny observed dryly.

"It would be my pleasure," Fournier said with that crinkly smile that Fanny loved so much.

And that was the last word they spoke. She held his arm as they walked to the road. The carriage was waiting where she had left it; Fanny got in and didn't look back, although she wanted to.

She had the driver take her to faubourg St. Antoine, to her parents. It was time she went home.

CHAPTER SEVENTEEN

"MOTHER, will you fasten my necklace," Fanny asked, and held up her Bastille pendant.

"I'm thinking this might be the only jewelry you'll ever wear after the stolen jewels affair," Martine said with a smile as she tied the velvet ribbon.

"I have no taste for diamonds, or the men who steal them, that's for sure."

"I know it's hard to believe, but you will love someone again. And think of it this way; You came out of this with your life. The chef and the maître d' certainly didn't fare that well, and Henri, but I thank the inspector for that."

"And whoever Fournier stole them from at the palace, I bet they're not around anymore," Fanny said with just a little bitterness showing.

"Fournier is gone. I heard on the street that there was more missing than just the jewels. I heard hundreds of thousands of livres were stolen, too."

"Well, I wouldn't put it past him. But as far as I know, it wasn't hundreds of thousands; it was just thirty-one thousand," Fanny said. "Livres, that is. I'm not sure about the other kinds of money."

Martine looked at her daughter intently. "Surely that wasn't in the spice box when you gave it to that murderous thief?"

"Mother, you raised a sensible daughter. A thief can't yell, 'I've been robbed,' very easily. That's how I got my restaurant."

"And the king's money looks like everyone else's when you spend it at Les Halles," Martine said with irony in her tone. "Well done, little one."

"I'm just sorry I didn't trust you to tell you about the jewelry sooner. I didn't know what to think about you making the march to Versailles. I guess I thought anything was possible."

"And it was. Your protector turned out to be a crooked policeman. Your teacher was his partner. Your boyfriend was a thief and a murderer, and worse, a greedy little bastard who double-crossed his own mentor. The only thing that wasn't possible was marching home from Versailles with thousands of other women, with my pockets laden with the queen's jewels. Why, I would have been lucky to make it back with one diamond, let alone a whole treasure box full of them."

Fanny laughed at that image. How had she imagined her mother carrying her newfound treasure back to Paris? Around her neck? It was absurd and she was ashamed to have to admit her suspicions now that she knew who the guilty parties really were.

Martine looked in the mirror that Fanny was sitting in

front of. She put her hands on Fanny's shoulders. "I'm just sorry that you were treated so badly by Henri. That kind of betrayal is hard to get over. It is not what a parent wants for her child. Your father is angry with himself that he allowed Henri to court you. But he was so sincere and you two shared a love of cooking."

Fanny smiled. "I was a fool about Henri. And Fournier, too. I never once suspected him. Even when he showed up at the Bagatelle, I thought he was there to arrest Henri, right up until he said the words 'my jewels.' I was such a, a girl."

"He was a handsome man. But, my dear, you are the one with the restaurant."

Fanny got up. She and her mother had on dresses made of silk taffeta the same color as their eyes. Martine had bought it years ago, when she saw it, knowing she would make something special for them someday. The styles were different; Fanny's was cut much lower at the bodice, but it brought out the color of both women's eyes very effectively. "We better go downstairs. This is probably the only time I'll get to be dressed up in my own restaurant and I want to enjoy it."

After much argument with her parents about living alone, an argument Fanny won, Fanny talked the landlord into throwing in the first floor of her building for a little more money in rent. It had been used for storage of vinegar and olive oil as the landlord was a broker in those two commodities. She persuaded him to move his storage to the second floor, the attic space, so she could make a simple bedroom–sitting room for herself on the first, above the restaurant. She didn't need a kitchen as she had a big one downstairs. The boys she had hired, Nicholas and Simon from the Place Royale, kept her water container full and her chamber pot empty. They slept in the kitchen on pallets under the worktables.

Fanny and her mother went downstairs to an elegant scene. It was the first of May and it had turned into a lovely spring evening. Tonight was the opening party for Chez Fanny and her neighbors had allowed her to make a long table out on the sidewalk in front of the restaurant. She wanted to give a dinner for all those who had helped her get the space ready. So she was the hostess tonight, having a party for her friends.

Violet and some of her employees from the boulangerie were helping serve tonight, as an opening gift, as well as provide the bread products. Lucy, who had cooked at number twenty-one, quit her job to work at Chez Fanny, something Fanny was especially excited about. It would be great to have another woman in the kitchen who loved cooking as much as she did.

Many of the cooks from Place Royale were in attendance, plus all of the Delarues' neighbors from faubourg St. Antoine, all of whom had contributed something to the restaurant's décor. Brother Albert and his family were there, as well as Violet's father, M. Lafarge, and other business owners on the street.

The restaurant itself looked magnificent. The dining room had a fireplace with beautiful gilded carving, à la Delarue, *père et fils,* and other touches that Fanny could never have afforded if she didn't have such a handy family. Martine had contributed the drapes, luxurious velvet ones. The tables had beautiful iron bases. There was linen to the floor, and plenty of candelabras, thanks to the supplies Fanny was borrowing from M. Monnard. Philippe Delarue had found a pair of ironwork chandeliers with a double tier of candle-holders, and he had painted them and rigged a pulley for each one so the women could change the candles without getting up on a ladder to do so.

Fanny picked up a wineglass nervously. "How's the lamb?" she asked toward the kitchen. The caterers who had rented the space before Fanny had been members of the ro-tisseurs guild, and their mechanical spit was still in the hearth oven. Fanny planned to always have at least one or two roasted meats every night. And she didn't have to worry a whit about the rotisseurs guild, or any other guild for that matter. The new government had abolished all guilds and corporations in March.

"I'm slicing it now. It looks great, still pink in the mid-dle," Lucy called back.

People were taking their places around the long table outside. "I'll take the *blanquette de veau,*" Fanny said as she picked up a big soup tureen full of veal stew.

Out she went and put the tureen in front of her father to serve. Lucy and the other two kitchen workers, women as well, brought out platters of roast lamb, green beans with hazelnuts, those braised leeks of Fanny's, and a mound of rice, something fairly exotic in Paris. Then Fanny went back in for something that she knew was going to cause the neighborhood to talk about Chez Fanny. She had tested and tested until she got it just right. Now if she could just get them to try it, she knew they'd love it as much as she did.

"This is a root gratin, with lots of cream and Gruyere cheese, and turnips and parsnips and something new, pota-toes," Fanny said proudly. "I know they used to be for pigs but all the chefs at the market are trying them. Taste it, please." And around the table the dish went, with much groaning from the men about trying new dishes.

Fanny herself didn't sit down; she was too nervous. She ran for more bread, poured wine, and walked slowly from one end of the table to the other, talking to everyone. After a while her father stood up. "Let's all raise our glass to my daughter and to Chez Fanny," he said. "Well done." Everyone toasted Fanny and she blushed and gave a little curtsey. "I hope you will all come back to my little tables. We want you to feel like you are at Grand-mère's house. But a grand-mère who may try something new. For instance, on Saturday and Sunday, we will serve a third meal, in the morning hours, omelets and ham and such. It is very popular in England. It's called breakfast," she said, and everyone laughed at the folly of such a concept. Fanny was going to shake things up, all right. Potatoes and breakfast, the very idea.

As Fanny went back inside to get more wine, she saw a delivery boy come around the corner. He had on the same fancy attire as the boy who had delivered a message from the supposed kidnapers that day that seemed so long ago. He entered Chez Fanny with a familiar object in his hands. It was the spice box.

"Fanny Delarue?" he asked. Fanny numbly nodded yes and the boy left. She even forgot to give him a tip. She felt an aversion to the box, once such a lovely gift from her father, then afterward the center of so much trouble and pain. Fanny still grieved over Henri and his treachery every day. She missed him, and she had to admit, she missed Jean Fournier as well.

Martine walked into the restaurant. "Fanny, are you all right? Come out to your party, sweetheart."

"Damn it. I wanted to ask where he came from."

"Who, dear?"

"The delivery boy. He just brought this to me," Fanny said and held up the spice box.

Martine recognized it, of course. But she didn't know how closely it was connected to the jewels or that Henri, then Jean, took it full of them. Fanny started to tell her the significance, but thought better of it. She opened the secret drawer instead. In it, on top of the recipes, were the sapphire necklace and the matching earrings. There was a note tucked under them, and Fanny pulled it out.

It read: *To match those eyes. Wait till the queen leaves town to wear these. Love, Jean.*

Martine looked at the box and the beautiful necklace, then at the note. She smiled at her daughter. "Good advice," she said and rejoined the party.

LATER that night, Fanny felt good about how things had gone. There wasn't a bit of food left, not even the dreaded potatoes. In the morning, they started cooking. Chez Fanny was open for business.

She sat down on a stool in front of her chest and the carved and gilded mirror. And with a smile on her face, she opened the box and tried on her new necklace. "Thank you, Jean. And you, too, Henri. If it weren't for you, I would never have started this journey. My own restaurant." Then she thought of something and rustled through the top drawer of her chest. She found the recipes she had copied at their cooking classes with Chef Etienne. Solemnly, she placed them in the box along with the other recipes. Then she took the note from Jean and put it in her drawer, lingering over the written words, outlining them with her fingers.

Tomorrow, she decided, she would give the spice box to Lucy. Lucy had always wanted to come to the cooking classes, so at least she could have the recipes. Fanny already knew them all by heart.

And tomorrow she would cut her hair, short, like a chef.

RECIPES

CREPES A LA MARTINE
(USUALLY SUZETTE)

For the crepes:
1 cup all purpose flour
3 eggs
2 tablespoons sugar
1 teaspoon vanilla extract
1½ cups milk
3 tablespoons melted butter

Combine the flour, eggs, sugar, vanilla, and half of the milk. Whisk until smooth. Add the remaining milk and let the batter sit for 30-60 minutes. This allows the flour to absorb the liquid and gives you a stronger crepe. Whisk in the melted butter right before use.

Heat a 6-inch seasoned crepe pan or a non-stick sauté pan to medium heat. Add about 2 tablespoons of batter at a time to the pan, turning quickly to coat the pan. Cook until the crepe starts to brown at the edges, then turn and cook the second side briefly. Slide onto wax paper or parchment paper and stack the cooked crepes with wax paper between each one.

Will make about 18 crepes

> **For the sauce:**
> 4 ounces butter (1 stick)
> ½ cup sugar
> juice of 2 oranges
> zest of orange and lemon mixed, about 2 tablespoons
> ⅓ cup brandy or a combination of brandy and Cointreau.

In a large sauté pan, combine the butter, sugar, and orange juice until the butter and sugar are melted and the liquid is bubbly. Add the zest and liquor carefully, as the liquor may flame up. Dip each crepe in this sauce briefly, folding the crepe into quarters as you work. I usually serve 2 crepes per person.

MUSICIAN'S TART

1 cup dried stone fruit such as pears, peaches, and apricots.
   Do not use apricots, which are easier to find, exclusively.
1 cup dates, pitted and chopped
½ cup pear nectar
⅓ cup packed dark brown sugar, plus 6 tablespoons for the
   nut topping
6 tablespoons butter
4 tablespoons light corn syrup
½ cup each of lightly toasted pine nuts, cashews, and
   slivered almonds
2 tablespoons heavy cream

Make your favorite pie crust dough, enough for a one crust
pie, and line a pie plate or 9-inch tart tin with the crust.
Cover lightly with foil and fill the foil with dried beans or
pie weights. Bake briefly in a 350 degree oven about 15
minutes, until the crust is set and starting to brown. Remove from oven and take out of the foil and weights.

Combine the dried fruits and dates with the pear nectar and
⅓ cup brown sugar in a heavy saucepan and bring to a boil.
Simmer for 5 minutes, stirring often. Take off the heat. The
original recipe called for puréeing this mixture now, but I
like the fruits still identifiable so I have omitted that step.
Smooth or chunky, as you wish.

Now, combine the remaining sugar with the butter and
corn syrup in a saucepan. Heat slowly to a boil and stir of-

ten. Simmer for 5 minutes, making sure your two sugar sources have dissolved smoothly. Remove from heat and add the nuts and cream.

Spread the fruit filling in your crust first, then the nut topping.

Bake at 375 degrees for about 30 minutes, until the filling bubbles and browns. Cool completely before serving.

MARINATED LEEKS

2–3 bunches young leeks
1 bottle white wine
Fresh thyme, tarragon

1–2 shallots
Kosher salt and ground pepper
½ cup sherry vinegar, or ¼ cup vinegar and ¼ cup wine
    verjus
salt
pepper
¼ cup mixed thyme and tarragon
1 cup walnut or hazelnut oil

Chose the smallest young leeks you can find and trim them to about six inches long. Soak them in cold water to remove the sand, and rinse. Do this at least twice. If the leeks are more than an inch across, split them in half lengthwise. In a fish poacher or a large sauté pan, heat the bottle of white wine and fresh herbs to a simmer. Put the leeks in this to cook, adding water if necessary to cover them, simmering gently. When leeks are tender to a fork, remove carefully so they stay intact and drain.

For the dressing: Mince the shallots very fine in a small mixing bowl. Combine them with the mustard, vinegar, and/or verjus, salt and pepper, and about ¼ cup mixed thyme and tarragon leaves. When you have all these ingredients mixed together, drizzle in the oil, stirring with a fork or whisk all the while, until the oil is all incorporated and emulsified.

Let the leeks sit with the dressing on them for at least an hour before serving.

VEAL BLANQUETTE OR WHITE VEAL STEW

Unlike most meat preparations, the idea of this dish is to keep the meat as white as possible, so no browning.

    5 pounds veal stew meat, cut into bite-sized pieces
    ½ bottle white vermouth
    ½ bottle white wine
    3 tablespoons flour
    3 tablespoons butter and 4 tablespoons butter
    1 medium onion, 4 stalks celery, and 1 lare carrot, all peeled
        and diced approximately the same size to make your
        mirepoix

1 pound crimini or button mushrooms
optional: ¼ cup dried porcini or other mushrooms
    reconstituted in 2 cups hot water
10-ounce package frozen pearl onions or 1 pound fresh,
    peeled and blanched
1½ cups each: chicken stock and heavy cream
kosher salt, white ground pepper
¼ teaspoon ground nutmeg
½ cup brandy

Preheat oven to 350 degrees. In a heavy Dutch oven that can go in the oven or on the stove top, place the meat and ½ bottle of white vermouth. Cook covered for about 1½ hours. Ideally this should be done the day before you are serving the stew. Remove the meat from the heat and cool. Heat 3 tablespoons of butter in a large sauté pan and sauté the mirepoix and the mushrooms. If you have soaked dried mushrooms, chop them coarsely and add, saving the liquid. Add the vegetables to the cooled veal, along with the onions. Now on the top of the stove, simmer the veal/vegetable mixture for about an hour on low heat, adding the mushroom liquid and the white wine. When you do this, make sure the last dredges of the mushroom liquid are not added as they usually contain grit.

Next, make a white sauce by melting the 4 tablespoons of butter in a heavy sauce pan. Add the flour and cook over low heat 5 minutes. Add the chicken stock and cream and let thicken slowly. When the mixture is thick and the veal is tender, combine the white sauce and the meat mixture. Simmer another 20–30 minutes until the stew is thickened. Remove from heat, season with salt, pepper, nutmeg, and add the brandy.